Sud

and switched his attention to the front door. *She* breezed in, hair like spun gold flowing to her waist, with a seductive yet regal body and a sway to her hips that should be illegal even in DC. She wore a snug rose and cream colored sweater, cut low enough he could see the swells of her rounded breasts, tailored black slacks that fit her cute ass like a glove and four-inch spike heels. She paused in the center of the salon, wet from the sudden spring storm, and lowered the briefcase she'd used as an umbrella. Her sparkling violet eyes glanced up to the mezzanine where Bruce stood watching. Blatantly her gaze wandered over his well-muscled body, undressing him piece by piece, until he felt naked. He shook his head slightly and smoothed his shirt and slacks with his hand, just to make sure he was still wearing them.

On the first floor, Owen, a stocky well-muscled man of slightly over six foot, with thick silver hair that fell to his shoulders, smiled and stepped toward her holding out a large towel. "Mother Nature frown on you?" His dark amber eyes twinkled as he watched water pool at her feet.

"It would seem so." She grinned and took the towel, dried off then knelt down to wipe up the puddle.

"Don't worry about it." Owen snapped his fingers. Mia came from the back room with a wheeled bucket and a mop. "It's been one of those mornings." He reached out, took the towel from her, and handed it to Mia. "Now, what can I do for you?"

*Jen,
Thanks for all your support & encouragement.
We did it!
Tena Stetler*

A Demon's Witch

by

Tena Stetler

This is a work of fiction. Names, characters, places, and incidents are either the product of the author's imagination or are used fictitiously, and any resemblance to actual persons living or dead, business establishments, events, or locales, is entirely coincidental.

A Demon's Witch

COPYRIGHT © 2015 by Tena Stetler

All rights reserved. No part of this book may be used or reproduced in any manner whatsoever without written permission of the author or The Wild Rose Press, Inc. except in the case of brief quotations embodied in critical articles or reviews.
Contact Information: info@thewildrosepress.com

Cover Art by *Kristian Norris*

The Wild Rose Press, Inc.
PO Box 708
Adams Basin, NY 14410-0708
Visit us at www.thewildrosepress.com

Publishing History
First Black Rose Edition, 2015
Print ISBN 978-1-5092-0308-6
Digital ISBN 978-1-5092-0309-3

Published in the United States of America

Dedication

To my friends, family
and wonderful husband
who believed in me and the magic
from the very beginning.
To my best friend, Lisa,
for her encouragement always.
We did it!
And to my editor, Lill,
a heartfelt thanks
for everything.
You Rock!

Chapter One

Flames exploded from a bowl of manicure solution, melted it right to the granite tabletop. Bruce Sahwyn watched from his glass office on the mezzanine, the activities on the first floor of his highly successful, Wycked Hair Salon. He touched a control panel in his office increasing the air filtration in the salon, then tapped the button on his head set. "Owen, what the hell is going on down there?"

Owen, the salon manager, craned his neck to look up at Bruce while walking into the manager's office. He shut the door and tapped the button on his head set. "Apparently Sage was upset with her mate when she came in this morning for her manicure. No one noticed the intermittent sparks emanating from her fingertips, 'til she put her hand in the solution." Owen wrinkled his nose slightly at the obnoxious odor that was beginning to fade.

"Did the senator's wife see what happened?" Bruce asked.

"Not exactly. Barbara was sitting in Toni's station across from Sage when the incident happened. Toni moved Barbara to your old station up front and finished applying her hair color. We explained that a faulty outlet caused a hair dryer in the next station to go up in flames. Barbara wasn't close enough to see where the flames came from, so she bought the story and watched us toss the hair dryer into the trash and take it out. To keep up appearances, I had maintenance replace the outlet to ensure her peace of mind and our reputation."

"Ok, good, and Sage?" Bruce asked.

"Riki took her outside for a walk to calm her down. When they returned, Riki took Sage to one of the stations in the back just as a precaution and continued her manicure, which is just about done."

"Good job. Comp the senator's wife a manicure anyway." Bruce ran his hand through his thick chestnut hair and blew out a breath, one side of his mouth curved in slight grin. B*usiness as usual.*

Keeping a lid on all the paranormal beings inhabiting Washington D.C. was a daunting job. However, Bruce a six hundred year-old demon, and Overlord of the Western Hemisphere was up to the task. The Wycked Hair Salon was his informational hub. It offered the finest hair stylists and nail techs in the area. Senators, Congressmen, their families, Secret Service, and even white house staff frequented his establishment. Usually, things ran smoothly at the multispecies salon, but occasionally…

Through these patrons, he kept abreast of the activities for all the movers and shakers on Capitol Hill, mortal or not. Even after all these years, it still mystified him that most mortals remained oblivious to the presence of magic and the creatures that wielded it. Within these walls, his anonymity was safe from mortals or magic beings alike.

Suddenly, he felt the magic aura shift and switched his attention to the front door. *She* breezed in, hair like spun gold flowing to her waist, with a seductive yet regal body and a sway to her hips that should be illegal even in DC. She wore a snug rose and cream colored sweater, cut low enough he could see the swells of her rounded breasts, tailored black slacks that fit her cute ass like a glove and four-inch spike heels. She paused in the center of the salon, wet from the sudden spring storm, and lowered the briefcase she'd used as an umbrella. Her sparkling violet eyes glanced up to the mezzanine where Bruce stood watching. Blatantly her gaze wandered over his well-muscled body, undressing him piece by piece, until he felt naked. He shook his head slightly and smoothed his shirt and slacks with his hand, just to make sure he was still wearing them.

On the first floor, Owen, a stocky well-muscled man of slightly over six foot, with thick silver hair that fell to his shoulders, smiled and stepped toward her holding out a large towel. "Mother Nature frown on you?" His dark amber eyes twinkled as he watched water pool at her feet.

"It would seem so." She grinned and took the towel, dried off then knelt down to wipe up the puddle.

"Don't worry about it." Owen snapped his fingers. Mia came from the back room with a wheeled bucket and a mop. "It's been one of those mornings." He reached out, took the towel from her, and handed it to Mia. "Now, what can I do for you?"

Smiling sweetly, she turned her attention to Owen, extending her hand. "Hello, I'm Angelique Shandie, the owner of The Krystal Unicorn down the street. Is it possible to leave flyers in your salon for the grand opening of my store?" She pulled a brightly colored brochure from her briefcase and handed it to him. Embossed gold lettering arched across the top of a shimmering silver unicorn at the center of the page, announcing the grand opening of The Krystal Unicorn, a new age specialty store.

Owen took her offered hand. "A pleasure to meet you, Ms. Shandie. I don't see a problem. I'll check with the owner and get back to you." He jerked his chin toward the mezzanine.

"Thanks. I'll be back this afternoon, if that's all right?" Angie sauntered to the door and paused as she reached for the handle. Glancing up at Bruce, her luscious, full lips curved into a slow sensual smile. She brought two well-manicured fingertips to her lips and blew him a saucy kiss.

"Sure." Owen licked his lips as she slipped out the door.

"Put your eyes back in your head and your tongue back in your mouth, if you want to keep em." Tobi called from across the room, the thin line of her lips curving at the corners as she chuckled and nodded her head toward the mezzanine. "I believe the boss wants to see you."

Owen shot an irritated glance over his shoulder at his wife and felt eyes boring through him. He looked toward the mezzanine. Bruce touched his headset. "When you get a chance, I'd like to talk with you."

"Sure thing." Owen quickly finished scheduling an appointment and climbed the stairs to the office.

Owen grinned as he climbed up the stairs. "Quite a looker isn't she?" He greeted Bruce coming to a stop just inside the open glass door of the office.

"I'll say. Who is she? I've never seen her here before. An aura of magic just rolls off her in huge waves."

"It should. Her name is Angelique Shandie. She's

Tristian's little sister and a very powerful witch." Owen paused and stroked his chin with thumb and forefinger. "Their lineage is traceable back to the Salem witch trials in 1692. I believe they are direct decedents of Abigail Faulkner. She was convicted and sentenced to death for witchcraft, then pardoned. The reason escapes me, at the moment."

Bruce's eyes darkened as his mind drifted back to that bleak era. "I believe Abigail was with child, so her sentence was postponed. Later the governor pardoned and released her from prison." He sighed and shook his head slightly. "Such a dangerous time for magic kind," he murmured.

"Ah, yes. It still is, in some ways." Owen paused, his forehead creased at Bruce's ability to recall such things. "Anyway, Angelique just opened The Krystal Unicorn, a new age store down the street. She came in to introduce herself and see if she could leave some flyers for our customers."

"Hmm, Tristian Shandie." Bruce tapped a finger to his lips. "Didn't know he had a sister. In fact, I don't believe he has ever mentioned any family, other than his father who is deceased." Bruce mused, then quirked a brow questioningly. "What'd you tell her?"

Owen frowned watching his boss carefully. "If you're thinking, what I think you are thinking, think again. She'll bring you nothing but trouble and Tristian would…"

Bruce raised his hand to silence Owen. "My business is my own. I don't believe I asked your opinion. However, be assured if I want it, I know where to find you. So is she bringing the flyers over?"

"Yes, later this afternoon. I didn't see the harm in

it…then." Undaunted, Owen narrowed his eyes in warning and stalked toward the door. "If we're done, I've work to do." He stepped silently through the door and closed it firmly behind him.

Bruce sat in his white leather chair with chrome accents and turned to the piles of paperwork covering the glass-top desk. *God I hate paperwork.* He'd considered hiring an assistant to handle it, but given the confidential nature of his dealings, decided it best to continue doing the work himself.

Owen and Tobi managed the salon business details and the paperwork that came with it. Bruce gave a silent thanks to the goddess for that. Owen had been his confidant and right hand man for centuries. The lines etched on his face and usual calm demeanor gave the impression that he was quite a bit older than Bruce.

When Owen married Tobi, a tall, auburn haired beauty with a wild streak, Bruce worried that things would change. The concern was unfounded. Tobi was as loyal as Owen and fit right into the business. They were demons he could trust with his life. Though for the life of him, Bruce couldn't figure out why Tobi streaked her gorgeous hair to match her colorful smocks each week.

The black laptop in the center of his desk chirped as the e-mail icon on the desktop blinked. "Damn. It never ends." He ran his finger over the touch screen and tapped the power button. The screen went blank.

Owen's stinging words still rang in his head. Centuries of existence had taught him most women were nothing but trouble. Tenting his fingers, he leaned back in the chair, ignoring the business at hand and let his mind wander back to Angelique. She'd been dancing around the fringe of his thoughts since he'd watched her saunter into the salon.

He shook his head slowly. "Women," he mused aloud. *Hell yes, I enjoyed them.* Lips curved as he thought of recent indulgences, and why not, he wasn't in any type of relationship. Those he entertained looked only for the fun and luxury his wealth afforded him, expecting he'd lavish it on them. For a time, he did, but none of the women held his attention for long. Admittedly, he preferred human females. They were so soft, fragrant, and willing to please. *But a witch, now that could be fun.*

The cell phone vibrated across the desk, yanking him back to reality. This particular female was the sister of his top enforcer and longtime trusted associate. *Owen was right. She was off limits.*

Irritably he scooped up his cell phone, slid the lock across the screen with a long slender finger, and held the phone to his ear. "This had better be important."

Chapter Two

Angie grinned outrageously as she sashayed down the sidewalk, glad to see the storm had passed. That was one handsome creature, and one she intended to get to know better, much better. She pulled on the curved copper handle and the glass door, with a white unicorn etched in the center, swung open. Sun streamed through the glass, rainbows bounced across the white walls and light oak floor as the door closed. Melodic chimes sounded in the back of the shop. A young woman with short spiked jet-black hair, dyed bright blue at the tips, slid her slender body between the crystal-beads hanging in the doorway, adjusting her narrow shoulders.

"Willow, how many times have I told you to tuck your wings in before you enter the showroom?" Angie laughed down at her partner, and life-long best friend.

"They were tucked by the time I came through the beads," Willow protested narrowing her ice blue eyes and giving Angie a thorough appraisal. "What have you been up to?"

"Enjoying the scenery down the street," Angie said with a smirk. "I asked the manager of the Wycked Hair to put some of our flyers in their store. He's checking with the owner, but didn't see a problem. I'll go back with some this afternoon."

"So he caught your eye." Willow shook her head

and waggled her index finger at Angie. "Owen is married and much too old for you. He is handsome with all that silver hair and rugged features. I bet he works out to keep those broad shoulders and narrow hips at his age. And those biceps." She pretended to fan herself with a receipt book, then burst into giggles.

Angie chortled. "Not him silly girl." She raised an eyebrow and grinned at Willow. "The owner, Bruce is his name, I believe. Now he's hot."

Willow scowled and her eyes widened. "Oh, Angie, that's not smart. I've heard about him. Tall, dark, handsome, and mysterious, just your type, but he's not human. The faery realm's heard tell of him, he's dangerous and vicious. He rules the Western Hemisphere with an iron fist, keeping magic folk honest and in their place. One misstep and you're history." She drew an index finger across her throat, flopped her head to one side. "It's also rumored that he controls those escaping the underworld as well. You know what that means."

"Willow, he isn't the devil himself. Although, demon he may be. Hmmm..." She pursed her full lips thoughtfully. "You know..." Her forehead creased in concentration as she said slowly. "I could see if my brother knows him."

"What? Ask Tristian, a dem...I mean warlock... your brother..." she stammered, "...about a demon you find attractive. Have you lost your mind?" She squeaked and drew in a deep breath, blew it out.

"Oh, give me some credit," Angie snapped, flipping her hair over her shoulders and narrowing her eyes at her friend who usually didn't fluster easily. "I don't know that he is a demon. I'll just ask Tristian to check out the businesses in the neighborhood near my new store. All very innocent."

Willow threw back her head and snorted in a very unfaery like way. "Tristan won't buy that for a minute, he knows you too well. You do what you damn well please and don't care what anyone else thinks. So why on earth would you care who or what your neighbors are here in this town of iniquity? You'd just bring trouble down on innocent people, and I use that word loosely."

"I would not," Angie retorted indignantly, whirling around and beginning to pace back and forth across the floor.

"Oh, yes, big brother would love to learn that you are infatuated with a…"

Angie interrupted. "Who said I was infatuated. I merely noticed he was a really hot guy. Besides, you don't know for sure what he is." Angie blew out a breath. "But you're probably right. Something, uh… someone that handsome, can't be human. Can you find out about him for me?" Her voice wheedling. "Please."

Willow crossed her arms across her chest, chin jutting out. "No!"

"Well, then I'll just have to find out for myself." Angie flounced out the door and called back over her shoulder. "I'll be back in a bit and relieve you for the rest of the afternoon. Fair enough?"

"Yeah, ok." Willow sighed and reached for the phone. She punched in a number and drummed her perfectly manicured, long, hot pink fingernails on the glass showcase waiting for an answer. "Hey, I need a favor."

****

The base of Bruce's neck prickled, announcing Angelique's arrival. *Why does she have that effect on me?* He wondered idly. A quick sidelong glance confirmed she was staring directly up at him. For a moment, he considered looking away but decided against it. If she wanted to play this game, he wasn't about to back down. If anything, he'd turn up the heat. His lips twitched in amusement considering his next move. Bruce pushed up from the chair and strolled across the room to prop the door open, then stood, one hand in his pocket watching through the glass.

Angie averted her eyes and sauntered across the floor to the desk where Owen stood. "Good afternoon."

Owen looked up from the computer and smiled. "That it is, Ms. Shandie." He waved a hand toward the desktop. "Leave the flyers here at the reception desk."

Angie reached into her briefcase and slid out a stack of papers. "Thanks so much for doing this. But could I trouble you for one more teeny tiny favor?" She peeked coyly from underneath her long blonde lashes. "Could you put a few of them on the tables with the magazines so your customers could peruse them while they wait?"

Owen nodded. "I suppose we could do that."

"Thank you so much. Would it be possible to thank the owner in person?"

"Afraid not, he is a very busy man. I will convey your appreciation."

"Ok, maybe another time. Thanks again." She strode toward the door and pulled it open, waited a couple of beats, then looked up, smiled, and blew another kiss to Bruce as he watched her turn and walk out.

Owen tilted his head up and glared at his boss. Bruce raised his hands, palms up and shrugged, then returned to his desk and the paperwork scattered across the top.

Tobi made her way across the floor to Owen. "What was that all about?" she demanded giving him the evil eye.

He glared in Bruce's direction. "Nothing." Owen growled. "Bruce is considering toying with Angelique. We disagreed about his intentions. That's all."

"Huh? Angelique? I was talking about you and that…" Her voice trailed off as what he said sank in. "She was flirting with Bruce?" Her voice softened, the angry lines around her mouth smoothed out.

"Yeah, and I don't like it." Owen stared at the computer screen slamming his crooked index finger down on the enter key.

"Since when did you start controlling Bruce's personal life? I thought his business entities kept you more than occupied." Tobi patted his arm affectionately. "Might want to take it easy on the keyboard. You don't want to replace another one this month. Do you?" Her eyes glittered with amusement as she glanced upstairs. "He'll start taking them out of your salary, if you keep it up."

"Like hell he will. It's his fault." Owen swore vehemently, swung out from behind the counter, and stalked over the tawny tile floor toward the employee's lounge.

Bruce laughed silently to himself at Owen's frustration then returned to his desk and the stacks of paperwork requiring his attention.

Chapter Three

It was long after closing when Bruce finished his paperwork and checked the e-mail reports of his Region Commanders for Greenland, Canada, and South America. He breathed a sigh of relief after reading the last report. Nothing in the reports required his immediate attention. He wasn't a micro manager and he'd appointed responsible, trusted confidants to the commander positions. He replied to the necessary e-mails, shut off the computer, and pushed back from his desk. It was a quiet ending to a hectic day at the salon and a brutal day as Territory Overlord.

He had sent Tristian cross-country to check on a rumor that demons in the South were setting up business as protection specialists. Allegedly, they were forcing their services on mortals with the threat of going out of business—or worse—if the mortals refused to pay. Evidence connected the same demons, assisted by vampires and a few shape shifters, to a politically motivated arson resulting in deaths, which the local police were currently investigating.

The situation made him cringe. Mortals investigating paranormal activity created a recipe for disaster or at the very least, discovery. It was against the code for otherworldly creatures to draw mortal's attention, be involved in their demise or intimidation, among other things. Tristian would verify the validity of the rumors and if true, neutralize the parties involved without a trace and alter memories of the mortals, if required. The necessary brutality of Bruce's position had never sat comfortably with him.

Bruce raked his fingers through his hair considering whether to contact Lady Rose, leader of the Vampire Council. Vampires were difficult creatures to control ordinarily, but once they went rogue, it was always a violent, bloody cataclysm. In his early years as Territory Overlord, he'd negotiated an agreement between the other Overlords and several high-ranking vampire officials allowing vampires to govern their kind, which had worked to the benefit of all concerned. He picked up his cell phone and scrolled to Lady Rose's number, his fingers hesitating. *Maybe it would be better to get confirmation from Tristian that a vampire was involved before contacting her.* A born vampire, Lady Rose's path to the top of the vampire hierarchy resulted in the death and destruction of her own kind, but her firm belief in a civilized vampire society won out and she was now a respected leader. Bruce exited the screen and pocketed the phone.

Reaching up he turned off the crystal light that hung over his desk and leaned back in his chair rubbing his eyes with a thumb and forefinger. He tapped the button under his desk closing the curtains around the inside of the glass office. An ornately carved, polished mahogany wardrobe stood in the back of his office. He reached in, plucked out a pair of well-worn jeans, black cotton t-shirt, and a pair of comfortable boots. Ready for a couple of days at his country estate in Virginia, he grabbed his leather jacket and keys. Took the stairs two at a time to the main floor, set the alarm, and walked out the back door, locking it behind him.

A red custom-built sports car sat in the parking lot. Yeah, it was an older model, but still one of the best vehicles ever built, in his opinion. He started across the parking lot and caught movement out of the corner of his eye, yet didn't sense any danger. Soon, he felt the surge of magic wash over him, along with something more subtle. *Faery dust? What the hell. Angie?* He continued his scan of the parking lot and adjacent buildings as a precaution. There was no one in the area.

A whoosh of wind rustled the dry leaves and the traces of magic and faery dust disappeared. Hair tousled by the breeze, he shrugged and walked to his car, folding his large frame inside then turned the key in the ignition. The engine rumbled to life, his foot hit the gas pedal and tires squealed as they spun, spewing gravel, and dirt in his wake. The vehicle barreled out of the parking lot and turned toward the beltway to pick up Highway 66 headed west.

****

Twin gaslights sat atop tall copper poles and framed the entrance to a driveway winding its way to his family's turn of the century Queen Anne Victorian home. The house was too large for just one, but he enjoyed the memories it held. He pulled into the four-car garage behind his home and parked, closing the door after him. Nostrils flared as he breathed in the fresh air, grateful to be out of the city at last.

The security alarm's red LED glimmered in the darkness. Pressing his left hand to the glass beside the panel, he waited for a key pad to appear, and then tapped in a code. The LED changed to green and a wall panel slid open. Light spilled onto the garage floor from the underground corridor as he stepped, inside and the panel silently slid closed.

As he wound his way down the passageway, he noticed a couple of the sconces remained dark and made a mental note to have them repaired immediately. Arriving at the house, a steady rainbow of LED lights on the security panel assured him it was safe to enter. He stared directly at the right top section of the panel, heard a click, and turned the door handle.

Megan, his housekeeper, had left a light burning in the kitchen to welcome him home. He tossed his worn brown leather jacket on the back of a chair. Kicked off his boots and stood, his eyes closed and listened. Nothing but silence, he loved it. He'd given his staff a few days off, so he could have the house to himself. They'd return upon his departure.

Tonight prowling the confines of his home, the peace, and relaxation he normally enjoyed here seemed to elude him. Finally, he slipped out of his shirt and into his running shoes. Mindless physical exercise would clear his head, drain his emotions, and banish that gorgeous blonde from his mind and body. He sprinted out the front door and ran laps around the perimeter of his 100-acre property until sweat trickled down his face and dripped off his chin, every muscle in his body screaming. At last, the driveway came into view and he slowed to a walk, rolling his shoulders and stretching his body. He raised a hand toward the front door, which swung open immediately. Usually, he didn't waste magic for his personal comfort, the cost was too high, but tonight…the devil be damned. He walked through the door, shut it firmly, and climbed the stairs to the master suite.

Stepping out of the shower, he felt renewed, relaxed, and ready to enjoy his time away from work. He toweled off, pulled on black silk lounge pants, and padded downstairs barefoot. Behind the bar, he poured a glass of red wine and carried it to his favorite recliner in front of the crackling fire. *This is more like it.* He sighed sipping the wine and reclining his chair completely to accommodate his six foot seven inch body. He leaned his head back and closed his eyes. *Damn it.* Angelique was back, dancing around the fringes of his mind. *What the hell was the deal? A woman never captivated my interest like this. Apparently, ignoring her wasn't going to be an option.*

He powered on the laptop that sat on the table to his right and moved it to his lap. For a moment his fingers paused over the keys, then typed Angelique Shandie in the search bar and hit enter. The screen filled with information. She'd graduated top in her class at Yale, a premed student with degrees in psychology and sociology. Accepted to Harvard Medical School and graduated with honors. She disappeared off the grid only to reappear a few years later in the residency program at John Hopkins. "What was a highly educated doctor doing as a co-owner of a New Age Store in D.C. of all places?" he mused aloud to the empty room. *Maybe it was a different Angelique Shandie.* He stifled a yawn and rubbed his eyes. *Further research could wait until tomorrow.* He yawned again, finished his wine, and trudged up the stairs to bed.

Warm sunlight streamed through ivory lace curtains that hung in large bay windows. Bruce rolled over and squinted against the brightness. Wound up in the patchwork comforter he'd crawled under the night before on his king size bed, he kicked his way free, and stretched his arms above his head as he let out a jaw-popping yawn. Sitting up he swung his feet to the floor and glanced at his cell phone on the nightstand. *No messages. Fantastic.*

His mother had decorated the house before giving it to him when she and his father relocated to Tahiti. Bruce never saw a reason to redecorate it, though it wasn't as masculine as he'd prefer. But since he rarely entertained guests here, the décor really didn't matter. Besides, he liked the homey look, feel, and scent of the rooms.

Foregoing a shirt, he pulled on jeans and riding boots. Truth be told, he liked the feel of the wind on his bare chest as he rode through the property, his shoulder length hair flying behind him. *Freedom*. That's what he liked, freedom from responsibility, and from the judgment of others for his behavior or attire. Not that he really cared one way or the other, but at least here, he could just be, pleasing no one but himself.

The aroma of fresh brewed coffee filled the house as he took the stairs two at a time, bouncing on the balls of his feet on the landing. He strode into the kitchen, surprised by the basket of huge blueberry muffins sitting on the counter. *Funny...I don't remember them being there last night.* Silently he thanked Megan, his housekeeper of many years, for her thoughtfulness. She'd served his parents and elected to stay on when they moved. He shrugged, grabbed a couple muffins, and poured a steaming mug of coffee. Glad he'd remembered to add water, a couple of scoops of Columbian, and set the coffee maker's timer last night. Rounding the breakfast bar, he reached out, snagged two apples from the fruit bowl, and pocketed them. He pushed the back door open as he took a big bite of muffin and ambled down the path to the stables. Further research on Angelique could wait.

"Morning, Jason." Bruce called out cheerfully, watching the tall, lanky stable manger stride toward him. Jason's bright red hair and brilliant blue eyes left no doubt of his Irish heritage. The freckles sprinkled across his face made him look younger than his forty something years. Bruce tossed the other muffin to Jason.

He stretched out a long arm and caught it in his large hand with little effort. "Thanks!" Jason grinned wide in appreciation. "And a good morning to you sir. Want me to saddle Satan for you?"

"Nope. Do it myself. Just go about your duties, as if I wasn't here. And drop the sir crap, when it's just you and me."

"You got it." Jason raised a bushy eyebrow, but turned back to mucking the empty stall.

Bruce strode into the tack room and threw a blanket over his shoulder, hauled his saddle from the rack, and grabbed a bridle. Satan snorted, pawing the ground with his hooves impatiently, flicking his ears back and forth.

"I'm coming, ol' boy," Bruce said with a smile.

A soft nicker came from the stall next to Satan's.

"Oh, I wouldn't forget you girl." Bruce leaned in and put his forehead against Harbor's cheek, as he drew an apple from his pocket and handed it to her. "You're free to join us," he said, unlocking her stall gate then walking to Satan's stall.

Harbor pushed the gate further open and followed

Bruce.

Satan stood obediently while Bruce settled the blanket and saddle on Satan's back, then checked the girth strap and adjusted the stirrups. He pulled another small apple from his pocket and offered it on his flat palm, while opening the paddock gate. He swung into the saddle and urged the horse into a trot with his heels, Harbor trailing close behind. *My own piece of paradise.* Contented, Bruce sighed, easing Satan into a canter down the path to the woods and twisted in the saddle to check that Harbor was still with them.

It was dusk before Bruce returned to the stables and handed the reins over to the waiting Jason. Bruce ran his hand over Satan's neck and patted his shoulder. "See ya in the morning, fella." He reached for Harbor and rubbed her cheek. "Good night, girl." Then Bruce turned to his stable manager. "Have a good evening Jason." Tired but happy, he trudged to the house, stretching his arms above his head and rolling his shoulders.

He toed his boots off and ambled across the hardwood kitchen floor to the frosty gray carpet of the family room. Bruce tossed several logs in the fireplace, with a flick of his wrist the dry wood burst into flames, then settled into a warm cozy fire. He descended the stairs to the wine cellar, pulled out several bottles before finally selecting a bottle of his favorite, a unique semi-sweet, light red, with raspberry overtones. A Colorado wine he favored. After opening the slightly chilled bottle and setting it on the table to breathe, he walked upstairs to shower. Feeling invigorated he returned to the kitchen, pulled out the meat and cheese from the fridge, and set them on the counter beside a loaf of home-made wheat bread. He sliced the bread, layered meat and cheese, mayo and spicy mustard, then put the sandwich on a plate.

Finally, settled in his recliner in front of the crackling fire, he poured the sparkling red liquid into a crystal glass, and sniffed appreciatively before taking a sip. *Ah, nothing better than an evening spent sipping my favorite wine by the fire and relaxing.* He bit into the sandwich and chewed slowly, idly wondering what Angelique was doing this evening. He shook his head, bemused at his fascination with her.

Chapter Four

Angie arrived at the store bright and early, unlocked the door, and flipped the sign to OPEN with flourish on her way to the backroom to prepare for the days business. Willow had the morning off, so it would be this afternoon before Angie could break away to deliver more flyers.

The front door chimed, and Angie emerged from the back room, rainbows danced on the walls as the crystal beaded curtain swung back into place.

"Mrs. Staret, how nice to see you. Did your daughter like the amethyst earrings you purchased for her birthday?"

Absently, Mrs. Staret nodded. "Oh, yes, yes she did. Willow called me yesterday and said my book on healing herbs had arrived."

Angie leaned down to look under the counter. There neatly wrapped was a book with Mrs. Staret's name on it. "Willow isn't in until this afternoon," she said, straightening up. "But I believe this is what you are looking for." Angie handed the package to her.

"Wonderful. Thanks so much." The impeccably dressed older woman paid for the book and continued to examine various items for sale in the display cases. She looked up at Angie and smiled, tucking a stray silver strand of hair back into her French bun. "I heard you created quite a stir the other day during your visit to the Wycked Hair."

"Now where did you hear such a thing?" Angie laughed, feeling the blood rush to her cheeks. "I dropped off flyers at the salon, but that's all." She turned away and placed the money in the cash drawer, glad to have a moment to compose herself.

"Not what my granddaughter said." Mrs. Staret shook her head. "No indeed. She said you flirted outrageously with the owner of that establishment." Clicking her tongue, she smiled knowingly. "He's a right handsome male, but dangerous. You watch yourself Angie. He's not one to be toyed with."

"Aw, Mrs. Staret, I'd never dream of doing such a thing. I was just having a bit of fun." Angie turned to face the woman and winked. "I'll keep your warning in mind, should I decide to visit the salon again."

Still considering Angie seriously over her half spectacles, Mrs. Staret lowered her voice to a whisper. "See that you do. Remember things are not always as they seem, young one. You may be a witch, but you're no match for the likes of him."

"What?" Angie sputtered. "Where'd you get the idea that…?"

"Oh, come now dear, I've seen this art practiced way too long not to recognize true magic when I see or feel it." She sighed and patted Angie's shoulder. "Your magic signature is very powerful. But don't worry, yours and Willow's secrets are safe with me. Though it may behoove you to disguise your magic signature a bit dear. If you don't want other creatures to know." She laughed quietly and turned her attention to the books on the shelf against the opposite wall.

The chimes rang out again, welcoming another

customer.

Huh, this town is full of surprises. Angie greeted the new customer, and then put the rest of the inventory away. She'd only met Mrs. Staret once when she sold her the earrings, but the woman had become one of Willow's best customers. Angie couldn't believe she'd failed to notice that the older woman was a witch.

****

Willow rushed in the door, cheeks rosy, eyes wide with excitement, and her short hair windswept, blue tips sticking out every which way. "Sorry I'm late. The cherry trees are in full bloom, and their fragrance is heavenly on the breeze. The sun is warm and it's way too nice out there to be in here working." She pirouetted across the floor stopping in front of Angie, her outstretched arms settling at her sides. Studying Angie for a moment she inquired, "What's wrong?"

"Your customer, Mrs. Staret, was just in."

Willow's forehead creased. "Oh, dear wasn't it the right book?"

"Nothing like that, it was her intuition that surprised me. I didn't know she was a witch."

Willow chortled. "She's not. Her husband, Paul, who served in the House of Representatives, was a warlock with substantial powers, so she claims. He passed a few months back, she misses him something fierce." Sighing, sadness crossed her ice blue eyes as she looked at Angie. "They were married for over fifty years. Her daughter and granddaughter inherited the magic and belong to a coven in Arlington, I believe. What made you think she was a witch? "

"Her observations that I was a witch and you had a secret. There is no doubt in my mind she knows you're a faery."

Willow's eyes rounded, and she blew out a breath. "Mrs. Staret came right out and said that?"

"Well, no, what she said was our secrets remain safe with her, but she acknowledged that I was a witch and in her opinion, no match for Bruce."

"Wow." Willow paused tapping her foot on the hardwood floor. "What brought him into the conversation? See, I told you he would be nothing but trouble."

"Apparently, Mrs. Staret's granddaughter was having her nails done at the Wycked Hair when I went in the first time." Angie rolled her eyes and pursed her lips, glancing at Willow, then at the floor. "Of all the luck."

"You didn't expect to go unnoticed did you? Especially not with your ability to create a scene with very little provocation," Willow said.

"It wasn't like that. I just walked in, searched for the manager, felt eyes watching me from above, took a quick peek and this gorgeous male stood staring down at me." She shrugged one shoulder nonchalantly and flipped her hair back. "So I blew him a kiss in fun and then asked Owen about distributing the flyers to customers in the salon. It was all very innocent."

"Oh, and I forgot your gift for understatement." Willows eyes sparkled in amusement.

Standing with her hands fisted on her hips, violet eyes flashing, Angie warned, "Don't go there. I left my brother's home in Maine because he kept riding my ass."

"With good reason. He was just trying to watch out for you, like he has since your parents died."

"I'm thirty-two and well able to take care of myself," Angie said, in a raised voice.

Arching her brow and glaring at Angie, Willow shot back, "If that was the case, we wouldn't be having this conversation. I'm not the one who created a scene in one of our neighbor's establishments almost before The Krystal Unicorn's doors opened for business. Nor was it I,"—she pointed her thumb at her chest—"who attracted the attention of the most powerful demon in the Western Hemisphere and Territory Overlord. Now was it?"

Angie sucked in a breath and let it whoosh out. "He's a what? So you did do some checking?"

"Well, I couldn't let you go chasing the first good looking hunk in D.C. who attracted your attention without checking him out. He's a bad one, Angie, and your brother would absolutely not approve."

"My brother never approves any of the men I date."

"Gee, I wonder why. Well in this case, you need to think very seriously about what you're doing. Don't mess with him, Angie. He's trouble, and he'll break your heart at the very least. I don't want to think about the worst."

"Ok, enough, I get it." Angie held one hand out in front of her. "You are not my keeper."

"No. I'm not. But I've been your best friend for most of your thirty-two years and now your business partner. Ange, I don't want to lose you."

Taken back by the sincere fear in her friend's voice, Angie said soothingly, "You won't. I'll stay away from him. Ok?"

Willow shifted in her chair so she could look Angie

straight in the eyes. "Promise?" There'd never been a promise broken between them. Would this be the first? Willow wondered.

"Yes," Angie said and added under her breath. F*or now*.

Willow shoved her toward the door. "Now get out there and enjoy this wonderful day. See ya tomorrow. Stay away from the Wycked Hair. I'll deliver more flyers to the salon on my way home today."

"Thanks, I think." Angie grabbed her sweater from the coat rack behind the door and walked out into the sun-drenched afternoon, inhaling deeply the fragrant cherry blossoms. The Wycked Hair was to her right and the boring rest of the world to her left. She turned left, strolled down the street, and crossed over to the park. She'd come back for her car later.

Chapter Five

Stacks of paperwork awaited Bruce as he breezed through the door of his office. The price he paid for a few days off. Resigned to the tasks at hand, he spent the entire day at his desk playing catch up. The time off was invigorating, after accepting the fact that Angie was just going to be a factor in his life. Rather than let it ruin his time off, he attempted to tuck her in the corner of his mind for later consideration, with less success than he'd hoped.

He shifted in his chair, fighting a feeling that drew him to the window. Finally, he stood and stretched his arms above his head, letting them fall to his sides, then shook the wrinkles from his tailored navy blue pants and sauntered over to gaze out the window. Across the street toward the park, light pink petals of cherry blossoms floated on the breeze. Spring could be a wonderful time in the city and then again, it could be deadly.

He switched his position and looked down the street to The Krystal Unicorn. Angie crossed the street from the park and was walking toward what he assumed was her car in the parking lot. If he left now he could surprise her at the car, as she had him the other night, though she hadn't made an actual appearance. He could mask his magical signature enough that she wouldn't sense him until he was beside her. Two could play this little game of cat and mouse. While his brain told him this was not a good idea, every fiber of his physical being was urging him on.

****

She reached out just as his hand covered hers, pulling on the handle to open the door. Spinning around, hand fisted and arm poised to punch, she found him grinning behind her. "W—What," she stammered as she stood gaping at him.

Reflexes faster than hers, he caught her delicate fist in his large hand. "Good evening, Ms. Shandie. How are you this fine evening?" His lips twitched in amusement, and the grin turned into a self-satisfied smile as he released her hand.

She gulped in air while her heart thundered in her chest. "I'm fine though you just scared ten years off my life. Where did you come from?" Her eyes narrowed scanning the area. "Were you spying on me?" Hands fisted at her sides, she waited for an answer.

He leaned into her, nostrils flared drawing in her scent, a mix of floral with a hint of citrus, very pleasant. Before he took a nibble, she got his attention with a firm strike to his solar plexus.

"Is there something I can do for you Mr...?" She hesitated, realizing that she didn't know his last name.

Grabbing her fist again, as he bent from the waist and wheezed, "It's Bruce, no Mr., just Bruce." He caught his breath, straightened to his full height and stared down at her. "Since you're asking, there is something you can do for me. Join me for a latte at the coffee shop around the corner. It's the least you can do, after attacking me for no reason."

"No reason," she squeaked. "I'm not the one who

came out of nowhere and scared the bejeebers out of me."

"The bejeebers. Huh." He bit back a grin.

"Yes, that's right," she said seriously while considering the ramifications of being seen with him by Willow or Mrs. Staret. Angie decided there was little chance of either one being out and about now. *What harm could it do in a safe public place?* She really wanted to get to know the man she seemed so drawn to against her better judgment. "I shouldn't. Everyone I've met recently has warned me about you. Besides, I really don't care for coffee."

Bruce quirked an eyebrow and said, "You don't have to drink coffee. There are lots of other beverages available. There is nothing wrong with a couple of people discussing business over a drink in a busy public place. Is there?"

She hesitated and looked around again. "No, I guess not. Business?"

****

"Yes." He took her hand, tucked it through his bent elbow, and guided her to the coffee shop. Just being near and her touch ignited something inside him. A female of any species never had this effect on him, and he'd experienced a wide range of female companions over the centuries. Puzzled, yet intrigued by this ability of hers, he decided it definitely would require he spend more time with her, something Owen would not approve of. For that matter, he was sure Tristian would do more than disapprove, if he found out. So, they'd have to keep an extremely low profile.

Away from the foot traffic, he led her to a table in the far corner and pulled out her chair. She looked surprised and pleased taking her seat primly while continuing to scan the area for familiar faces.

"What is your pleasure?"

"A hot chocolate with lots of whip cream."

"Your wish is my command." He bowed deeply and took her hand brushing his lips over it softly, and then gently laying it back on the table. "I'll be right back."

****

At his touch, a jolt of desire shot through her, which left her, trembling inside. She brushed her hair from her face and smiled, hoping he wouldn't notice how off balance she felt when he was around. He made her feel special and very female; she liked that, maybe too much. Not that the rest of him was bad either, tall and confident with chiseled facial features that should belong to a model, and gorgeous shoulder length hair, chestnut with just enough highlights to look kissed by the sun. She'd love to run her fingers through that hair. But, he was off limits, she reminded herself as a little voice in her head wondered. *Well, what could it hurt to just...*

"Hello Angie, are you waiting for someone?" Mrs. Staret asked, looking over her half-spectacles at Angie.

Caught up in her own thoughts, Angie startled. "Oh, hi there, Mrs. Staret. No, uh, a business associate of mine is getting our drinks. Are you here by yourself?"

"No just passing by, I'm having dinner up the street with my daughter and son-in-law. I saw you sitting alone and thought maybe you'd like..." She glanced up at the counter and back to Angie, Mrs. Staret's pale blue eyes narrowed in disapproval. "Heed my warning young one." She turned sharply to leave, nearly colliding with Bruce.

"What a pleasant surprise, Mrs. Staret. I was so sorry to hear of Paul's passing, please accept my condolences. If there is anything I can do?"

"Thank you, Bruce. I'm sure you've done enough," she said icily.

Ignoring her sharp tone, he continued. "Would you care to join Ms. Shandie and me, we were discussing business strategies and maybe a revamp of her flyer. Have you seen it?"

"Yes, yes I have and thought it was quite appealing."

"True, but a discount coupon or offer of a free gift, might add more interest, don't you think?"

"Perhaps. I have to go, I've a dinner engagement." She nodded curtly to Bruce and shot a warning glance in Angie's direction before hurrying up the street.

Angie rolled her eyes and looked skyward. "Oh, great. Just what I need, now the whole magic community will know I was seen alone with you."

"Oh come now, that's not such a bad thing. I am a successful businessman just helping a new proprietor. Relax." He sat the drinks down on the table in front of them, patted her hand reassuringly, and eased into his chair.

"What did she mean, you did enough?"

"I'm not quite sure. She's very bitter over her husband Paul's death, seems she thinks it could have been avoided. He led a double life, one as a legislator, the other undercover—a dangerous life."

"How? What happened to him?"

"Those are questions you'd have to ask her. Now

let's enjoy what's left of our evening. Tell me about yourself and what brought you here." He smiled and leaned toward her to catch every word.

She considered pushing the issue, but the determined look on his face, decided against it. Maybe another time, after she'd had a chance to gather more information. "It was time to get a life of my own." Angie paused and felt a twinge of guilt. "No that's not exactly right. My brother raised me after our parents died. Made sure I attended the best colleges for his career plans for me. In fact, he controlled every aspect of my life. He claimed it was too dangerous for me to be out on my own. The final straw came six months ago. Tristian left on business, and I moved out without telling him where I was going." Angie paused. *What am I doing telling a stranger my whole life story? Especially him.*

Bruce frowned. "That was a little harsh. Don't you think? He is all you have, right?"

"Yes, but I called him a week later and told him, that Willow and I had decided to start a business in D.C., and would check in from time to time. He wasn't happy, but there wasn't much he could do about it."

"Willow?" Bruce asked his brow arched.

"Oh, we grew up together. She is my best friend and always the cautious one. My brother thought I was wild. So he feels better she is here to watch out for me."

"Now, how about you? What brought you here?" Angie leaned her chin on her hand and gazed up at him from under long golden lashes.

****

He craved to reach out and put his hand over hers, caress her soft skin, but thought better of it. It would only fuel the fire inside him that burned out of control, when he was close to her. He didn't want to let her go, he wanted to continue seeing her, but knew it was a bad idea for all the reasons Owen stated. "I've owned The Wyked Hair for several years. Owen manages the salon for me along with his wife, Tobi, whom you enjoyed irritating during your second visit." A chuckle rumbled deep in his chest. "She was ready to shred your face, until Owen explained it was me you found intriguing. She's a possessive little creature."

Lips forming a pout, Angie cooed, "I never said I had designs on anyone, you were available and attentive. Owen's reaction was an inadvertent benefit."

"You really need to be careful. Things are not always as they seem in this city, and you could find yourself in a dangerous situation," Bruce said.

"You sound like my brother." Angie blew out a breath and rolled her eyes. "Always doom and gloom. Now back to you, do you have family?"

"No." This was a discussion he wasn't ready to have with her, probably never would. "It's getting late Angie. May I walk you back to your car?"

Surprised at his sudden icy tone, she remained seated and continued to watch him, deciding she'd touched on a sensitive subject.

Bruce stood, placed the empty cups on the tray, and took it over to the trash, returning to stand behind her chair. Apparently, as far as he was concerned the evening was over.

"Was it something I said?" she asked jokingly, feeling more uncomfortable by the minute.

"No, not at all. It's just that I still have work to finish up and an early morning tomorrow." Continuing to see her would be a mistake he should end it tonight. But he wasn't going to, after spending the evening with her, he was more attracted to her than ever and not just her beautiful body, it was more. "Is there a cell phone or number I could reach you directly?"

"Yes. If you'll give me yours?" She smiled mischievously, batting her long lashes.

Raising a brow questioningly, he smiled and jotted his personal cell number on the back of his business card, as he watched her out of the corner of his eye doing the same. He curved his arm and started to reach for her hand, but she had already slid it through the crook of his arm and intertwined their fingers. That quick jolt of intimate awareness was back and none too welcome.

****

Arriving at the salon an hour before dawn, Bruce climbed the stairs to his office to find the door open just as the desk light flicked on. He stepped silently through the doorway and let out a breath in relief. "Owen what the hell are you doing here on your morning off?"

Owen's eyes blazed as he swung around to face Bruce. "Just couldn't control yourself? Wouldn't listen to me? Now look at this." He flung a photograph toward the desk. It fluttered in the air and came to rest on the glass top.

Flipping on the main light switch, Bruce walked over and calmly picked up the picture. Apparently, someone took the photograph last night as he and Angie walked back to her car. "So I had coffee with a business associate. We discussed her new endeavor and I escorted her back to her car. What's the problem?"

Owen snarled and pointed to the picture. "Last time

I went out with a business associate, we didn't hold hands, or stroll close together. What do you think Tristian is going to do when he sees this picture? There'll be bloodshed and it'll be yours."

"I don't really care what Tristian thinks. Like I indicated before, there is nothing going on," he said curtly. We had a business discussion and I walked her back to the car, she was chilled, so I drew her in close. If Tristian wants to call me out on it, I'll tell him the same. Though, I usually don't explain my actions to anyone, much less employees." He narrowed his eyes and glared at Owen. "By the way, who took this picture?"

"I don't know. It was taped to the front door." Owen snorted loudly. "To discuss your supposed business meeting."

Chapter Six

As Tchaikovsky's 1812 Overture rose to a crescendo, Angie sat upright in bed, slapping the snooze button on her alarm. She cursed her brother even as she fondly remembered the day he'd given her the alarm. Her love of classical music motivated the gift, but she wondered now if it had actually diminished her love of that particular overture, once her very favorite. She placed the clock far enough away on the nightstand that she had to sit up to turn it off. A deep sleeper, she many a time slept through the alarm or hit snooze never really being awake, and had been late for school or work. That was unacceptable now that she was a business owner.

Sleepily she padded barefoot into the bathroom and turned on the shower. Cool water splashed on her face and streamed down her naked body as she reached for the soap. She felt better already. She hopped out of the shower and dried off.

Sitting on the edge of her bed, she wiggled into tight blue jeans, pulled on over-the-knee black leather boots, and layered a soft burgundy V-neck sweater over her favorite pink lace tank top. Springtime mornings in DC still held a chill. Resting her hand on the hope chest that her parents had given her on her tenth birthday, she shoved herself upright. A little sigh escaped her lips as she thought of the wonderful time she'd had last night.

The healer talent she inherited allowed her to feel Bruce's strength, but unexpected was a deep sadness and loneliness. She sensed none of the pure evil that everyone warned her about in him. Demon he may be, but he wasn't what she expected or what others claimed. She realized that exercising the power necessary to become and remain Territory Overlord, he'd probably done heinous things. She sighed again, *Oh hell, who am I kidding, the danger was a turn on.* But something more drew her to him and until she discovered what it was, no one would dissuade her from seeing him. She'd just have to figure out how to skirt the promise she'd made to Willow, no one else really mattered.

Sneaking around wasn't something she wanted to do. Any relationship with Bruce needed to be up front and honest from the beginning. The thought of exploring that possibility left her breathless and her pulse racing. Regarding her brother, that was a different matter, he wouldn't approve, but she'd cross that bridge later.

Angie strolled into the kitchen and found Willow sitting at the table with a cup of steaming hot chocolate. "Is there more where that came from?" Angie asked, inhaling deeply of the warm chocolate aroma that wafted through the room, a smile turning up the corners of her mouth.

"Good morning to you too, and yes, over on the stove." Willow grinned as her best friend reached into the cupboard pulling out a large mug with 'I Think I'm Allergic to Morning' emblazed across the cup in bright red letters. "You were out late last night. Did you have a good time?"

Angie poured the hot chocolate into the mug, added a dollop of whipped cream, and settled into the seat across the table from Willow. "I did."

"Not going to tell me about it, huh?" Willow gave her a sideways glance.

"Just had coffee with a business associate." Angie shrugged, her hands wrapped around the warm mug. "That's all, nothing to tell."

"Oh, really?" Willow eyed her suspiciously. "You don't like coffee. Someone I know?"

"No, not really. I'll introduce you soon." Angie waved her hand in a dismissive gesture, then lowered her eyes to the mug as she reached for a spoon and stirred the whipped cream into the smooth dark liquid.

Willow sipped her hot chocolate and frowned but said nothing more.

Holding her steaming mug in one hand, Angie stood and turned to Willow. "I've got to go. Enjoy your day off." Angie looked closely at her friend and seeing the concern, smiled, brushing her other hand over Willow's spiked hair affectionately. "Don't worry about me, I heard your warning. See you tonight." She stepped toward the door then paused. "How about we have a girl's night in tonight, movie, popcorn, and some of that decadent chocolate fudge ice cream in the fridge?" She walked through the doorway then spun around grinning mischievously. "Unless you got a hot date."

Willow sighed and looked up at her friend. "No hot date." Hesitantly, she smiled. "But I'm working on it." With that, she got up, washed her cup in the sink, dried, and returned it to the shelf. "See ya tonight." Willow said over her shoulder and left the kitchen.

****

Over the next few weeks, The Krystal Unicorn saw a flurry of new and return customers. The sustained business allowed them to add a part-time clerk to work Saturdays and fill in when needed. Autumn was a young witch from an old political family looking to break with tradition and find her own place in the world. From Angie and Willow's point of view, Autumn was perfect for the job, bubbly personality, dependable, and well connected in the community.

Angie stood at the store window, flipped the OPEN sign to CLOSED, moved to the door and held it open for Autumn. "Good Night, thanks for your help today, see you next week." Angie locked the door behind her. Leaning back against the door, Angie let out a heavy sigh. "Wow, what a week. Those redesigned flyers brought in lots of new customers."

Willow smirked and conceded. "Ok, so your mysterious business associate might know a thing or two."

"Hey, I created the flyer. Don't I get some credit? Not to mention I haven't had a day off in two weeks."

"Sure you do and deserve a day off to boot. So take Sunday off, we're closed anyway. I'll come in, do inventory, then order the items we are out of. Fair enough?"

"Sounds good to me. Now get out of here, I'll close up." Angie gave her friend a little shove.

A loud rap on the window made both women jump. A tall young man with sandy blonde hair and large dark eyes stood at the window smiling at Willow.

"Who's the handsome guy?" Angie wanted to know.

"My date." Willow said airily, grabbing her coat and pushing past Angie, who unlocked the door.

"Hey, aren't you going to introduce us?" Angie grabbed Willow's arm before she could escape out the door.

"Nope." Willows eyes sparkled with mischief. "Not until you introduce me to your mysterious business associate." She smirked, wrenched her arm free, and flounced out the door.

I don't think you want to know who that would be. Angie shut and locked the door again then slumped down in the nearby chair. She'd not heard a thing from Bruce since they went for coffee that night. Maybe he wasn't as attracted to her as she had thought. There was only one way to find out she decided and pulled out his business card. She reached for her cell phone and dialed the number written on the back of his card. It rang several times.

****

"Good Evening Angelique, how are you?" His deep, smooth voice flowed seductively through the phone.

"I'm fine, what ya doing?"

"Just finishing up some paperwork that I have ignored all day."

"So you're still at the office?"

"Yes."

"How about we grab a bite to eat, I'm just closing up the shop, and can be there in a few minutes."

He paused, blowing out a breath and running his fingers through his hair. "I don't think that's a good idea. I enjoyed your company the other night, but there are things about me that will cause problems and could actually put your life in danger."

"Geez, you sound like my brother. I'll tell you the same thing I tell him. I'm a big girl, make my own decisions, and can take care of myself. Now how about that meal?"

"No. I'm sorry, I can't." He clenched his fingers into a fist on his desk.

"Why, because you are looking out for my best interests, even though you are attracted to me?"

"Something like that. Now there is nothing more to say. I'm sorry if I hurt you, but believe me it's better this way." He disconnected the call and threw the cell against the wall, watching it shatter into a million pieces and scatter all over the polished floor. He stood and swept the remaining paperwork off his desk and watched it flutter to the ground. Slamming his fist on the top of the desk, he shoved away and paced back and forth across the room. Feeling like the room was closing in, he strode to the door and yanked it open, coming face to face with Angie, her mouth set in a thin line, cheeks red with fury.

"How did you get in here?" He demanded blocking her way into the office.

"Through the door downstairs," she said airily.

"That's not possible. I locked and dead bolted it myself."

"Well either your locks are bad or your memory is. One wave of my hand and I was in. Now…we have things to discuss. You don't brush me off like a piece of lint on that expensive suit of yours."

Being a petite woman, Angie swiftly turned sideways and slid under his arm deliberately brushing her body against his. He spun around and grabbed her arm preventing her from continuing into the room. She raised her other hand in a quick, sharp flick, an unseen force sent Bruce sprawling against the white leather sofa, shoving it hard against the wall.

"I don't like to be manhandled." Indignantly, she straightened her sweater then glanced around. "Geez looks like a tornado hit your office." Angie sauntered across the room, careful not to step on the papers scattered around the floor. She sat in one of the sleek navy blue leather chairs facing the desk, crossed her legs, and rested her arms on the chair. She swiveled the chair around to face him, the corners of her mouth curved up in a sweet smile. "Won't you join me over here and we can have that discussion?"

Bruce bounded off the sofa prepared to retaliate, his normally soft dark amber eyes turned hard with bright orange whirling through the amber. *Get a grip man. This is no way to treat a beautiful woman. Especially one that has those kinds of powers and isn't afraid to use them, you'll only escalate the situation.* He stopped, took a deep breath, and he stood for a moment as if counting to ten, then strode by her, rounded his desk, lowered himself into the leather chair, and glared at her. "There is nothing to discuss," he said flatly,

"Oh, that's where you're wrong." Her eyes caught sight of a picture on the corner of his desk. "Then why do you have a picture of us?" She cocked her head to get a better look. "Lying on the corner of your desk." She reached across and snatched the picture.

"That's just one of the reasons this won't work," he said, voice void of all emotion.

"Why? What does that picture have to do with anything? I think it's quite good of both of us, and the background lights are spectacular."

"Yes, but your brother won't be thrilled."

"Who I see is my own business. He has nothing to do with this."

Bruce leaned back in his chair, closed his eyes, then ran his fingers through his hair to the nap of his neck, rubbing at the knotted muscles. "Ok, I guess we'll have to do this the hard way." He straightened and turned his cold piercing eyes on her. "You know what I am?"

A chill prickled down her back, she shook it off, put her game face on, and said smugly, "Yes, I did a little digging, appears you are a powerful demon, the Overlord for the Western Hemisphere, if I'm not mistaken."

"Then that makes two of us, my informants tell me you are Tristian Shandie's little sister. A powerful witch, as you demonstrated. Tristian is a long time trusted business associate of mine and I don't want to cause problems by dating his little sister."

"Why? What does it matter? He doesn't like any of the men I date anyway. What makes you so special?" She smiled coyly and looked up at him from under her long blonde lashes. "He wouldn't have to know," she paused, "at least right away."

"You're not going to make this easy. Are you?"

"No. It appears the big bad demon is afraid to tell a little ol' witch what the real problem is."

Bruce shoved up, nearly knocking over his chair, then stalked to the window and stared out, hands behind his back. "I didn't want you to hear this from me. My associates tell me that Tristian went to great lengths to keep what he does for a living from you. But it appears you are determined to enter our world."

He returned to stand in front of his chair leaned over the desk his face inches from hers and said, "The choice is yours. You can either call your brother and talk with him, or learn the truth from me." He shoved the telephone console across the desk toward her. "Be forewarned, he will be furious when he finds out I've told you. Still we can't explore a relationship, no matter how much that might please us, until you understand the situation." He paused. "Now, which will it be?" Tristian is on speed dial, just tap #2," he said.

****

Shocked at his cold demeanor, she sat silent, running over in her mind other alternatives or explanations. *What did her brother do that was so horrible he'd felt it necessary to keep from her? Their world? What the hell did he mean by that?*

"Well?" Bruce drummed his fingers impatiently on the glass desktop. His piercing eyes staring at her relentlessly.

The person sitting in front of her was certainly not the man she'd flirted outrageously with at the salon, nor the proper gentleman she'd accompanied to the coffee shop. *Had Willow and Mrs. Staret been right*? "I need time to make that decision." She shoved the phone back at him and got shakily to her feet, hoping he didn't notice. "I'll let you know." She took a deep breath and strode determinedly out of his office, without a backward glance.

****

He relaxed against the chair closing his eyes, something was breaking apart inside him, but he'd done what was best for both of them. Positive she wouldn't return he was surprised at the feeling of loss filling his chest. God, he'd only known her a few weeks. What was wrong with him? Whatever it was, he had to get it under control.

Chapter Seven

Fingers of fiery orange and red fanned across the bright blue sky as the sun peeked over the treetops. At the kitchen table Angie sat, head propped in her hands, replaying her conversation with Bruce. She wondered what services Tristian preformed for Bruce, and how to find out without alienating one or both. Most of the night, she tossed and turned, considering her options and didn't like any of them. A slight breeze from an open window brushed across Angie's face as Willow slid, face beaming, into the seat across the table from Angie.

Willow took a good look at her friend and asked, "You look like you've lost your best friend. What's up?"

"Oh, nothing." Angie smiled at her best friend. "Look at you, you are absolutely radiant. Tell me all about last night. Was he wonderful?"

"Oh, yes, he is fantastic, in more ways than one," she said grinning, red patches blooming on her cheeks. "We're going out again this evening. Would you mind closing up tonight?" Willow asked, getting up to fill the kettle with water and sat it on the stove. She reached up into the cupboard and got out two mugs.

"Sure. I am so happy for you. Now, when do I get to meet him?"

"How about you bring your man of mystery and

we'll have dinner together on Saturday night?" Willow set the mugs on the table. "What kind of tea do you want?"

Angie peered into the tin of tea bags on the table and selected the spiced orange tea. "I'm afraid that's impossible." Her brave façade slid away and she turned her glistening eyes on her friend. The feelings she'd kept walled up all night threatened to burst. She viciously willed the tears away, but one trickled down her cheek.

Willow immediately was at Angie's side, arm wrapped around her shoulders. "What happened? Did he hurt you?"

"Oh, it's a mess and I don't know which way to turn. You warned me, but I didn't listen."

Willow put her hands on her friend's shoulders and pushed her away to get a good look at her. "What have you done? It's Bruce, isn't it?"

"Well, not exactly. He's the one I met at the coffee shop and that night he was so kind and proper. We had a wonderful time, I felt a connection to him I've never felt with anyone. Last night when I went to talk to him, he was someone completely different, cold, and distant. He cares about me. I can feel it and he had a picture of the two of us on the corner of his desk."

"Demons are like that. I told you they are not to be trusted. Wait a minute. You had a picture taken of the two of you?" Willow asked her eyes rounding in surprise.

"No, it was lying on his desk. I didn't get a chance to ask where he got it. Apparently, someone took it when he walked me back to my car from the coffee shop."

"Oh, Angie," Willow said with a sigh, then jumped up to take the whistling teakettle from the stove.

"The problem is that Tristian is a business associate and that whatever he does for Bruce is something that my brother has deliberately kept from me. Then Bruce said something about me being determined to join their world? How crazy is that?" Angie asked.

Willow shook her head and sighed again. "Oh, honey, it's not crazy at all. You need to have a heart to heart conversation with your brother." She poured the steaming water into the mugs and returned the kettle to the trivet in the middle of the table.

"No way, somehow that would involve Bruce, and then I'll never get to investigate this connection I feel when I'm with him." Angie narrowed her eyes. "What do you know Willow? Spill it," she demanded, dipping her tea bag savagely in and out of her mug.

"Not enough to keep you safe and too much to tell you. Call your brother," Willow said stubbornly, arms crossed over her chest.

"No. Bruce said he'd tell me, but indicated that if Tristian found out, he would be furious and no telling what he'd do."

"Bruce is right. Can't you just leave it be? There's lots of other good looking and powerful males in this city. Besides how do you know what Bruce feels, he's probably just playing you." Willow stirred a little sugar into her mug and took a sip of the green tea.

"He's not, I can feel it. I want a chance with him, but first I have to talk to Tristian. There's the caveat, I can't talk to Tristian because he'll demand to know how I found out. Which will lead right back to Bruce.

Help me, Willow. Tell me what you know. Please."

"He's a demon, Angie, pure evil, don't you get it? No matter how good looking he is or how chivalrous he can be, he's evil." Willow took another sip of her tea wishing she'd opted for Irish coffee instead. This conversation wasn't headed anywhere good.

"He's not pure evil. Trust me on this." She gripped her friend's forearms and gave her a little shake. "Help me. That's what friends do, remember?"

"Ok, here's the deal. I'll tell you part of it, so you'll know Bruce is telling the truth. The rest you'll have to get from Bruce or Tristian. And there will be dire consequences when Tristian finds out about our treachery, which could be deadly for all of us." Willow shook her head and solemnly began. "Tristian is an enforcer. I imagine Bruce employees him to handle the demons or dark ones that don't abide by the rules of their world and endanger the humans living in this one." Willow took her hand. "Remember when mom told you never to use magic around mortals? It was forbidden."

Angie nodded her head. "My mom told me the same thing, before she died. But your mom was emphatic about the dangers and lectured me repeatedly.

Sadness reflected in Willow's eyes. "That's probably because your mom thought she had time to influence your behavior."

"So what does that have to do with Bruce and me?"

"He is the judge and jury when magical creatures break the rules in his territory. You are not allowed to use mortals for monetary gain. Magic creatures cannot hold an elective office procured by magic in the mortal world. A magical being can't do anything that would draw attention to itself or other magic creatures in the mortal world, There are more rules, but those are the biggies."

"Wow," Angie murmured.

"As you can tell, some of the rules are ambiguous, Bruce decides whether a law was broken and how severe the punishment. The mortals are happy to believe magic and monsters are things of nightmares and fairytales. We are expected to maintain that status quo. Can you imagine what would happen if mortals found out otherwise? Chaos would rein." At an end of her tirade, Willow fell back against the chair and blew out a breath. "And that's only the beginning."

Angie sat upright and considered the implications. "What do you mean? How do you know all this, and why wasn't I told?"

"As faeries we don't get involved in the two worlds, we live in this one and let the others take care of their own. My mother told me of the two worlds, because of my friendship with you and your family. After your parents died, mom tried to help with your magic education, but Tristian was adamant you never know and swore my family to secrecy. He promised when the time was right, he'd tell you. Obviously, he didn't keep his promise."

"Why would he do that? He's a warlock with magic of his own."

Willow shrugged. "I guess that was his way of protecting you. When you went off to college and medical school, he felt justified in his decision to set you up in the mortal world. Now it's backfired on him because you've fallen for a demon and not just an ordinary demon." Willow waved her arms in the air.

"Oh, no not you. You fell for one of the most powerful demons in the world and if that's not bad enough, one that employs your brother. See the problem?" Willow finished with a hiss.

"Clearly." Angie sat there shell-shocked. *Maybe everyone was right. I should just walk away.*

****

Owen shoved open the door that was rarely closed and stepped inside. "Morning boss, how's it going?"

Bruce raised his head and glared over his laptop at Owen. "Hello, Owen, what can I do for you?" he asked, his voice curt.

Owen stood behind one of the chairs in front of Bruce's desk, his hands resting on the chair back. "Oh, nothing, just checking to see if you were still alive up here. Haven't seen you on the floor for over two weeks. You didn't even do a cursory round while Tobi and I were off yesterday. The employees are worried that something is brewing, if you know what I mean." Owen said, with a raised brow.

"I've been busy. Sorry. Everything is fine. Tell them there's nothing to worry about, unless they have picked up something from our clientele." He turned his attention back to his computer screen, letting Owen know the conversation was at an end and he was free to go.

Owen deliberately moved from behind the chair and sat down, a booted foot resting on his knee. "Ok, let me put it another way, I'm not leaving until you tell me what's going on?" He settled into the chair and flipped through a magazine he'd snagged off the table as he entered the office.

Looking up again his brows raised, Bruce's amber

eyes tinged with orange. "Excuse me, what did you say?" He closed the laptop and turned his undivided attention to Owen,

"You heard me and I'm not putting up with this bullshit anymore. Although, I must say it is nice to have all the supplies replenished in a timely manner and the invoices approved before the due date." Owen ducked and caught the cup that Bruce hurled at him without spilling a drop of coffee, setting it lightly down on the desktop. Owen rose. "Come on let's go down on the floor, reassure the troops, and take a walk outside. You can't sit up here and brood. Either take action or walk away."

"It's not my action to take. I gave her a choice and I've heard nothing." He glowered at Owen. "And I don't brood."

"Then it's time to move on. We are talking about Ms. Shandie?"

"Yes, we are and it's not that easy. She knows who and what I am, and she didn't even blink an eye." Bruce shoved away from the desk. "I told her Tristian worked for me and that if she needed to know more she should ask him. Since I've not heard from him, I assume she hasn't talked with her brother. The other alternative I gave her was that I'd tell her, but that there'd be hell to pay if Tristian ever found out and he would."

"Oh, good job, you're going to have your own assassin looking to take you out. Nice!" Owen said.

Bruce got to his feet and walked to the door, with his foot he flipped the doorstop down propping it open. "Let's walk the floor and ease the nerves of the staff. I could use some fresh air. You're free to join me, but keep your mouth shut. I don't need advice, I need to clear my head and think."

"Ok by me, boss." Owen said.

They spent an hour walking the floor of the salon, visiting with staff and customers. With a friendly wave, Bruce walked out the door and turned down the sidewalk toward The Krystal Unicorn.

Bruce gave only a fleeting glance at the glass door of Angie's store as they passed and sprinted across the street into the park. The cherry trees were in full bloom, and their sweet fragrance filled the air.

Bruce stopped and leaned against a gnarled tree looking skyward. Heaving a sigh, he closed his eyes and waved Owen on. "I'll catch up with you in a minute."

It was quite some time before he joined Owen again. Something had changed. A spring in his step and lips curved in a smile, Bruce said, "If she comes to me again, I won't turn her away. We'll just have to face Tristian when the time comes and hope it is a long time coming. Did you find out who took that picture?"

"No. I didn't try. Customers mentioned seeing the two of you that night, but I merely explained it away as a business meeting. Some raised their eyebrows at that, most just nodded when I handed them a flyer. You know how the clientele loves to talk about your conquests. If you intend to pursue a relationship with her, out in the open, then we'll have to come up with another plan."

"Why do we need a plan? My personal life is just that, mine."

"That would be fine, if you hadn't gone to bed with nearly every woman that you found attractive and if you didn't hold the position you do."

"Oh, come on Owen that's business as usual in D.C."

Owen's eyes widened and his brows rose nearly to his brow line then he continued. "At one time, the staff, as well as, the clientele took wagers on whom and when. Granted you've toned it down quite a bit, but once you and Angelique are together frequently, people will notice and talk. It won't take long for Tristian to get wind of it, which I assume you want to avoid for as long as possible. Then all hell will break loose, literally."

"We'll be discreet, but I won't sneak around looking over my shoulder. She deserves better than that. Besides, this may all be a moot point, since I've not heard from her and I won't force her hand." He glanced toward the darkening sky and watched the wind whip the petals of the cherry blossoms. "Let's head back. We both have work to do." He clasped Owen on the shoulder. "Thanks."

Owen smiled wide. "You got it, anytime."

Returning to his office, Bruce reached for his new cell phone lying on the desk. When he checked the phone log and messages, there was one call from Angie, but she didn't leave a message. He swore. Deciding to wait until she called again, Bruce stuffed the phone in his pocket to make damn sure it was with him.

It was late evening when he turned off his laptop and called it a night. He locked up the salon and sprinted across the parking lot. The silence inside his car was refreshing. He savored it for a few moments before starting the engine and heading home. A glass of vintage wine and his lounge chair in front of a blazing fire sounded like a piece of heaven. Just has he was about to turn onto the highway, his phone lit up and chimed on the seat beside him, it was the ring tone he'd set for Angie. "What a pleasant surprise, I've missed you."

"Me too. We need to talk, somewhere private and it could take a while," she said.

"I'm headed home. It's just West of Falls Church in Virginia. How about I turn around, pick you up, and take you with me. I've my heart set on a nice quiet evening, a glass of wine, a comfortable chair in front of a roaring fire. Join me?"

She sighed into the phone. "Sounds wonderful. I'm just leaving work. You can pull up to the back door. I'll be waiting."

"See ya soon." Flipping a U-turn, he punched the gas pedal. The car spun neatly around tires spewing gravel in all directions. She wouldn't wait long.

The ability to disrupt electrical current in a limited area for a short period came in handy. He made a habit of using magic sparingly, but felt this time it was absolutely necessary to maintain privacy, both his and hers.

Darkness enveloped the entire block as he pulled into the parking lot behind her store. He flipped the high beams on once then shut off the headlights, hoping she could see in the dark as well as he could. A little twinge of discomfort curled in his chest, a reminder of the cost of using magic for personal benefit.

Precisely at the moment she stepped out, turned and locked the door, he pulled the car beside her and reached across the seats to push open her car door, making sure the interior lights were off. She slid deftly into the seat and quickly closed the door

"Another transformer must have blown," she remarked absently fastening her seat belt.

He made a noncommittal sound and they disappeared into the moonlit night.

****

As he pulled off Sleepy Hollow Road, lights came on illuminating the long winding driveway and extinguished as his vehicle passed each one.

The lights at the rear of the Victorian mansion switched on automatically as he pulled around to the four-car garage. The first bay door opened, lights flickered inside the garage as he parked beside the midnight blue luxury SUV. Angie reached for the handle, but he was already opening her door, and offered his hand. When she put her hand in his, he helped her out then raised it to his lips kissing each knuckle and brushing his lips slowly over the back of her hand. He released it and placed his hand at the small of her back guiding her by the security panel that glowed green indicating there had been no intrusion.

He waved his hand over the panel and touched his left index finger to the screen. A door slid open revealing the well-lit underground corridor. Angie blinked and peered in hesitantly. Bruce took her hand and tugged lightly. "The corridor leads to the house, keeps the elements at bay, and protects my privacy."

Once they reached the entrance way into his home another security panel displayed a rainbow of LED lights up the left side of the panel, again indicating the house was secure. Rather than use his handprint and the key pad, this time he looked directly into the right top section, retina scan matched, the door opened into a warm state of the art kitchen. On the granite counter sat two trays, one with cheese and crackers, another with finger sandwiches, both covered with crystal domes. China plates sat beside them, along with silverware and neatly folded cloth napkins.

"Wow, nice place," she said turning slowly in a three hundred and sixty-degree circle then peering around the corner into another room where a fire crackled merrily in the hearth.

He watched her closely, as a slight smile curved his lips. "In case you are wondering, the staff has already left for the evening after fulfilling my requests. They have Saturday evening, Sunday, and Monday off to spend with their families. Good domestic help is hard to find. Mine have been with me for years and know my preferences. I like that, so I do what I can to make sure they are happy and I enjoy time alone."

The archway where Angie stood gave way to a large living area, paneled in warm oak and solid hard wood floors polished to a gleam. A recliner and sofa of chocolate brown leather and cream accents faced the fireplace. Wood crackled and snapped as orange and blue flames flickered between the logs. On the table in front of the sofa and chair sat two crystal glasses and a bottle of wine chilling.

"Are you hungry? We can take the plates of food with us to enjoy with our wine, if you'd like. Or eat at the breakfast bar in the kitchen and retire to the other room for our wine. I'm sure I can find soda or iced tea to drink with our food, if you'd prefer."

The deep, smooth, seductive tone of his voice had lulled her into a state of relaxation. Alone with a Demon Overlord, her senses should be screaming for her to get out of there, but they weren't. Actually, she appeared quite safe. She stood staring at him as he awaited her answer and shook her head as if to clear her thoughts. "Oh, sorry, my mind wandered. It doesn't matter to me, whatever you like will be fine. I'm starved. Now that I think about it, I don't believe I've eaten since breakfast."

"Well by all means let's get you fed. We'll eat here in the kitchen, I'll get some drinks, and we'll have the wine later. I understand you want to talk, but we have plenty of time and privacy, we can do that comfortably seated in the living room. Will that work for you?"

Standing in the doorway, still taking in her surroundings she answered. "Sure."

"You don't have to work tomorrow, do you?" He asked watching for any signs of discomfort or anxiety.

She chewed on the side of her bottom lip. "No. But I'll need to return home or Willow will worry."

He nodded. "Of course."

During the meal, Angie told him about her day and the steady stream of customers that collected their gift, but also made several other purchases. The store was doing well and would turn a profit sooner than anticipated, thanks in part to his suggestions. She told him about hiring Autumn and a little of her background. His ears perked up at the thought of another potential source of information. They laughed over his telling of Owen's little tirade this morning in Bruce's office and his failure to mingle among his employees and customers. He'd never considered what affect his absences had on them, a mistake he wouldn't make again.

When they finished eating, she helped him clear

away the dishes, cover the food, and put it in the refrigerator.

"You don't just leave things for the staff to clean up?" She questioned tilting her head to get a good look at his face. It was ruggedly handsome with high cheekbones, large dark amber eyes that sparkled when he laughed, a straight nose and long scar running under his chin, which had a small cleft in it. The two small dimples low in his cheeks seemed completely out of place. Except for the amber eyes, no one would believe he was a demon.

"I wouldn't dare. If I entertain on their days off, it's up to me to clean up. Otherwise, Megan will have my head and Sena will lecture me. Since I don't care for either, I do as requested. I like to keep my staff happy, as I said before. Now, shall we soak in the warmth of the fire while we discuss the reason you called?"

Enjoying herself immensely, Angie hated to ruin the wonderful mood, but she had to have answers on which to base her decisions. However, by calling him she'd already made one of her decisions clear. She curled her feet underneath her on the corner of the couch closest to his recliner. "Ok, tell me what you meant when you said, I was determined to enter your world. How is your world different from mine?"

He considered moving over to sit beside her, but remained in his recliner instead and reached for the bottle of wine, filling first her glass then his. The glasses rang melodically as they touched rims. "To us," he said quietly and she echoed his words. They each took a sip and he put his glass on the table.

"My world consists of demons and creatures of the

dark that for the most part follow the rules and coexist amicably with mortals in this one. Unfortunately, there are times when they go rogue and cause harm to mortals or risk exposure of our world to them. This is not tolerated and is dealt with harshly, by mortal standards." He lifted his glass and swirled the burgundy liquid watching it wink in the fire light. Taking another sip, he considered his next statement carefully.

"So you are saying that I live in the mortal world and by gaining knowledge of your world, I endanger my existence? It would seem they are one and the same." She twisted a strand of her hair around her index finger waiting for his explanation.

"Not exactly, but by pursuing a relationship with me, you are putting us both at risk of experiencing your brother's rage. And believe me, he is not one to be taken lightly. But we can address that situation when it arises. Others will try to use our relationship to undermine my position and put Tristian and I at odds against each other which is unacceptable. I depend on him to help keep magic kind in order and the mortals oblivious to our existence."

She took a deep breath and blurted out. "What exactly does Tristian do for you?" There it was hanging between them, the silence deafening.

This was the question he dreaded most. He studied her. This was going to destroy her world...for a while. *Could she handle it?* He saw no way around it, unless he refused her and that wasn't an option. She'd made her decision and he wouldn't push her away this time.

"I assume that by calling me you haven't discussed this situation with your brother. Correct?" He kept his eyes locked on hers.

She searched his face. A cold chill had returned and traveled the length of her spine. She shivered.

"Are you cold?" he asked, wishing like hell, he wasn't the one that had to tell her.

"No, just answer my question. I haven't talked to my brother."

Bruce swirled his wine in the glass and watched it sparkle in the firelight. He stared at her over the rim of his glass for a beat. "Tristian is my hired enforcer. He takes care of those who get out of line. Permanently." He let the words sink in then continued. "Truth is, sometimes he is, well, part of his job…he is my hired assassin, one of the best."

The blood drained out of her face, and she shivered harder. "No…No…you are lying," she said as tears trickled down her cheeks.

Bruce put his glass down on the table. "Why would I lie, I've nothing to gain and everything to lose." He moved beside her on the couch and put his arms around her as she pounded her fists against his chest. Once the initial shock wore off and she calmed, he tried to explain it again. "Think of it like this. Tristian is the police in my world. In the mortal world, police keep the order and arrest those unwilling to abide by the laws, using deadly force when deemed necessary. If I call on Tristian, deadly force is necessary to contain the situation. Otherwise someone else handles the problem."

"So Tristian is in danger every time he goes to work?"

"Yes, but he knows the risks and has done this job for years. He is the very best." Bruce released her and leaned back against the sofa, his arm resting across the back, hand draped around her shoulder.

She shifted on the sofa to face him. "This is how he provided for us as I was growing up?"

"Yes, he is well compensated. In addition to his more than adequate salary, if the demon he takes out has property it automatically becomes Tristian's possession. This job has made him an extremely rich man and he enjoys keeping our world safe as possible and the mortal one oblivious to us as required by our laws"

"So why would I be at risk?"

"Since we met, I've done some investigating. Apparently, when you were under Tristian's roof, the family home was protected by the strongest spells ever cast by your mother and father then maintained by Tristian. It's impervious to the outside world. No one in our world knew where Tristian went when the job was over, nor that he had a little sister. That is the reason he kept you under his thumb or immersed in the mortal world of education and unaware of how he made a living. Otherwise those obsessed with revenge could exact it against you."

She raised a brow questioningly. "Then how did you find out who I was?"

"When you insisted on going out on your own, Tristian called in a favor of my right hand man, Owen. He arranged for your real estate agent, who found the empty building for your store and your apartment. Then Tristian made sure there were protections in place."

"So all this time, I thought I was on my own, I was still under my brother's protection." The blood returned to her face in a flash of fury. Her fists clenched in her lap and her mouth formed a thin line as the muscle in her jaw worked overtime.

Anticipating her reaction, he reached for her hands gently coaxing her slender fingers to relax. "It all unraveled the day you came into the salon and commandeered my attention. An immediate intimate connection crackled between us like nothing I've ever felt."

"I felt something too, but Willow said it was my imagination." Angie snorted.

"When I asked about you, Owen insisted you were absolutely off limits and even went so far as to threaten me with bodily harm." The corners of his lips twitched with amusement. "Such behavior is usually punished severely but Owen has been my trusted advisor for centuries. I gave him the benefit of the doubt and demanded that he tell me what he knew or suffer the consequences."

"And he did?"

"He did, knowing I could be trusted and hoping to avoid what we have now. Owen thought I would come to my senses." Bruce shrugged, brushed her hair out of her eyes with gentle fingers, and leaned into her whispering. "He was wrong." Angie tilted her face up toward his and he touched his lips softly to hers. A bolt of lust zinged through him. Bruce pulled away and stood up abruptly. "This is the wrong time and place. It's time I take you home."

"I'm not ready to go home," Angie protested, grabbed his shoulder, and spun him to face her. "You tell me my brother is an assassin, and there's another world out there, and they could be gunning for me. Then you want to take me home?" Her voice edged up a notch with every word. "How do you go about your business knowing your life is in danger?" She added extra emphasis on the word you.

He rubbed his chin and thought for a minute. "It's really no different than the mortal world. They kill each other, die in car wrecks, kill themselves, and you are subjected to the crossfire every day. How do you survive?" He used her same vocal emphasis.

"I never considered it." Her eyes widened in realization while her body relaxed just a bit.

Smiling, he sat down beside her. "Exactly, and mortals don't have magic at their disposal. While it takes a toll on our physical well-being and energy, we can use magic to protect ourselves, and the ones we care about." He noticed the normal color had returned to her face and she'd quit shivering. "Feel better?"

"I think so, but I'd like to stay a while longer, to decide what to do next. I shouldn't, but I feel safe here with you. May I stay until I can get my head around all you've told me? Could we return to the city on Monday morning? I don't have to work until the afternoon."

He raised a brow and looked down at her. "You told me earlier, Willow will worry."

"I'll call her. She's probably worried by now, unless she's out with her hot new boyfriend. She doesn't know what I decided. In fact, I wasn't sure until I called you the second time, and your voice felt so soothing. You're not using your power on me, are you?"

A chuckle rumbled in his throat. "No. But I'm not sure spending the night with me is all that great an idea." He wanted to wrap his arms around her, feel her body pressed against his and... *That wouldn't be a good idea, at all.* Even the thought had him nearly hard again.

"You have more than one bedroom in this beautiful home. I could borrow one of your shirts to sleep in." Angie said blinking coyly up at him.

"And if Tristian finds out? Not only am I dating his little sister, but she has spent two nights with me alone at my secluded estate."

"I guess we'll have to handle that when it happens, because I intend to spend more than two nights alone with you and possibly in your bed next time." She smiled wickedly at him as he raised his eyebrows, shook his head. "I have spent the last two weeks worrying and stressing over this whole situation. I need a little down time to come to terms with it all. Tomorrow, could we relax and get to know each other better? Unless you have other plans?"

"No other plans, but I have one stipulation. Don't tease me." He arched a brow. "You are a beautiful woman and under any other circumstances, you'd already be in my bed. What you are asking is a first in my long life. Fair enough?"

"More than fair." she nodded her head. "Now, if you'll show me to my room and lend me a shirt, I need to call Willow. Angie winced. "She's not going to be happy, but she'll understand…eventually. By the way how old are you?"

He stared fixedly at her, his lips twitched and one side turned up in a lopsided grin. "Does it matter?"

"Not really. Just curious."

"Thirty-eight with six hundred years experience." He smiled and tucked her hand in his and led the way up a spiral staircase to her room, which was next to his. Bruce found a soft well-worn t-shirt as she requested and tossed it on a chair in her room, while she sat curled on the bed, her back to him, talking with Willow.

He showered and dressed in black silk lounge pants, he didn't own a pair of pajamas. Never saw the need for them until now and crawled into bed, emotionally exhausted as well as physically.

Chapter Eight

A woman's piercing screams and hysterical pleas brought Bruce straight out of bed. Bleary eyed and fuzzy brained he wondered who or what had managed to break through his failsafe security system. He grabbed the gun from its niche in his bed's massive mahogany headboard and flipped the safety off. Then he remembered the evening's events and his houseguest.

He hit the floor running and burst through door to find Angie soaked with sweat in her bed pleading for someone's life. Her pillow and face covered in tears and her whole body quaking uncontrollably. He lowered to the edge of the bed rubbing her back and shaking her gently. "Angie wake up, you're having a nightmare."

Her violet eyes flew open and she threw herself at him flinging her arms around his neck in a chokehold.

Pushed backward by her unexpected force, he righted himself while murmuring, "Angie you're safe, I'm right here." Reaching behind his neck, he pried her fingers apart gradually. "Now if you'd just loosen your grip a bit, I might be able to breathe."

She let out a sob and loosened her hold. Her face buried in his warm bare chest. He gathered her onto his lap and held her until the shivering subsided, her body relaxed as she cuddled against him. Leaning back against the ornately carved oak headboard, he drew in a deep breath and let it out slowly while the adrenalin in his body dissipated and his nerves settled. He silently cursed his involuntary erection as she sat quietly in his lap until her ragged breathing became shallow and even.

Red patches bloomed on her cheeks as she blew out a breath, leaned back and her eyes meet his. "Having second thoughts?" she asked softly rubbing the back of her hand across her puffy eyes. "Sorry about that, I guess I should have gone home. Willow's used to my nightmares. Seems to come with the territory of empathic healer."

Shaking his head slowly, dark amber eyes full of concern. "No second thoughts. Wished you'd warned me, so I'd known what to do. You all right now?"

Brows knitted together, she rubbed her temples. "Yes, I think so." She let out a sigh and gave herself a little shake. "This one was different, probably brought on by my own insecurities and fears after our discussion."

He stood up, took a robe from the closet and wrapped it around her, rolling up the sleeves until he saw her hands, then tied the belt around her waist. "There that'll keep you warm, and for my benefit, covered, making it harder for you to tease me with that beautiful body of yours." He picked her up putting her feet on the floor. The hem of the robe covered her toes.

She reached for him tracing the contours of his bare, muscular chest with her fingertips. "And what about me?" Angie cooed and smiled seductively, though a slight nervous tic remained below her right eye.

With a wicked grin, he growled playfully hoping to take her mind off the nightmares. "The way I see it, turnabout is fair play." Disappearing out the door, he took the twisting stairs two at a time until he reached the kitchen landing.

By the time he stopped and looked up the open spiral staircase, she was only half way down and muttering curses. The long robe hampered her steps.

In the kitchen, Bruce popped mugs of hot chocolate in the microwave along with a plate of cinnamon rolls. Then he placed the warmed food and drinks in the center of the massive oak table and winked at Angie as she entered the kitchen.

"How'd you do that so fast?" She narrowed her eyes at him suspiciously and sniffed the air for traces of magic.

"It's called a microwave, ever hear of it?" He teased ignoring her inference of misused magic. "Now sit and enjoy. Then maybe we can still get some sleep tonight."

She sat on the bench seat behind the table. "I'm not sure closing my eyes again is an option." She shivered as she bit into the warm gooey roll and sipped at the steaming mug of hot chocolate, topped with a swirl of whipped cream.

He slid in beside her, put his arm around her, and picked up his mug of hot chocolate. "Nothing will happen to you while you are in my house and under my protection."

"Apparently, you can't control nightmares."

"No, that's one thing I didn't think to protect against." He bit the side of his cheek trying hard to look serious. "Sorry about that. I do have a couple of large dream catchers given to me by an old trusted friend. Would you like me to hang one over your bed?"

She surprised him by nodding. "Native American magic is very strong and real dream catchers are quite powerful."

"Done." He watched her blink slowly and stifle a yawn. "Want to head back to bed?"

"Yeah, I'll give it another try." She tilted her head and smiled weakly. "Could you stay with me?"

"If that'll keep the gremlins away…sure," he said hesitantly. "But I'm going to put you in my bed. There is a lounge chair in my room that I can sleep on." He smiled sheepishly. "And one of the dream catchers I mentioned already hangs above my bed."

Ascending the steps was slow going until he picked her up and carried her to his room. Gently he laid her on the bed and pulled the comforter over her tucking it around her. She grabbed his hand, curled it to her chest sighing contently. As he sat on the bed beside her, waiting for her to fall asleep, exhaustion overtook him and he slumped down beside her. His arms snaked around Angie in a snug embrace.

Golden slivers of warm sunlight spread over the bed and woke them. The clock on the nightstand indicated they'd slept the morning away.

Angie pushed the comforter to the side and rolled over to face him, still in his embrace. "One more reason for us to sleep together." She smiled and sighed contently.

"You are going to be the death of me in more ways than one." He groaned tightening his hold on her and felt the soft, round mounds of her breasts against his naked chest through the worn t-shirt she wore. His body's reaction was immediate as he nuzzled her neck, breathing in her scent.

She snuggled closer to him, her soft breath caressing his chest, her fingers tangled in the hair at the nape of his neck. With a curse, he pushed her away and sat up. "You're playing with fire li'l witch. I'm not known for my control." He swung his feet to the floor and stood, his back to her, while he reached for the clothes he'd had on the night before. "Come on, I'll show you around the place and we can walk or jog the acreage." *I need exercise to cool my desire for you, before things go too far.*

She rolled over and moaned in frustration. "Ok, but can we eat first? I'm starved."

"You got it. I'll see you in the kitchen." He finished tying his shoes and disappeared quickly out the door, shutting it quietly behind him.

Chapter Nine

She arrived in the kitchen in a pair of jeans, a sweatshirt and her tiny feet were clad in running shoes, rather than the business clothes and heels she'd worn the night before. He made a sound of approval, and raised one eyebrow.

She followed his glaze. "I always carry a change of clothes and running shoes with me. Just in case a handsome demon offers to whisk me away to his country estate."

He frowned at that. "And just how many of these demons did you go home with?"

Putting her finger under her chin she looked at the ceiling, her lips curved up at the corners. "Let me see, to date…one." She smiled innocently batting her long eyelashes at him.

Amused, his eyes danced with mischief. "If I have my way, that's all there will ever be." He prepared two plates of eggs, bacon, hash browns, and biscuits and sat them on the kitchen table. Bruce took a pitcher of orange juice from the refrigerator, poured the yellow liquid into their glasses, without spilling a drop, and left the pitcher in the center of the table.

"Really. Kinda bossy in the morning, aren't ya?" Taking a bite of bacon then a sip of orange juice, she chewed slowly and watched his reaction as she placed her hand over his. "Really, I carry a change of clothes and shoes with me so I can walk or run the days stress off after work. Business attire isn't appropriate for that."

"Agreed. Me too, only the clothes and shoes are in a wardrobe in my office. I usually run or if I am here, I ride the stress off."

"Oh, that's right you mentioned horses this morning." Eyes bright with excitement she got up and walked to the window. "I love to ride. Haven't done much since my parents died."

His eyes clouded for a moment wondering how long ago she lost her parents. His attention turned back to her shoes. "You can't ride in those. You'll need something with a heel to keep your foot in the stirrup."

"No, I rode bareback and barefoot most my life. These will be fine." She insisted then eyed his running shoe clad feet.

"Not on my horses, we'll see what we can find in the stable. The horses are a Gypsy Buckskin named Satan and Harbor is an American Paint. Both were rescues, so I am not one hundred percent sure of their heritage. Satan is large for a Gypsy but with the feathering that starts at the knees in front and hock in back that nearly cover the hooves, Jason says he has to be part Gypsy. Harbor is white with patches of maroon and a black tip on her tail. Again, she is larger than an average Paint. We can go out there after breakfast and you can meet them." Following her gaze, he said flatly. "My riding boots are in the stables."

"Rescues? So you are not what people perceive you to be." She returned to the table scraped a bit of egg onto her fork and finished the last bite of toast.

"Oh, I am everything people perceive me to be, but

that isn't all I am. I just don't let others see the part of me that you are seeing now. Few people know about this place. I maintain an apartment in the city for appearances and when I don't have time to come out here."

"So tell me about your horses." She forked the last bite of hash brown and slid it in her mouth, chewing slowly.

"Satan is the Buckskin, he was a difficult horse, beaten and trusted no one, but they couldn't break his spirit. He was scheduled to be put down when I came across him. Took me over a year to bring him around, but now he's a great horse, single footed too, which makes for a very smooth ride."

"Can anyone else ride him?"

"No. He still has trust issues as far as others are concerned."

"And Harbor?"

"She is the sweetest horse you'd ever want to meet. I found her one day when Satan and I were out riding several miles from here. Apparently, someone had abandoned her quite a while before we found her, you could see every rib. Satan tried to coax her to follow us but she was too weak. We rode back to the stable and got the horse trailer."

"How did you get her in the trailer? She didn't even know you." Her eyes wide with amazement, she rested her chin in her hands, watching him intently.

He smiled fondly remembering the events. "It was Satan. When I returned for the trailer, I tried to leave him in the stable here. He wouldn't have any part of that. So I put him in the trailer, added hay, and grain to the feed bins, grabbed a couple bunches of carrots and went to get her. By the time we found her again, she was lying down in the grass, too weak to stand. It was a good thing that I brought Satan, he nudged her to get up, and then she followed him into the horse trailer. I had to secure her with straps that I brought to keep her upright for the ride back to the house, but she made it."

"Wow, that's unusual for a horse to voluntarily go into a trailer, let alone a strange trailer with someone she doesn't know."

"I know it sounds crazy, but I think they knew each other on some plane of existence. They have been inseparable since that day. If I ride one, the other always comes along."

"You must have had huge vet bills between the two."

"Not really. Jason, the stable hand I hired to care for Satan is a former Vet Tech, so he tended to Satan's wounds with my assistance. When we brought Harbor back, he single-handedly nursed her back to health. It was nine months before she was strong enough to ride. Jason keeps the horses healthy and cares for them as if they were his own. Like I said, I have a great staff." Bruce pushed up from the table and picked up the plates and glasses, put them in the dishwasher then turned to her. "Ready to go meet 'em?" He flipped the dishwasher to on and started for the door.

She nodded and followed him out the door "No one has discovered this side of you, other than your help. How did you keep the secret?" From what she could see, the security at his estate was impenetrable, but what about his horses and stables, she hadn't noticed them when they drove in last night.

"I value my privacy." The chirping of his cell

phone interrupted the peace and quiet as they walked toward a huge building. He checked the caller ID and cursed, increasing the speed and length of his strides. "We need to get to the security of the stable compound so I can return this call."

Puzzled, she matched his pace to the building. Another security panel glowed green as he passed his open hand impatiently across the panel. He placed his arm around her shoulders pulling her in close and walked right through what appeared to be a solid wall. Once inside Angie turned and ran her fingers over the wall, it felt solid.

They'd stepped in an enclosure with stables, exercise and training rings and pasture area complete with grass. The air was fresh with clean earthy scents wafting on the light breeze flowing through the area. From the inside, she could see outside through strategically placed panels, yet she was positive when she stood outside there was no evidence of windows.

She turned to Bruce in amazement. "How is all this possible?"

"State of the art building material, air filtration systems, and a little ingenuity make all this possible."

A man with red hair, a friendly smile and a lanky build, dressed in jeans, well-worn boots, and t-shirt strode toward them. "Morning boss. Going for a ride?"

"Not sure, Jason. I need to return a phone call then I'll let you know our plans. This is Angie. She is my guest for a few days."

Jason's eyebrows shot up to almost his hairline, but he said nothing. In all the years, he'd worked for Bruce he'd never brought a guest here, especially not a female.

"Angie, if it's all right with you, Jason, my stable manager, can show you around the place and answer any questions. Maybe find you an acceptable pair of boots. Megan keeps several pairs in the tack room. See if any of them will fit you. Megan exercises Harbor when she feels the need to escape her household duties. I'll catch up as soon as I handle this call. Ok?"

She nodded in agreement, still overwhelmed by what she saw. "Magic?" she whispered.

"No, at least not what you see." The phone beeped urgently again, Bruce checked the screen and frowned. "I'll explain later." He continued through the rough wooden doorway into the stable office and turned toward her. "Just be a minute." Holding up one finger, he sent her a smile meant to reassure, and then closed the heavy wooden door behind him.

"Well, looks like we got a few minutes. Let's check out the tack room, see if any of Megan's boots fit, then I'll show you around." Jason stuck his thumbs through his front belt loops and waited a beat, stealing a glance at the closed door. "This way." Once inside the tack room, Angie found a pair of boots that fit. She glanced at Jason. "I think these will work. "Let's go meet Satan and Harbor, if that's all right."

"Follow me, but keep your distance from Satan, we don't get many guests and he's skittish. I assume Bruce told you about them."

"Yes." She glanced nervously toward the door before following him.

****

Bruce sat down in the well-worn brown leather chair and picked up the phone in the office. It was a secure line just like his computer servers and all communications on the estate. Signals were scrambled and encoded for safety. He dialed Owen's private line. It rang only once.

"Well, it's about time. I've called you several times."

"I know that. Wasn't at a secure location to take your call. What's up?" Bruce's voice was smooth and unconcerned.

"Tristian dropped off his reports in person. I stopped by your apartment to deliver them. Where are you?"

"I told you I was leaving town for a few days."

"Oh, yeah…I forgot. Anyway, after Tristian dropped by, he decided to surprise Angie, take her to lunch, check out her new business venture, and spend some time with her. They parted with such animosity, he wanted to apologize, I guess. Hell, I don't know. Bottom line, she's missing and he's worried."

"Did you talk to Willow?"

"Yeah, she was of no help. She's spending the weekend at her boyfriend's house and hasn't seen Angie since Friday evening, when Angie volunteered to close, so Willow could leave with her boyfriend. Angie is not due back to work until Monday afternoon. By that time, Tristian will be insufferable. Not to mention, what if she is in trouble?" Owen asked.

Bruce ran fingers through his hair and blew out a breath, rubbing the back of his neck he sat back in the chair eyes closed. "She's safe," he said flatly then hesitated for a couple of beats. "Angie's with me at my estate. We'll be back sometime late Monday morning."

"Alone. Shit, Bruce, didn't we discuss this?"

"Yes, and I told you what I was going to do if she

called and she did on Friday night. We talked well into the night.

"Yeah, I'll just bet you did," Owen grumbled. It was well known Bruce slept with every woman he'd found attractive given the chance.

Bruce ignored Owen's comment and continued. "We decided to see where this relationship leads. She knows everything. Tristian will just have to learn to live with it. Although, I was hoping for a little more time before he found out."

"It's not his living with it I'm concerned about; it's your living through it." Owen swore. "I can tell you where it will lead and it's nowhere good. I suppose you expect me to run interference for the two of you?"

"I do."

"Great!" Owen heaved a long sigh into the phone.

"Talk with Willow, get her to back you up. Tell Tristian Angie went on holiday with friends and will be back sometime Monday afternoon."

"You know we don't lie to our business associates, especially Tristian. Your scent will be all over her, especially if you were intimate."

"We weren't. Not that it's any of your business. And it's not a lie. We're friends. I'll figure out how to get her back to the shop without running into Tristian, Monday. If we can't, we'll simply face the consequences."

"Good point. I'll do what I can from here, but it would help if you'd keep me in the loop as to your plan, when you have one," Owen said.

"Fair enough. I'll be in touch. Probably won't be today, we're going riding and will be out of range most of the day."

"Ok, I'll handle it. But when you get back, we need to talk."

"Sure." Bruce returned the handset to its cradle, fingers drumming on the receiver for a moment.

Relieved there was no dire emergency, Bruce stood and strolled out of the office, looking for Angie and Jason. Figuring they went to see the horses first, he hurried to the stables where Harbor nuzzled Angie's hand and Satan watched with more interest than he'd ever paid to a stranger. Jason was standing protectively between Satan and Angie.

"Thanks Jason, I'll take it from here. Sorry to take you away from your duties."

"Not a problem, boss. Do you want me to saddle 'em up for you?"

"Go ahead and saddle Harbor, I'll handle Satan."

"Right away. Nice to meet you Angie." He nodded to her then strode quickly to the tack room followed by Bruce.

"Be right back." Bruce smiled turning back toward Angie. "Then we're off."

****

The concern he'd displayed earlier was gone, much to Angie's relief. Apparently, the phone call was not what he'd expected. It had been years since she'd been on a horse and she was really looking forward to it. Tristian sold the horses after her parents died because there was no time or money to care for them. Taking care of her and the family business, as he'd called it took up all his time. She wondered if her father had also worked for Bruce in the same capacity as Tristian. But that was a discussion for another day she decided. Today she was determined to enjoy being with Bruce and riding carefree, if only for the next twenty-four hours.

Bruce and Jason returned and saddled the horses. Bruce grasped her calf and put his hand under the sole of her boot boosting her into the saddle, checking her stirrup length and cinch strap then mounted Satan leading the way across the pastured area.

"Jason, open the west door, we are going to ride around the property." Bruce shouted over his shoulder. A wall to the side of the area they occupied simply disappeared and horses turned in that direction quickening their pace, heads and tails held high ready to burn off some pent up energy. Bruce let Satan have his head and Harbor tested Angie's tight hold on the reins following at a slower pace.

****

Once outside, Satan took off at a canter straining to make it a full gallop. Bruce reined him in, turning in the saddle to watch Angie's fluid movements atop Harbor. It was as if she was one with the horse. *Yes, she'd ridden before and often.* He made a mental note to order her a pair of riding boots for the next time she visited.

He waited for her to catch up and asked, "You up for letting them run? It's been a while since they have been outside and allowed a full gallop. Jason takes them out every day, but keeps them close to the enclosure."

"Sure, I'll just hold on tight and hope you and Satan know where you're going." Angie said with a giggle as she loosened the reins and tightened her knees against Harbor's sides.

"We'll keep it controlled and slow down after they begin to tire. They'll be happy to walk after a good run.

Then I can show you around the acreage and we'll be able to talk."

****

Bruce loosened the reins and Satan took off, Harbor right behind and Angie holding tight to the saddle.

Heart pounding, breaths coming in fast gulps, the exhilaration of riding horseback again was wonderful. She hadn't felt so carefree in years. The sun in her face, the wind in her hair, a confident horse beneath her and most of all a man with whom she was free to be herself. One that knew her secrets, heck, knew more secrets of her family than she did and really cared for her. Her terrible nightmares caught him off guard but he seemed unaffected by them.

****

Watching her laugh, face flushed with excitement, his head conceded what his heart already knew. This woman is his soul mate, created just for him. Granted, there were going to be a few formidable obstacles, Tristian being one of the biggest. There seemed to be a force stronger than either of them bringing them together, so who was he to question it.

Was this how his father felt when he'd taken his mother as his mate? An action that shook both heaven and hell to their very core. Facing insurmountable obstacles, his father managed to rule his territory with an iron fist, earn respect, and make their relationship work, even to this day. Though now his father was retired and his parents live in Tahiti.

After about fifteen minutes, the horses slowed to a canter on their own and then eventually were contented to walk alongside each other.

He reached over and caught Angie's hand. "You look radiant."

"Thanks, I'd forgotten just how much I enjoyed horses. Not only the riding, but just being around them."

"I see you spending much more time with them and me in the future."

She laughed. "So now you are a fortune teller, also?"

He rolled his eyes and smirked. "I wish." His mood turned somber as he brought the horses to a standstill.

"What is it?" She asked frowning.

"The phone call I took earlier was Owen. Angie, your brother is in DC. He came to deliver some reports to me and surprise you. Apparently he is feeling bad about the way you two left things. Naturally, he can't find you, he's worried, and Willow isn't talking."

The corners of her lips curled up in a half-smile. "Willow won't either. We knew he'd find out eventually. I was just hoping for the later. But it is what it is and I am ready to face him."

"As am I, but hopefully it won't come to that…yet. Owen is running interference and will get with Willow to sidetrack Tristian until Monday afternoon. I'd planned for us to return mid-morning Monday, so you could get to work on time. Unless of course you want to leave earlier."

"I'm good with Monday morning. We agreed not to hide our relationship, but be discreet for the time being. Right?"

"Yes. When we get back to the stable, I'll let Owen know we'll return day after tomorrow. If he can work something out, he will. If not, we'll face Tristian together when I drop you off at the store. Or do you need to go home first to change?"

"No the store will be fine, I'll call Willow later and have her bring me a change of clothes. Boy am I going to owe Willow big time after this."

"Yep, ditto for Owen. He doesn't like to get involved in my personal affairs and normally I like it that way. Now let's head back to the stable. We'll get the horses taken care of and have the evening to ourselves, before the staff returns in the morning." He nudged his heels into Satan. "Home boy."

After they groomed and fed the horses, Angie and Bruce walked toward the house. Angie grabbed his hand and spun him around to face her. "When I asked about the magic use around here, your answer was pretty cryptic. Not what I could see? What kind of answer was that? Care to explain?"

"No…not really. But I suppose you're going to insist." He stuck his hands in his pockets and rolled the ache out of his shoulders.

Expecting the return of his cold, distant demeanor, he surprised her with pleasant forthright answers.

"It was a gift from my parents. I bought this place from them when they retired to Tahiti."

"Oh, so it's not your magic."

"No. My father thought I'd need extra protection as I asserted myself and proved worthy of claiming his place as Territory Overlord. There were others that felt entitled, in the end I won, but the costs were steep." His shoulders slumped and eyes saddened as he remembered close friends that had his back during that time and paid the ultimate price. Owen still bore scars of those battles. "This," he stood stretching his arms open wide turning to survey his estate, "has always been my sanctuary."

Angie didn't take her eyes off him, but lightly touched his shoulder and changed the subject. "Ok, so what kind of magic was used?"

"Much like the magic that protects the family home you and Tristian shared. As well as the magic that protects your apartment and store. It's impervious to outside magic, but allows the use of magic by the protected inside its walls."

"You were serious about that? Wouldn't I know if there was magic protecting my apartment and store?"

A wicked grin curled his lips. "That's a question you can ask your brother on Monday." He slid an arm around her waist, while directing his gaze into the security panel. The door swung open allowing the wonderful aroma of baked ham, sweet potatoes, and apple cobbler to surround them.

An older woman with dark hair flowing down her back, dressed in a white shirt and tan slacks bustled around the kitchen, glanced over her shoulder as they entered the room.

"Megan, what are you doing here? You're not due back until tomorrow." He raised a brow and smiled warmly at the woman.

She narrowed her laughing hazel eyes at him then winked at Angie. "What are you doing entertaining this lovely young woman without proper supervision and a culinary expert? She'll think you're a heathen, and she won't be far from the mark. Now go wash up and relax in the living room, dinner will be ready in forty-five minutes." She glanced at Angie's feet. "Nice taste in riding boots."

"Thanks. I guess we wear the same size, or almost. Bruce said you wouldn't mind."

"And he'd be right." She nodded grinning.

"I hate to interrupt, but how'd you know I had a guest?"

"I have eyes and ears all over this house, even when I'm not here." She laughed then opened the oven door to check on the ham. "Now get out of my way." She mimed putting her foot to his ass as she shoved him toward the arched doorway to the next room.

Back in the living room, Angie collapsed on the couch in a fit of giggles and wincing at the same time, partly due to fatigue, and the events of the past few minutes. "Every muscle in my body is screaming."

Looking back into the kitchen a smile danced around his lips. "I guess we'll have dinner and then see what can be done about that. There's a hot tub on the lower level. I have a few swimsuits down there I keep for guests, you can see if anything fits. Or you can conjure up one, if you are so inclined."

"I don't waste magic like that, but the tub sounds great. Are you just trying to get me out of my clothes?"

"Oh, li'l witch, if I wanted you out of your clothes, you'd be naked right now. Though the idea is very appealing after sleeping with you last night." He smirked letting his gaze wander over her. "So I guess the third choice could be naked?"

"I…we…we weren't sleeping together like you're insinuating and you know it. And that would be a resounding no to the third choice." Then she narrowed her eyes suspiciously. "Just how often do you entertain female guests in your hot tub?"

The question caught him off guard. The swimsuits

had been his mother's idea. She hoped her son wouldn't spend his life alone, that he'd find someone that mattered, and bring her here to enjoy what was his. He'd never entertained his conquests here, they'd just never mattered that much and he was unwilling to share his private estate with anyone who didn't. This was his paradise. The only woman to grace these premises at his invitation, sat beside him, her full bottom lip stuck out in an adorable pout, waiting for an answer.

"I don't kiss and tell," he said smugly.

****

She suddenly had a desire to hit him with something…anything within reach. However, she refrained, she wasn't sure of his limits and wasn't comfortable testing them, yet. She merely nodded and glared at him. "I see."

He slid closer to her and wrapped his arm around her shoulder, kissing her lightly on the nose. "I don't believe you do." But he was unwilling to elaborate.

She slipped her shoes off and curled her feet under her, snuggling into him as they both enjoyed the fire Megan had coaxed to life again sometime after they left this morning.

"Dinner's ready, would you like it in there or in the dining room?" Megan announced primly.

"The kitchen table will be fine, no need for formality, though I appreciate the effort. Won't you join us?"

She shook her head and removed her white apron. "You know that is not proper etiquette."

"To hell with etiquette. You came in on your day off, cooked a wonderful meal for Angie and me. We want you to share it with us. It would be bad manners to turn us down under these circumstances. Don't you agree Angie?"

"Oh most definitely." Angie nodded her head vigorously.

Megan smiled appreciatively and set another place at the table in the dining room.

After the dinner dishes where cleared away, Angie and Bruce returned to the living room couch and Megan silently disappeared to her room.

"Alone at last." Bruce leaned over and nibbled lightly on Angie's neck. "How about a dip in the hot tub? Clothes are still optional," he murmured seductively and offered his hand to help her up off the couch.

"Would they be optional for you as well?"

"Always. Whatever you desire."

"This early stage in our relationship, I think swimsuits would be appropriate. Don't you?"

He pulled her against him and brought his lips down on hers, hot, demanding, and proprietary, then his tongue slid between her lips twining with hers in a sinuous dance.

She felt his erection press against her as moisture gathered between her thighs, preparing for the next step. Her bones felt as if they were melting and knew her legs wouldn't hold her up, if he let go. No one had ever made her feel like this and it was only a kiss. Just what could she expect in a more intimate joining, she wondered, surprised by her desire to find out.

He trailed his lips down her neck to the rise of her breast and murmured, "I intend to have you, but it will be consensual between us and you'll agree there will be no other, as will I. This is forever or not at all. As for swimsuits, I've already stated my opinion."

The fire he'd lit burned slowly through her, Angie could do nothing but rest her head against his chest and wish it were bare. She breathed in his delicious scent and tried to come to terms with what this man could do to her. Forever, oh yeah she could live with that. Nevertheless, she wasn't naive enough not to realize there would be others that would try to tear them apart. She wouldn't let that happen.

"Ok, so are you going to show me where you hide the swimsuits?" Angie inquired her violet eyes sparkling with mischief as she glanced toward the stairs.

"Certainly, but it's still against my better judgment." He laughed and turned her toward the stairway as he moved his hand to the small of her back letting it slide lower as they descended the steps.

At the bottom of the stairs, he pointed to a curtained off area to the left of the hot tub where tendrils of steam wafted above water and bubbles floated on the surface. "There should be several styles and sizes in the wooden chest against the wall. I'm going to dash up to my room and get mine, if you are ok here alone?"

"I'll be fine." She lifted the lid on the beautifully hand carved oak chest and found an astonishing variety of swimsuits with the price tags still attached. Either he'd been telling her the truth about never entertaining women here, or they didn't wear swimsuits. She'd seduce the answer out of him later, if she had her way. Picking through several in her size, she decided on a turquoise string bikini that barely covered her assets and was designed to tease a man. She'd just wrapped a towel around her and sat on the edge of the tub when he strode back into the room.

Her eyes traced the contours of the male body in a swimsuit that barely covered the essentials, and Bruce's essentials were impressive. His long powerful legs and tight ass just added to the delectable package, not to mention washboard abs and wide muscular shoulders.

Using one hand, he swung into the tub barely making a ripple entering the water. "Are you going to sit on the side of the tub all night wrapped in a towel or are you going to join me in the warm pulsating H2O?" He raised a brow and one corner of his mouth curved up seductively.

Shrugging off the towel along with her inhibitions, she slid into the gloriously warm bubbling clear water.

He let out a low appreciative whistle as his dark amber eyes devoured her. The swell of her firm round breasts, tiny waist, and the curve of hips caused the intended results. Her full pouty lips issued an invitation all their own as she straddled him and slithered against him. Accepting that invitation, his mouth covered hers hungrily forcing her lips apart, and thrusting his tongue inside as his hands gripped her hips holding her tight against him.

She succumbed to his forceful domination, enjoying the sensation and nipped at his bottom lip just before he moved down to explore her soft flesh. His mouth covered her breasts through the thin fabric and he tongued her nipples until they were hard. She bucked up against him, even as he drew back.

Breath coming in gasps, he said in a husky voice, "Unless you want me to take you right here, right now, we best divert our energy in a different direction."

Paying no attention to his words, she wrapped her arms around him burying her face in his neck as she breathed a kiss against the bare flesh, then ran the tip of her tongue along his strong jaw line. His hands caressed her hips and untied the strings that held her bikini bottom on, letting it float to the surface, long fingers exploring the area between her legs he'd just uncovered. That action was enough to bring her out of the sexual haze that enveloped her brain.

"No. Not here, not this way, we're not ready." She shoved at him even as he positioned himself between her voluntarily spread legs.

"Maybe you're not ready, but I'm way past ready." He growled but reluctantly eased away, floating to the corner seat still panting with a raging hard on. Vaulting out of the tub, he wrapped a towel around his waist and sprinted upstairs.

Appalled at her lack of self-control, she floated to the opposite corner to cool off. After he disappeared up the stairs, she let the warm water cascade over her sore muscles wondering what to do now, and then climbed out of the tub, dried off and dressed. She wandered back to the living room and sat in front of the comforting warmth of the fireplace, the fire now reduced to embers.

****

After a long cold shower, he dressed in jeans, a loose knit copper sweater and went to find her. Slouched in the doorway of the living room, his shoulder leaning against the doorjamb, one bare foot crossed in front of the other, he watched her. His blood stirred and his body ached for her like none other. *Steady ol' boy, this is going to be a long journey, which has just begun, control yourself, the reward will be worth the wait.*

Logs were stacked neatly in a stone recess a few feet from the fireplace. He sauntered over, picked up a couple large logs, and tossed them effortlessly on the fire, as if they were twigs. "We'll have a roaring fire in no time to warm you." He smiled tentatively and sat beside her, sliding his arm around her shoulders. "I'm sorry for my behavior in the tub. I'll try to refrain from doing it again. But I have only so much control and taunting me isn't a good idea."

She relaxed against him and sighed peering up at him, her eyes gentle and full of understanding. "I was as much to blame as you. I dressed deliberately to seduce you. I didn't expect… I just wasn't ready for the raw sex appeal you exude in that tiny piece of fabric you call a swimsuit. When you touched me, control went out the window. Wish I could say I am sorry, but I'm not. Just not ready to take it as far as you apparently are."

"Li'l witch, I'm male and seeing you in next to nothing stirred my blood and aroused my body. We are just going to have to keep our clothes on until you're ready."

"I'm afraid so," she reluctantly agreed.

"Now what are we going to do about sleeping arrangements. We both need to sleep tonight. Will the nightmares return, if you sleep alone in your room?" Bruce asked gently tucking a wayward curl behind her ear.

"Not usually, but it's hard to tell. Those last night were different from any I've had before. I should be all right in my own room, besides it'll give us space we need."

Separate bedrooms fit with his feelings. He was a male demon with carnal needs far beyond the mortal male. Controlling them until she was ready was already a challenge. Once that connection happened, there was no turning back for either of them. He had to be sure this was what she wanted.

He offered his hand, she took it getting to her feet and starting toward the stairs. He followed her, took her face in his hands, and kissed her forehead leaving her at her bedroom door, continuing on to his. The hallway light remained on in case of nightmares.

At two in the morning he awoke feeling her restlessness, listening he heard her soft sobs. He pulled on his black silk lounge pants and grabbed the robe from the foot of his bed. Padding silently in his bare feet down the hall, he paused at her bedroom door just as her anguished scream filled the room. He was at the side of her bed a second later. Gathering her onto his lap, he held her unyielding body to his until her flailing limbs quieted and her troubled violet eyes opened. Cognizant of where she was now and with whom, she flung her arms around his neck and clung tight as shivers racked her slight frame.

Megan came running from the other wing of the house where the staff lived during the week. "Is everything all right?" She peeked inside Angie's bedroom door.

"Just a nightmare, nothing to worry about. She's awake now.

"Oh no my Lord," Megan said in a low frantic whisper.

"Don't call me that," he growled, his amber eyes

tinged with orange glowed in the dark room.

"Sorry. There's something dark and dangerous chasing that one." She nodded in Angie's direction. "It's not of this world."

He lowered his voice and spoke kindly. "Go back to bed, I've got this handled." He paused for a beat exhaling slowly. "For now."

Megan stepped into the room and leaned toward Bruce. "Your witch is a seer as well as a healer. Then she turned her attention to Angie. Was your mother a healer and empath as well?"

Angie nodded, loosening her grip on Bruce.

Megan turned to go, then looked back. "What a rare gem you are." She closed the door quietly behind her and padded down the hallway.

One of the few paranormals on his estate staff, Megan was a witch-angel who had been with his family for centuries.

Quiet now, Angie laid her face, moist from tears and hair damp from sweat, against his bare chest. He dabbed at her face with the side of his open robe. With her still in his arms, he stood. "I guess we'll spend the rest of the night in my bed, it's much bigger than yours."

"Thanks," she whispered against his neck, a weak smile forming on her trembling lips. "So it's true, size matters," she said in an attempt to dispel the somber mood.

He gave her a tight-lipped smile. "You tell me." Laying her gently on the bed, he pulled the sheet and comforter over her. Then grabbed the blanket folded neatly at the foot of the bed and yanked it over him as he slid his arms protectively around her, hoping to silence her demons.

The sun shone brightly through the lace curtains when Bruce rolled over to watch Angie sleeping. He gently brushed a golden strand of hair from her face. She blinked and looked at him.

"Morning already?" she rubbed her eyes and yawned wide.

"More like afternoon, my li'l witch."

She stretched arching her back and winced. "Ohhh, I feel like a stomped on toad frog."

Bruce chuckled. "What a way with words you have. Maybe we'll take it easy today, a leisurely walk, relax on the porch, wine by the fire and an early night."

"Sounds wonderful." She sighed.

****

Megan served apple cinnamon oatmeal hot off the stove and fresh baked blueberry muffins when they entered the kitchen Monday morning.

"Mmmm, that smells absolutely heavenly," Angie said licking her lips.

"Come sit and eat, then you'll have time for a morning horseback ride before returning to DC to face whatever awaits you," she said knowingly.

They ate quickly and enjoyed their morning ride, returning just in time to leave for DC.

Megan kept an eye on Angie while packing the rest of the muffins and sandwiches prepared for their lunch. "You have a good trip into the city." She patted Bruce's arm fondly, handing him the basket of food and surprised Angie with a hug. "Take care."

A steaming mug of hot chocolate frothy with whipped cream sat on the counter. Megan handed it to Angie then turned to grasp a full mug of hot coffee, handing that to Bruce. "You're going to need this." She leaned into him and lowered her voice to a whisper only he could hear. "Take care of your li'l witch, she's special and dark times are ahead."

He nodded, then ushered Angie out of the house.

The SUV sat in front of the house idling. Bruce opened the passenger's door for Angie, waited for her to get in, and walked around to the driver's side. The ride to DC was quiet. Finally, Bruce broke the silence. "Those are some nightmares, still different?"

"Yes."

"Just started while you were staying at my place?" Bruce asked his eyes scanning the road.

"Yes. I've had nightmares since my parents died. They happened frequently when I was a child, but now not often and nothing like this. It's strange the only way to keep them away is with you beside me. It feels like a premonition, but I've never had the gift. My mother did." She turned to watch out the window then looked back at Bruce. "What will I tell Tristian when I see him and what if he's at the store when you drop me off?"

"We'll face him together and tell him the truth. We're dating. I don't think that will be a problem though. Owen assured me Tristian would be waiting in my office to go over the reports."

"Does he usually bring them to you personally?" Angie shifted in her seat to face Bruce.

"Sometimes when he's in town or something about the reports bother him." Bruce slid a glance at Angie.

"These reports, are they on the jobs you've given him?"

"Yes." He looked over at Angie again. This time gauging her reaction, then turned his eyes back to the road. "I'll drop you off at the back door of your shop. Then I'll go to the salon and meet with Tristian. That will give you a chance to shower, change into work attire, and talk with Willow before facing him."

Angie chewed on her bottom lip. "I'll just tell him I was with friends. I don't think he'll question me further, not after our fight when I left. It was all about his constant invasion of my privacy."

"Sounds good," Bruce said with a wink.

"If you have nightmares tonight, I want you or Willow to call me, I'll port over. I've a feeling these are more than just nightmares."

"And if Tristian stays the night?"

A little furrow dug itself between his brows then he shrugged. "I guess he'll have to handle it, huh? Unless… Well, he's handled them before."

"Yes," she said quietly.

****

The back door to The Krystal Unicorn was open when Bruce drove up and Willow waited just outside. He dropped Angie off without incident and no Tristian in sight.

Bruce strode into the salon, acknowledged the staff with a friendly smile, and nodded to Owen who looked sullen and glanced meaningfully up at the mezzanine.

Bruce gave a thumbs up and sprinted up the stairs two at a time. He strode through his office door to find Tristian seated on the leather couch reading a new copy of Money magazine. "Sorry, I wasn't in town this weekend. Sometimes I just need to get away. If I'd know you were coming, I'd stayed." Bruce settled in his leather chair, and flipped the laptop open.

"It's all right," he muttered closing the magazine

and laying it on the table. "I should've have called before I came. I missed Angie too." Tristian shifted in his seat and stared at Bruce. Tristian didn't like to discuss personal matters with Bruce, but Tristian already knew that Owen had discussed the situation in detail with Bruce.

"That's too bad. My customers are thrilled with her store. They claim to spend way too much money there. So, I assume it's doing well. Owen put her flyers at the front desk, to kinda help her get started." The leather creaked as Bruce leaned back in his chair waiting for Tristian to get to the point of why he was here. The reports were just an excuse.

Tristian stood up pacing back and forth in front of the desk. "Yeah the girls are enjoying their adventure, and business is good according to Willow. She met a new guy that she really likes. He seems nice. I met him when she invited me to have dinner with them last night. Angie was off with friends for the weekend. So I guess they've settled in."

"That's a good thing. Right?"

He sat down in a chair at the front of Bruce's desk. "Yeah, I guess. I was hoping they'd fail miserably and come back home. I should have known better, those two have always been successful at whatever they set out to do. Angie is supposed to be back this afternoon. I'll ask her to dinner tonight and try to work out our differences. I guess it's time to let her try her wings."

"Sounds like a good plan. Now is there anything unusual in the reports, or everything up to your standards?" Bruce shoved his laptop to the side of the desk and looked directly at Tristian.

Tristian met his gaze unwavering. "That's what I

wanted to talk to you about. On the surface, everything looks good. My assignment is complete without complications. However, there's rumblings of another powerful dark demon, a higher up, escaping when the tear in time opened up and he's out for revenge. I'm trying to ferret out more information, but my sources say this one's bad and they're scared to talk. Have you heard anything?"

"No. But, I just got back. I'll check into it and let you know." Bruce glanced at his laptop. "Otherwise things seem quiet?"

"Yeah, kinda, like the calm before the storm. That's another reason I came to check on the girls. I don't like it," Tristian said shaking his head slowly.

"Well, let's hope not, I could use a few months or even years of quiet."

Tristian's eyebrows shot up. "Seriously."

Bruce laughed. "I know, just wishful thinking."

Tristian stood up to leave. "Me too." Then he shoved his hands in his pockets and turned back to Bruce. "Uh, there's something else. Oh, never mind, I need to work it out in my head first."

"If you need to talk, you know where to find me." As soon as the words left his mouth, he thought better of it.

Tristian raised a brow questioningly and said with a sneer. "Right."

Smiling sheepishly, Bruce countered. "Usually."

Bruce rose and walked Tristian to the door. They shook hands and Bruce handed him an envelope. "Talk to you soon. I'm sure everything will work out with your sister." He watched Tristian walk down the stairs and ran his long fingers through his already tousled hair. Telling Tristian about his relationship with Angie was going to be more difficult than he first thought.

****

"Don't you ever do that to me again. I was worried sick." Willow stood toe to toe with Angie, finger in her face. "You weren't home when I came home from my date. Then you call me and you're alone with Bruce at his estate." Willow took a couple of steps backward as the color in Angie's cheeks rose to a bright red. "After you promised not to do anything stupid. Then Tristian shows up as I am locking up, searching for you." Willow huffed out a breath and threw up her hands. "As if that wasn't enough, Owen stops by shortly after that demanding to know where you are. All this time, Caleb is standing in the store watching this scenario play out."

"I'm sorry. I told you that already," Angie said, examining her fingernails and tamping her temper down. She hated lectures. "Who's Caleb?"

As if Angie hadn't said a word. Willow continued to rant. "Then Owen's back with a plan to save your sorry ass and wants me to go along with it. Which I did." Willow narrowed her eyes and glared at Angie.

"Thank You. I said I'm sorry. What more do you want?"

Willow paced back and forth in front of Angie. "Then your brother shows up again just before closing hoping you've returned. I tell him you're gone 'til Monday afternoon with friends, just like Owen said. Tristian looked so miserable I invited him to dinner with Caleb and me. Tristian and Caleb got along real well. In fact, he seemed more relaxed than he'd been all day. We had a nice dinner then dropped Tristian off at the hotel. Caleb asked me to his house. I spent the night there, just to avoid the craziness."

Angie nodded, "I understand."

Willow's temper appeared to have run its course, she sighed. "Caleb is the new guy in my life, if you're interested. I'm surprised he hasn't dumped me after what went on the last couple of days," Willow said with a pout, crossing her arms across her chest.

"I'm always interested, Willow, you know that," Angie said patiently, laying a hand over her friend's hand. "Now, tell me all about Caleb. Is this the handsome guy you left with Friday night?"

"Oh yes. He's wonderful. The art gallery on the other side of the park is showing his work. You gotta come see. It's selling really well. Caleb's offered to give us a painting to display on the wall of The Krystal Unicorn. I told him I had to ask you, but I was sure we'd be honored. Right?"

"Of course." Angie winced and hesitated. "I gotta ask, his paintings aren't abstract or something weird?"

"Nooo..." Willow said.

"I'd like to meet him first. I'll apologize for the chaos I've caused, if you think it'll help."

"I think we're all right, especially since he is offering to give us one of his paintings to hang in the shop. I was angry with you because I had no idea where you were, or what happened to you or if you were safe." Willow sighed, walked over to one of the chairs in the books section, and sat in one of the wing backed chairs. "Now tell me about your weekend. Is Bruce really the Demon Overlord?"

Angie followed her and eased into the other chair. "Yes, but he is also a wonderful man. At least when he's with me, he's not dangerous or pure evil. I'd feel it. He's a gentleman. There's a connection between us like I've never felt with anyone. When he touches me…well let's just say I don't want him to ever stop."

"Angie, you didn't." Willow squealed. "Not with a man, ah, demon you don't even know, very well."

"Hey look who's throwing double standards around. You spent a couple nights with Caleb."

"Yeah, but we've been talking for weeks. Besides that's different."

"How?"

"It just is. I don't have a brother that will kill us both when he finds out. You do. He's not a Territory Overlord. Bruce is."

"Well. Just to ease your mind, I didn't sleep with him, but I sure wanted to. He has the most incredible body and built to please a woman." Angie fanned herself with her hand.

"Really?" Willow's eyes grew big. "How would you know that if you didn't see him naked?"

"We relaxed in his hot tub and the swimsuit he wore left very little to the imagination."

"Oh. What did you wear, you didn't have one."

"He had some for guests, so I wore one of those. It was brand new, still had the price tag on it." Angie giggled and leaned into her friend. "It didn't leave much to his imagination either."

"So you had a good time. Will you see him again?"

"Yes. But while I was there, my nightmares, well let's just say Bruce was surprised." Angie took a deep breath and leaned toward Willow. "Willow, they were different than the ones I've had before. These were like a warning that something bad was going to happen to Tristian and Bruce."

"Duh, you were worried about Tristian trying to kill Bruce when he finds out. It was just your subconscious addressing your fears."

"No, I'm serious, Willow, I'm worried. The weird part is that the only way I could sleep without the nightmares was with Bruce wrapped around me."

"What! You said you didn't sleep with him."

"Don't be silly, I'm serious. We didn't have sex. It was as if the nightmares stayed away because of him being close enough to protect me from them. Sounds crazy, doesn't it?"

"No it doesn't, your mom was a seer, maybe you are just coming into that part of your talents. What did Bruce say?"

"I didn't tell him, yet. I will. I think he suspects there's more to the nightmares than I'm telling him. I wanted to get your take on it, and you said what I expected."

Willow tilted her head and stuck out her tongue. "I'm glad I'm predictable. But you better tell him and soon." A tinkling chime came from Willow's cell phone. She glanced down to check the text. "Now get your clothes changed, Tristian will be here any minute. Owen just texted me he's left the salon."

While she was changing, Willow hollered to Angie. "Hey I just got a super idea. After Tristian leaves town, why don't you and Bruce join Caleb and me for dinner. We can all get to know each other."

"Sounds great. I'll check with Bruce. We want to keep our relationship low profile until Tristian catches wind of it and we have to face him. But, we aren't hiding it either, so I imagine that will work. One more thing, Bruce wants you to call him if I have another one of those nightmares. He'll come right over."

"And if Tristian is here?" Willow asked.

"Don't call Bruce unless you or Tristian can't wake me. Then I guess that's how Tristian will find out about us. Not a scenario I want to face."

"Bruce's place is where they started. Maybe you won't have them here."

****

From the back room, Angie heard the front door chimes. She poked her head through the beaded curtains in time to see her brother amble through the door.

"Angie, are you here?" Tristian called as he stood in the middle of the show room where rainbows danced across the floor. Angie watched as he surveyed the showroom filled with glass cases of crystals, statues of wizards, faeries, water nymphs, dragons, and every kind of mythical creature.

The crystal beads tinkled as she stepped through the curtain, catching Tristian's attention. "Welcome to The Krystal Unicorn." She sauntered past the bookcase on the far wall that held shelves of how to books, for magic, growing medicinal herbs, horoscopes, and tarot cards reading.

In front of the main counter, she greeted Tristian with a hug and kiss on the check. "Sorry to have worried you. I had a couple of days off and decided to get away for a while."

"I know, Willow told me." He glanced over Angie's head to the mirrored wall behind the main counter "I didn't notice all those." Tristian motioned to the glass shelves of crystal apothecary jars filled with a wide variety of herbs, lotions, and miscellaneous ingredients. Then he glanced at a sign on the counter written in a purple flowery script that said, "If you don't see it, we will be happy to order it, just ask." Tristian smiled at her and pointed to the sign. "Cute sign. Nice place you got here."

"Thank you, we're proud of it." Angie knew he was doing his avoidance thing, so she cut to the chase. "If you'd called, I would have stayed here," Angie said.

"I wanted to surprise you. Wouldn't be a surprise if I called," he said, then hesitated. "Hell Angie, I wasn't sure you'd agree to see me."

One of several large crystals hung strategically in the front window cast a rainbow over Tristian's face. He frowned and moved out of the crystal's trajectory.

Angie smiled remembering when they chased rainbows as children. "Of course I would. You're my big brother." Angie reached up and threw her arm around his shoulder. "So where are you taking me to dinner?"

He grinned down at her. "Anywhere you want."

Once seated in the Italian restaurant, Tristian put his hand over his sister's. "I want to apologize for the things I said before you left. I know you're grown up and I have to let you go, but it's not easy, with all the things that could happen to you."

"I know. I'm sorry too for some of the things I said. But you have to trust me. There are a lot of things you should have told me for my own protection. Willow and I have had long talks about the things you wanted kept from me."

Tristian's mouth was set in a firm line, his dark eyes flashing.

"Now don't get mad, I just want everything out in

the open, and I mean everything, since all of it could affect me someday. Then we start with a clean slate and rebuild our relationship. Fair enough? I will always love you, but respect on both sides is important." As she said this, she thought about Bruce and how that would affect anything they decided. She had to trust that it would all work out somehow.

"Sounds fair."

"One more thing, my private life is just that, private. If I decide to share any of it with you, that's my decision, not for you to snoop."

"But how am I supposed to protect you?"

"I believe the spells you arranged on The Krystal Unicorn and my apartment will be of help in that area."

The shock and confusion on Tristian's face made Angie burst out laughing. "I am a witch with pretty good command of the powers I possess, no thanks to you."

Sheepishness now replaced the confused look crossing his face. "It was supposed to be undetectable by any magic source. Apparently, something went wrong. I'll have to work on that."

Recovering from her fit of laughter that left tears streaming down her face, Angie suggested. "Maybe you should mind your own business. Honestly, I have friends that were aware of your desire to protect me. Thanks for caring, but could you just consult me next time?"

"Yes, I see that you are all grown up and I have to let you go. It's not easy, you are all I have, but I'll try. I love you, Angie, and don't want anything to happen to you."

"I know and I won't take unnecessary chances."

Chapter Ten

It had been slow all day. The trickle of customers appeared to stop at midday. Everyone was preparing for the Cherry Blossom Festival gearing up for the weekend.

A brief glance at the salon, told Bruce there were two customers left and it looked like they were about finished. With one thing and another, he'd not had a chance to see or even phone Angie all week. Leaning back in his chair, rubbing his eyes with thumb and forefinger, he made a decision. The computer indicated no new e-mails, so he turned it off and reached up to turn the desk lamp off as well.

Bruce stood, shaking the wrinkles out of his slacks that formed from sitting so long and walked to the stairs, taking them two at a time he landed on both feet at the bottom. A grin spread across his face, one of the staff near him glanced over amused.

A quick scan of the salon found Owen at Tobi's station. "Hey Owen," he called as he crossed the floor. "Let's close the salon and let everyone join the Cherry Blossom festivities." His exuberance had everyone raising his or her eyebrows. Known for his quiet, controlled demeanor, this was anything but. "With pay of course."

Owen grinned. "You heard the boss, clean up your stations, finish up your customers, and get out of here before he changes his mind." Owen stepped to the OPEN sign, flipped the switch to CLOSED and locked the door, but stood there to let out the last customer.

Finally, Owen came back to Tobi's station and put his arm around his wife. "Let's go. We can finish up the close out paperwork tomorrow."

Grinning Bruce called out, "Owen, you and Tobi take the weekend off. I'll I handle the salon. I don't want to see or hear from you until Tuesday morning when you open. Got it?"

"Sure thing, I'll just finish up the little paperwork left from today, and close out the cash drawer. It'll only take a minute. It's been so slow I got most of it done already."

"Good man. In that case, close up, I'm going for a walk, see you Tuesday, and have a great weekend."

Owen followed Bruce to the door. Bruce turned, a slight smirk on his face, "I can let myself out, I have keys you know."

"I know that. I just wanted to update you on the rumblings. Tristian's info is correct, but I'm hitting a brick wall with our sources. You may want to touch base with the other Overlords and see what they know."

"Good idea. I'll get on that first of the week. I plan to enjoy the weekend too, around the work schedule, of course." He turned the key in the lock letting himself out and disappeared down the street toward The Krystal Unicorn.

****

The glass door to The Krystal Unicorn opened wide enough to let a person in sideways, but not enough to trip the chimes. Bruce grinned. There were no customers in the store. Silently, he crossed the show room floor and saw Willow and Angie in the back bent over a large box, checking its contents.

He slipped to the side of the beaded curtain, the women still unaware of his presence. Willow glanced up and spied Bruce peering through the beads. He put a finger to his lips with a pleading look. Raising a brow, she smiled slightly and returned her attention to the box, Angie's back was still toward him.

As he glided up behind her, grasped both of her arms, and nuzzled her neck. The scream she let out deafened his right ear and rattled the windows. He spun her around then his mouth covered hers hungrily, intending to arouse her.

Raising his mouth from hers, he gazed into her violet eyes. "I've missed you."

Willow stood with her hands fisted on her hips. "So much for keeping your relationship low profile or low key. Either get a room or let her get back to work." Willow laughed. "Good to see you again Bruce, I think."

In an exaggerated motion, he lifted his arms and spun around checking around the room and through the beaded curtain. "Hey there's no one here but you two, same as when I arrived." He pointed a long slim index finger toward Willow. "And you already know about us. Angie claims you can be trusted, so I saw no reason I couldn't kiss my li'l witch." Still holding her against him, he laid his head on the top of hers, letting her warmth and floral scent envelope him.

"I missed you too. It was a crazy week though. After Tristian left Wednesday morning, it's been nonstop from opening to close, until today." She threw her arms out, then let them drop. "It simply died."

"The salon too. How'd your visit with Tristian go?" Bruce asked.

"Not bad, we set boundaries for our relationship. I let him know I had an inkling of what he did for a living and that I knew we had to be careful. Also informed him I knew that he had protection spells for the shop and my apartment. I let him leave those in place, after all the things you told me. I feel safer and understand my brother's concern. How'd your meeting with Tristian go?"

"No indication that he knew anything about us. Just business concerns but I admit being relieved when he left. Now, about us, would you like to go to the Southwest Waterfront on 600 Water Street tonight, enjoy live music, cuisine from local restaurants, and huge fireworks display?"

"Are you sure? We'll be seen by hundreds of people."

"As we said before, we are not hiding our relationship. Though we can't be as affectionate as when we're alone, you understand. The nature of our relationship is what I want kept unknown."

"I'd love to go. I'll close the shop at four-thirty, change into my jeans, sweater, and running shoes, and meet you out back?"

"That works. I need to go back to the office and change also." Sending a sidelong glance at Angie, he winked and turned to address Willow. "If you and your guy don't have plans for this evening, would you like to join us?"

"We don't have any plans tonight. I'll call him and see if he wants to spend the evening with you and Angie. I'm sure it'll be fine." Willow grabbed her cell phone off the counter and hurried into the other room.

Angie tried to wriggle out of his grasp, but Bruce was too strong and she really liked the feel of him against her. But she wasn't getting the inventory counted or up on the shelves. "Bruce, I gotta get this stuff checked off and put away before I can leave tonight. So let go."

Reluctantly, he released her, breathing a kiss on her neck. "Next weekend, you off?"

"Yes, that's the current schedule." She raised her brow in question as she looked up at him.

"I'd like you to spend the weekend with me, we'll leave town as we did before, if you're available."

"Not only am I available, I would love it." She stood on her tiptoes and wrapped her arms around his chest, kissed his cheek then brushed her lips slowly over his, nipping at his bottom lip. "I can't wait."

"I told you guys to get a room or let her get back to work. Now out of here, Bruce." Willow pushed him toward the door. "Caleb and I will meet you two here between four-thirty and five?" She glanced between Angie and Bruce for confirmation of the time.

Bruce nodded. "That'll work fine. With the crowds that will already be there, it may be wise to take just one vehicle. I have the SUV today that will seat all of us comfortably, unless you and Caleb would rather be on your own, which I totally understand."

Willows eyes rounded. "I'm sure that will be just fine. Though you'll need to bring us back here, I'm spending the weekend with Caleb at his place."

The chimes rang cheerfully as Caleb entered the front door. Willow greeted him with a quick kiss as they inclined their heads together murmuring.

Leaning close to Bruce, Angie whispered, "The demon recluse seems to have turned into a social butterfly."

"You're good for me in a lot of ways. Though more social the setting, less questions asked."

"Smart idea. You'll have to bring me back to get my car too, so I can drive home."

"Well, that depends on where you want to spend the night, li'l witch," he said suggestively.

His seductive smile and possessive touch as he rubbed her lower back made her want to purr among other things. "Oh, does it."

"Didn't I just hear Willow say she was spending the night with Caleb? That leaves you all alone in your apartment."

Willow came bouncing in. "We'll ride with you." She waved her hand in the vicinity of Bruce and Angie. "Caleb this is my best friend Angelique and her companion, Bruce. Guys this is my friend Caleb."

Caleb nodded to Angie and offered his hand to Bruce. "It's a pleasure to meet you both. Don't you own the Wycked Hair salon down the street?"

Shaking his offered hand, Bruce said, "Yes I do."

"A lot of clientele from the art gallery, where my work is shown, patronize your salon and say it's the best in DC and surrounding area."

"We try. I think all our clients deserted us today in favor of the fun and festivities. I closed the salon early and came down here to visit these two lovely young ladies. I understand we are to meet back here and join the festivities ourselves."

"Yes, we'll see you two soon." Willow took Caleb by the hand and pulled him out of the shop.

"I'm going to go change my clothes and set the alarm on the salon, then I'll be back and help you with whatever you have left to do, since I have distracted your from your job." He ran his fingers slowly through her long golden blond hair, reclaiming her lips as he crushed her to him, and then held her tight against him before slowly releasing her.

Her body screamed for more when he released her. "You intended to stir me up on purpose." Angie accused, her lower lip stuck out in a pout. .

Bruce leaned over and kissed her pout. "Sure did. Didn't want you to forget me while I'm gone." He chuckled.

"No danger of that with or without that sort of incentive." She slithered against him then shoved him out the door. "Hurry back, you've caused me to get way behind in my work." Angie stood at the door for a moment and watched him walk down the street. *That is some kind of man.* The door closed.

****

Bruce didn't mention the nightmares and assumed that since he didn't receive a call, the nightmares had ceased. He'd check with her later tonight, but didn't want to ruin the evening festivities with the question. It would wait. Her frank discussion with Tristian had probably put her mind at ease and the nightmares to rest.

Seducing her at his apartment was not what he had planned. Keeping her close to him and safe was the goal. At least until he received more information about the high-level demon. He expected to see Tristian again soon, for no other reason than to check on his sister. If confronted, Bruce intended to explain his relationship with Angie and defend himself against Tristian, if necessary. But he'd prefer to avoid the situation.

Angie checked off the rest of the items in the box with the packing list and put them away. Then turned the OPEN sign to CLOSED, locked the front and back door. Her body was still tingling from Bruce's touch, a sensation she'd begun to enjoy. Obviously, they were meant to be together, but at what cost? He was so evasive about his life that she considered asking about it, but decided to wait until he was ready to share it with her.

A light knock on the back door at the same time her phone vibrated, told her it was Bruce. She answered the phone before opening the door. Security was foremost on her mind these days.

"Nice. You checked to make sure it was me before you opened the door. Good job."

"Since I seem to have forced myself into your world, I'd better learn to survive there." Angie said flippantly.

"Agreed. I'm sure Tristian, as well as, myself thank you for your efforts. Now, what I can I do to help so we can get out of here and enjoy the evening? It's a bit chilly, but beautiful for an early spring night, so bring a coat."

Several empty boxes littered the floor and she nodded in their direction. "Would you mind gathering those up and taking them to the dumpster? It's across the parking lot. I'll get my coat and meet you at the SUV out back. Willow and Caleb will be along shortly."

"You got it." He gathered the small boxes, put them in a big one, started to pick it up, then looked around. His dark amber eyes glowed orange and the box incinerated leaving only a trace of ash on the floor, which he wiped up with a damp paper towel and tossed in the trash. Sometimes you have to release a little magic just to keep in practice, he reasoned. The days of her standing in the dark alone, even for a minute were over, at least until the recent unknown demon threat was neutralized. Bruce had a bad feeling in his gut about this ever since Tristian brought it up.

Her coat stuffed in her bag, she bounced into the room. "I'm ready." She nearly collided with Bruce who still stood in the middle of the room. Sniffing the air, Angie narrowed her eyes at him, "You didn't."

Bruce shrugged. "I don't know what you're talking about." His arm around her shoulder, he turned her toward the door. "Come on, Willow and Caleb just pulled up." They hadn't reached the door yet when Willow rushed inside. "Sorry we're late, traffic was terrible. Glad you two are still here. Tonight is going to be fun." She turned right around and bounded out the door in front of them.

Bruce raised an eyebrow and looked questioningly at Angie. She shrugged. "It's Willow." He walked Angie to the door and waited for her to set the alarm and lock the door. They stepped outside where Willow and Caleb waited next to the only SUV in the parking lot. Bruce took the key fob out of his pocket and pressed it to unlock the vehicle for them. He opened Angie's car door, waited for her to settle in before closing it, then walked to his side of the car and got in.

"Wow, this is really nice. Thanks again for inviting us," Willow said. Caleb slipped his arm around Willow in the back seat in an effort to quiet her for the short drive.

Apparently, Caleb was the quiet type, or appeared that way because Willow was doing all the talking. Bruce noticed Caleb watching him several times during the night, Caleb seemed almost nervous.

Willow and Caleb went their own way and promised to meet back up by the music arena. Bruce and Angie wandered the area, her hand through his arm. As it grew cooler, she entwined her hand with his and slid them into his pocket for warmth. After sampling various foods that restaurants offered, they met up with Caleb and Willow and found seats for the four of them from which to enjoy the live music.

Bruce glanced at Caleb. "Tell me about your paintings. I'm looking to spruce up the salon with a few new pieces of art. Maybe I'll come by the gallery."

"Let me know when you plan to stop by. I'll meet you and see if any of my paintings would fit your decor." Caleb shifted in his seat and pulled out his wallet. "Here's my card, it has my cell phone and e-mail on it."

"Thanks, I'll be in touch."

The music was an eclectic mix of everything from Rock and Roll to Classical. They sang and swayed to the familiar songs, then a rousing rendition of the 1812 Overture brought a loud boom, and fireworks lit up the night sky in a brilliant array of colors. The fantastic display lasted thirty minutes, then the crowd began to disperse. The four of them headed back to the SUV and got inside. Bruce threaded the vehicle through traffic back to the shop.

Only two cars remained in the parking lot when Bruce turned in. "Is that your Charger, Caleb?"

"Sure is."

"Nice ride." He pulled along side the car, Willow and Caleb got out. Angie rolled her window down. "You staying with Caleb this weekend?"

"Yes for part of it, but I'll be around. Call if you need me."

"Don't worry." She shot a look toward Bruce and winked at Willow. "I'll be fine."

Willow raised her eyebrows, wrinkled her nose, and wagged her finger at Angie. "Don't do anything I wouldn't do." Then she burst into giggles.

Angie pretended seriously to consider her remark. "Ok, so that means that absolutely nothing is off limits. Right?" Her eyes danced with amusement as she succumbed to a fit of laughter.

Bruce leaned over Angie and looked out her open window where Caleb stood beside Willow. "I think the girls are tired and had a bit too much wine with dinner. Maybe we should take them home before they embarrass themselves further."

"Couldn't agree more. Thanks again for the invite, see ya later." Caleb grinned as he wrapped his arm around Willow's waist and guided her to the car. He opened the door and tucked her inside as she continued to giggle.

Bruce couldn't help but smile watching Angie try to compose herself. He pushed the button and brought the dark tinted window closed. "Ok, if nothing is off limits, is it your place or mine?"

"Your choice." She leaned over and slid her hand around his neck, bringing his lips to within a whisper of hers.

He moved the seat back and angled his body

toward her caressing the sides of her face with his hands, he laid his mouth on hers, parting her lips with his tongue, gently exploring and enjoying the hint of wine still on her tongue. This is what he'd wanted to do all evening.

The touch of his lips on hers sent waves of lust crashing through his entire body. He pulled her tighter as she arched up to meet his continued caress.

Stroking the side of her neck as his mouth grazed her earlobe, he slowly traced the hollow of her throat and feathered his fingers at the side of her breast, his thumb teasing her nipple every so lightly through her sweater.

She gasped softly and skimmed her fingers in his hair encouraging him, as his mouth trailed down.

He wanted to leave his hand there, even slide it under her sweater to cup her full breast, remove the lace bra holding them, but again this wasn't the place or the time. The excitement of having his way with a woman in a vehicle, even one this comfortable, had passed long ago. Bruce wanted to take his time with Angie. Naked in his bed, he'd slide between her legs, explore, arouse, and pleasure her until she succumbed to sleep enveloped in his arms. "Angie, lets continue this somewhere more comfortable," he whispered, his finger traced the inside edge of her low cut sweater. He brushed his lips over hers once more before starting the SUV and pulling out of the parking lot.

The secure entrance to his apartment complex loomed ahead. Iron gates drawn across the entrance gave the modern building a medieval appearance. He stopped at the key pad, lowered the dark tinted window, and punched in his security code. With a groan, the large wrought iron gates separated and rolled to each side allowing the vehicle inside. Once the vehicle passed through the gates and crossed the sensors, they closed immediately. His eyes flicked up to the rear view mirror confirming the gates returned to their closed position, before he continued on to one of his assigned but unmarked parking spaces.

The building housed D.C.'s elite politicians and offered the best security available in the mortal world. Even so, Bruce preferred the relaxed drive and safety of his estate. Tonight it was more convenient to stay close since both he and Angie needed to be at work early. It had been almost a year since he'd performed the opening procedures at the salon. He'd never hear the end of it if he didn't have the Wycked Hair ready when the staff arrived.

"This place looks like the setting where all the attacks and murders take place in underground parking lots on TV." She caught herself and grimaced. "Sorry, what a thing to say. I guess the wine loosened my tongue just a little too much."

"Let me be the judge of that," he said seductively

"Just like a male, add a sexual twist to a simple innocent statement."

"I'm a male and thanks for noticing." He raised a brow and smiled reassuringly. "I can assure you that nothing like you see on TV has taken place here. If it would make you feel more secure, I can port us both to my penthouse." He opened the car door and in a whisper of movement, he was at her side opening her door and extending his hand to assist her out of the car.

"No, no, I'm fine, the penthouse? Wow, look a camera in every corner and two in front of the elevator.

What if we are seen together going up to your penthouse? Won't that blow the low profile we're trying to keep?" She took his arm as offered and walked toward the elevator.

"I've taken care of the cameras while we go to my apartment. The cameras never photograph my coming and going. On the outside, it looks like a selfish use of magic, but it's necessary to keep my personal habits and locations a mystery." He stepped into the elevator first, giving the inside a sweeping glance then tugged her quickly in beside him. The plush carpeting under foot and soundproof tiles overhead quieted their steps and hushed their words.

"Ok, I'll buy that, but how?" She stepped into the elevator.

"That's a question I am not at liberty to answer. The lives of many depend on my secrecy, yours included. Now, shall we exit to my apartment and entertain ourselves in a more pleasurable way?" The air whooshed out of her as he swept her up in his arms and carried her through the door.

She wrapped her arms around his neck and sighed. "That was so romantic. You take my breath away."

Lowering her down lightly on her feet, his hands glided down the length of her back ending at the small of her waist. He curved her into his body and whispered, "There is nothing I'd like to do more than take you to bed with me tonight and show you what romance is all about. But, I fear the wine has lowered your inhibitions. When I make love to you the first time, it will be slow and gentle and with your complete consent, because after that there will be no turning back for either of us."

She pulled away, her violet eyes blazing. "I am not drunk. I only had a couple of glasses of wine."

"I know, but for some reason it affected both you and Willow. Maybe it was the wine tasting at the end that did you both in." He moved around the room turning on soft music and starting a fire in the stone hearth.

"Fine, I'll just go to bed by myself. Where is my room?" Her arms crossed over her chest, she glared at him.

"Let's not end this wonderful night with a disagreement. Come sit with me on the couch while I enjoy my glass of wine along with your warm fragrant body curled against me. Then I'll carry you into our room and share my bed with you, without the intimacy we will save for another time. Perhaps at my estate."

The gentle nature of his request and the faint twinkle in the depths of his dark amber eyes, made her relent and follow him to the couch. She settled next to him and rested her head on his shoulder. "Would you like a t-shirt to sleep in? Or are you going to lay naked all night, just to tease me with your sensual body?"

"My first instinct would be to sleep naked, just to get back at you. But I'd be mortified to wake up naked next to you in the morning."

"If it would make you feel better, I'll sleep naked too. I've no inhibitions about naked flesh. Just not under the covers with you. Even I have my limits of self-restraint." He cradled his arm around her and sipped his wine as they enjoyed the soothing music and crackling fire. "Would you like some sparkling juice, hot chocolate or soothing tea?"

Angie shook her head.

Chapter Eleven

As they wound their way through the DC morning traffic discussing the anticipated day's events, his cell phone chirped. Bruce checked the caller ID and looked over at Angie. "Excuse me, I have to take this."

"No problem," she said quietly.

"I'm on my way to the office now, can it wait?" He hesitated and listened intently before responding. "I understand. I'll call Bobby. See if his team can handle the situation. If not, then we'll need to call in Tristian. I'd rather discuss any further details from my office, security you know." He disconnected the call and glanced over at Angie. "Sorry about that."

"No problem. Sounds like your day is starting off with a bang."

"Yeah." He stopped the car at the back door of The Krystal Unicorn. Unfastened his seat belt and leaned over to brush a kiss across her lips, then laid his cheek against hers. "Do me one favor, please be locked in your apartment before dark."

"You're worse than my brother." Angie gave an exaggerated eye roll and felt for the door handle.

Bruce shook his head. "Nope, pro-active and maybe a bit protective. There are issues we're trying to settle, and until we do, extra caution is required. I may not see you for a couple of days, depending how my day sorts out and I don't want to worry about whether you're safe or not."

"You won't tell me what's going on. You're sheltering me just like my brother," she sputtered, bristling with indignation and hurt.

Keeping his anger and frustration under control, he said in a low composed voice, "No, I'm not. I just don't have time to go into it all now. I will soon and maybe by then we'll know more. What we know is even our well trusted sources are afraid to talk and that concerns me greatly."

"What about Willow?" Angie asked.

"Willow grew up aware of my world. She knows. However, I'm going to check out her boyfriend anyway. Please let Willow know to be extra vigilant, until we know what we're dealing with."

Angie reached into her bag for the keys to the shop, then opened the car door and stepped out. Bruce appeared beside her as she turned the key in the lock and shoved the heavy wooden door open. Peering in cautiously, he held it open for her as she entered and deactivated the alarm. He followed her in then walked the entire shop. Sensing no danger, he kissed her forehead as he ran his fingers through her hair and was gone.

Bruce left the blue luxury SUV parked in the lot behind The Krystal Unicorn. He decided to walk the couple of blocks to the The Wycked Hair, and check on her store before he got in his vehicle to go home tonight.

****

The alarm's LED light glowed steady red indicating no intruders during the night. He unlocked the door to the salon and entered the disarm code, then closed and relocked the door. The salon wouldn't be open for a couple more hours and the employees had their own keys.

He'd forgotten how well he liked the quiet of the salon before anyone arrived. Bruce filled the glass coffee pot with filtered water and slid it under the coffee system, poured beans into the grinder and pushed the button. He sniffed and sighed, the aroma of fresh ground coffee beans, nothing better in the predawn light. He took the cash drawer out of the floor safe and slid it into place under the counter next to the computer. Owen made the bank deposit when he left yesterday, so there was only a couple hundred in small bills and coin to make change for the early customers. Reaching across the counter he pushed the power button on the computer and monitor watching as they came to life, ready for a new day.

Finished with the opening duties of the salon, Bruce climbed the stairs to his office, with his steaming mug of black coffee, to continue the business that had interrupted his morning commute. The only sound in his office was the rustle of the leather as he sat in the chair, leaned back, and took a sip of the fresh brewed coffee. He closed his eyes and took a deep breath, letting it out slowly, turned the laptop on, and prepared for a busy day.

The cell phone he'd laid on his desk was the first intruder in his quiet world. It emitted two different tones, letting him know there were callers on both lines and the computer chimed the arrival of over eighty new e-mails. Yep. It was going to be a long day, he'd be lucky to get out by midnight.

As he picked up his cell phone and tapped the

green button to answer, the salon phone on his desk rang. He watched all seven lines light up. "Hang on a minute Cade."

Where the hell was Reka, she was supposed to answer the phone while Owen and Tobi were gone. A quick glance at his watch, told him she wouldn't be in for another half hour. He flipped the phone switch to silent, routed the calls back to the night answering service, and returned his attention to the call on his cell phone.

"I'm sorry Cade. It's crazy around here. Owen and Tobi have a few well-deserved days off, I'm paying the price already, and it's only the first day." He blew out a breath. "Now bring me up to speed on what's happening down south."

Bruce listened intently, eyes narrowed. "I see. But I still want to give Bobby and his team a chance to see if they can straighten it out without bloodshed, if not then we'll call in Tristian. I'll have Bobby down there by midday. Good enough?"

"There's a vampire involved? That's just great, I'll call the Vampire Council and see if they want to handle it or leave it to us. I'll be in touch." He ended the call and dialed Bobby's number. He rubbed his temples to ease the throbbing headache and the salon wasn't even open yet. Then he remembered there'd been a call on the other line, he checked the ID, it was Tristian, probably just checking in. *I'll have to get back to him.*

A deep voice answered on the second ring. "Morning boss. To what do I owe the pleasure?"

"Bobby, I have a job for you."

****

All the opening duties done, Angie sat down to

peruse a book she'd just unpacked, The Latest Healing Power of Herbs. The door chimes rang as Willow flitted in.

Angie chuckled. "Can't stay away even on your day off, huh?"

"Caleb had to go to the gallery to finish the sale paperwork for several of his paintings." Willow leaned on the counter, glancing around the store to make sure they were alone. "So…how'd it go last night? Did you go home with him?" Willow raised her brows.

"Yes, I did. His apartment is in the penthouse and security is tight, cameras all over the place. Although he still uses magic to cover exits and entrances."

"Well…did you?"

"Willow." Angie let out an exasperated breath. "We're not teenagers any more. I'm not going to tell you what did or didn't happen last night." Angie's violet eyes snapped with impatience.

"Why not? We've shared most everything all our lives. I didn't ask details, it just requires a simple yes or no answer."

"Well, did you?" Angie shot back at Willow.

"You know the answer to that, I told you the next day. So there's nothing new with me. But you, a handsome, powerful demon…well, you know kinda like your prince? So you're really not going to tell me?" Willow's shoulders drooped and her gaze dropped to the floor.

Angie relented. "No, ok, we didn't. Happy? We spent the evening in front of the fireplace cuddling and talking. I fell asleep and woke up in his bed, dressed in one of his t-shirts with him beside me on top the covers. At least there were no nightmares."

Willow's face clouded with worry when her gaze met Angie's. "Glad there weren't any nightmares. The one you had while Tristian was here, scared the shit of out me. Not your normal night frights. Did you tell Bruce about it?"

"No, I figured if I had another one, then I'd tell him. I think it was just the stress of learning about Tristian and being with Bruce, then worrying about Tristian finding out. I've come to terms with all of that now, Bruce and I will deal with it together when it happens." Angie shrugged. "No more nightmares, so that must have been it."

"I hope so." Willow lifted a black eyebrow. "Enough trying to side track me, let's get back to the more interesting subject at hand. Why didn't you? If it was me, I couldn't keep my hands off him. He's absolutely gorgeous and so sensual."

"If you must know, it's because he felt the wine clouded my judgment, and he was right. I vaguely remember offering to sleep naked beside him, if he'd do the same. He agreed, but I must have fallen asleep before the discussion was finished, because I woke up in his t-shirt." She sighed just a little. "It smelled so good. I just love the way he smells."

"Ohhh, now were getting somewhere. Was he naked?"

"None of your business. Except." She giggled feeling silly about admitting it. "I stuck his t-shirt in my bag. I love his spicy scent. When he's not around, I feel safer wrapped in his shirt."

"How romantic." Willow rested her chin in her hands and her eyes went dreamy.

"He also keeps mentioning that once we commit,

it's forever, there's no turning back." Angie tilted her head. "Strange huh? There's always a choice."

Staring openly at her, Willow swallowed hard. "Not if…that depends on if you believe in destiny, fate or whatever you want to call it, and apparently he does."

"That stuff is just fairy tales." Angie flipped her hair over her shoulder and turned the book she'd been reading over in her hands.

"Think about it. After six hundred years, he's never found a woman he wanted to commit to or spend his life with. He must feel pretty strongly about your relationship to risk Tristian's wrath, possible betrayal, and not to mention his position as Overlord." Willow picked at the edge of her blouse. "Not that I think your brother would carry it that far, but he's gonna be pissed."

Angie sobered and she grasped her friend by the arm. "Are you serious?"

"Yes. When you're in Bruce's position, there is always someone waiting in the shadows to take advantage of a weak moment, seize the opportunity to kill him then take over his position."

"I'm kinda expected to have his back?"

"Sorta. It's not likely to happen because he was born and bred to be Overlord, as his father before him. Just the same, you shouldn't take the responsibility and dangers of being his mate lightly."

"Then why doesn't he just say what he means, instead of being so cryptic?" Angie tilted her head questioningly at her friend. "And when did you become such an expert in all things demon?"

"When my best friend became involved with not

only a demon but a demon Overlord much to her detriment," Willow countered. "If your feelings are the same, it must be your decision without any influence from him. You said from the very start that the connection between you two was like nothing you'd ever felt. Right?"

"Yes, I still feel it every time we're together and it's getting stronger. What do you think?"

Willow shook her head. "I've said too much already, these are things your mother should have told you."

Angie glared at Willow. "And she couldn't, she died."

Willow winced. "I know, I know, she died before she had the chance. Instead, you're difficult, hardheaded, jackass of a brother chose to disregard the possibility something like this could happen. Left you naive to the magical world and mistakenly felt you were safer in the mortal world."

Angie's brow creased in confusion. "Something like what? I don't have a mother or a sister. You've got to tell me how this works."

Willow grimaced and drew in a breath, letting it out slowly. "I think you are his predestined mate, he's waited a long time to find you. I see it in your eyes when you look at him, so does he…believe me. The fact he hasn't seduced you yet, shows great self-restraint on his part. He wants you to come to him. It has to be your free choice."

"Ok, so let me get this straight. If you were in love with Caleb, not just lust, and he's from the mortal realm or raised there, you couldn't just tell him how you felt?"

"First of all, I'm not royalty in the magic realm, so different rules apply, and I'm female so I'm allowed a certain amount of latitude. But for your question, no, it's forbidden. We have to let our actions speak for us." Willow waved her hands over her head then let them drop to her sides.

A half smile crossed Angie's face. *Willow couldn't talk if someone tied her hands.*

Willow frowned then continued. "Then it's up to the mortal or in your case, a witch raised in a mortal world, to decide if what they feel is strong enough to want to be with that person or demon forever. There are no divorces in the magic world, only by death and that's more common than you'd like to think." Willow studied the floor then slowly brought her eyes up to meet Angie's.

Angie sat silently taking it all in and staring at her hands clenched on the top of the glass showcase. Willow covered Angie's hands with hers. "Sorry I didn't tell you sooner, but I promised my mom and your brother I'd not interfere in how he wanted to handle it. I just had no idea he wouldn't tell you this stuff or at the very least release me from my promise or send you to talk with my mom."

"Wow, Bruce warned me when he thought I was trying to force my way into his world. I just didn't see how different our worlds could be."

The door chimes sounded announcing the arrival of a customer. Angie turned her attention to a well-dressed middle-aged man and Willow slipped into the back room.

****

It was past midnight when Bruce walked down the

steps from his office, set the alarm, and locked the door, thankful for the end of a brutal day. The volume at the salon dictated that he help customers too, which he'd not done in years. Truth be told, he enjoyed the couple of haircuts he'd done. One customer looked so much better, in short, shaped hair than the long stringy style she'd come in with. He'd never enjoyed coloring, but the older woman looked ten years younger when he was done. She was thrilled with the highlights and he enjoyed the satisfaction of making his customers look their best.

On the opposite end of the spectrum, it looked like he'd have to call Tristian to neutralize the situation in the south. The Vampire Council already sent their envoy who took out the rogue vampire leader quickly and quietly, but the remaining changelings, demons, and werewolf were determined to control the election outcome, and remained his responsibility. The independent candidate disappeared and the front-runner of the election was in hiding. Bobby planted a news story cover implicating terrorist factions, but no one had taken responsibility nor demanded a ransom.

This has gone far enough. He pulled out his cell phone and called Tristian.

"Well it's about time, wondered if you were going soft on us, not a good message to send," Tristian said tersely.

Bruce didn't rise to the insult, but gave it consideration. "We didn't know a candidate had already been taken out when I sent Bobby to investigate. Besides last time we talked it seemed you needed some time to sort out a personal matter."

"Personal matters don't interfere with the ability to

do my job. You know that better than anyone," Tristian shot back irritably.

"I do, and never question your abilities. I was merely giving you a chance to take care of your personal situation. Assignments have been back to back recently, everyone needs down time. So take care of this and take some well-deserved time off."

"Thanks. You'll still be able to reach me by phone in an emergency."

"That'll work." His demon blood reveled in the thought of taking out the brazen offenders. Though Tristian would make it swift, painless, and leave no trace. He didn't have the stomach or time for torture. "And Tristian the official report can wait until you return from personal leave. Just give me a verbal by phone when you're done."

If it came down to it, his mother's blood kept him from enjoying the consideration of such an act. There'd been times he'd overrode her blood influence and done what was necessary. That was a long time ago, when he battled for his position, now he preferred to let Tristian handle the situation however he saw fit.

Bruce glanced down at the phone, which still held Tristian's number. Dreading the conversation he needed to have with Tristian. He'd already decided to attempt to keep his relationship with Angie from her brother, until he'd taken her as his mate.

After that there would be nothing Tristian could do and most likely the fight between them wouldn't be to the death. Bruce wasn't willing to kill his mate's brother, but felt sure Tristian would have no qualms attempting to kill him. It wouldn't be easy, but he was confident he'd be the victor in such a battle. What concerned him most was the pain it would cause Angie. Her mate and her brother would be mortal enemies, not to mention the political ramifications.

Owen would need to issue Tristian the assignments for a while. The less contact Bruce had with Tristian the better, until he came to terms with his sister's choice. There was no doubt that Tristian would eventually accept it and they would began to rebuild the working relationship. Hopefully, that would include some semblance of friendship they'd enjoyed for years.

It was a good idea for him to park behind her shop. The walk had given Bruce a chance to sort out the day and his personal issues. More certain now than he'd felt since she came into his life. It was time to make his move. If only it would be as easy as he envisioned.

She was aware of the connection between them, as he was, only she didn't have any idea how that connection could change her life forever. He cursed out loud. *I shouldn't be the one to explain it to her. Her parents should have taught her as she grew up. Instead, Tristian directed her life to the mortal world without teaching her to navigate the magic one. She should've learned to wield her power in that world and protect herself when necessary.* That was enough thinking. His head was beginning to ache.

Walking past the back door to her shop, he checked the light on the alarm, it still glowed solid red, no breach in security since she set it. The area seemed calm and peaceful. He hoped it stayed that way. At his car, he opened the driver's door, slid into the seat, and closed the door. He reached into his pocket for his phone and keyed in her number. At least he would hear her voice before heading home to an empty apartment.

****

She answered at the first ring. "Hi Bruce. Are you just now leaving work?"

"Yeah." He closed his eyes letting to her melodic voice wash over him.

"Rough day, huh?"

"You could say that. How was yours?" He turned the key in the ignition and the engine roared to life.

"Enlightening and busy. Want to come over?"

"I do, but it's late and you have to work tomorrow." His heart quickened at the thought of seeing her tonight.

"I don't have to go in at any set time. I just have to check the inventory and e-mail orders to our suppliers, so they'll ship Monday morning. The salon is closed tomorrow. You don't have to go in, do you?"

"I hope not," he said wearily.

"Come on over."

"I'll be there shortly. Is Willow there?"

"Nope. We have the apartment all to ourselves until tomorrow night. It's not as grand as yours, but it's cozy."

Dressed in only his t-shirt, she greeted him at the door with a warm, affectionate touch of her lips to his, wrapping her arms around his waist drawing him against her.

He rested his arms on her shoulders letting his hands caress the back of her neck and down her spine breathing in her essence. This was just what he needed after the day he'd had.

She gazed up at him, tenderly brushing the blonde streaked hair out of his eyes. "You look like hell."

"And you are the most beautiful woman I've ever

seen. Leaning over slightly he massaged little circles at the small of her back with his fingertips as she curved into him. "Nice t-shirt."

Angie's cheeks reddened. "I guess I stuck it in my bag by mistake. Want it back?"

"That depends on what you have in mind. You look good in it."

"Have you eaten?"

He hesitated and considered for a moment. "Not since sharing breakfast with you."

"Have a seat." She pulled out one of the old wooden chairs at the kitchen table. A pot of steaming Chamomile tea sat on the stove. Angie reached for the kettle, poured a big mug, and placed it in front of him. "Drink up, it will make you feel better, relax you."

She popped two pieces of prairie bread into the toaster and pressed the lever down, then grabbed a jar of peanut butter from the cupboard. "Nothing makes you feel better than a warm piece of toast, covered in melty peanut butter with just a touch of honey."

The aroma of warm toast wafted through the room, the toaster clicked and bread popped up an even golden brown. She whisked it out of the toaster, spread a bit of butter, then slathered her special mixture of peanut butter and honey on top.

Angie handed him the piece of toast. He held her wrist and licked the peanut butter from her thumb and little finger, released her, bit into the toast, and closed his eyes savoring its flavor and texture on his tongue.

"Good huh?" She stood behind him letting her arms wander down his neck and shoulders, undoing the first few buttons of his shirt, and sliding her hands inside, her fingertips caressing the contours of his muscular chest.

He opened his eyes and grasped her arm spinning her so she stood in front of him. Staring hungrily at every curve and angle of her shapely little body, he whispered, "I like the way my t-shirt fits your curves."

She tugged the neck of the shirt over her nose and mouth. "I like the way it still has your scent, it makes me feel safe. That's why I stole it this morning. You don't mind, do you?"

"No, but I'm not sure how much longer you are going to be wearing it, if you continue to let your hands roam over my body." He caught her hand as it slid beneath the waistband at the front of his jeans. "Before we go any farther we need to have a serious discussion."

She wound herself around him and settled in his lap. "So talk."

"What you think you want with me comes with serious consequences and responsibilities." He took a deep breath and blew it out. How could he give her a lifetime of knowledge in a couple of hours or even a couple of days? Maybe she instinctively knew, but he couldn't assume that. It all had to be laid out before her, so her decision was based on cold hard facts. Not some fairy tale fantasy woven by a naive young woman meant to be his mate, forever.

"You're exhausted. Why don't you spend the night here and we can finish this conversation in the morning, when we've both gotten a good night's sleep. I've had quite a day myself. I'll take Willow's bed and you can have mine."

"Are you sure?" He laid his cheek on the top of her shoulder and let out a breath.

She brushed a kiss across his other cheek. "I'm sure."

****

Slivers of yellow sunlight streamed through a crack in the curtains and warmed her face. Angie opened her eyes to discover sometime in the night he'd rolled over and banded his arm around her. They lay face to face. His impressive erection seated comfortably between her splayed legs confirmed what she'd always heard. Testosterone was highest in the morning and here was proof, it didn't matter whether the male was demon or human. *Where the hell did that come from?* She stifled a giggle.

She hadn't noticed he was naked, when she slid into bed with him last night. *Must have been more tired than I thought.* Then it hit her, this was not where she wanted their first time to happen, not in her apartment, where her brother cast a protection spell without her permission. Not in Bruce's apartment, a place he spent very little time in and kept only for convenience. She wanted it to happen at his estate, so lovingly protected by his mother and father. A place he considered a sanctuary. The first time, she wanted to be in his king size bed when they made love that would bind them to each other for eternity.

Gently she loosened his arm, wriggled ever so slightly out from under his hold and slipped out of the bed, padding silently through the doorway.

The corners of his lips curved again in an unseen smile as she closed the door quietly. He had to quit letting her do this to him or he was going to explode, not to mention being on a sexual edge all the time. Stretching his arms, he sat up and swung his legs out of bed, looking around. Thank the stars her room had its own shower. He turned it on full cold and stepped under the spray. He'd taken more cold showers in the last few weeks than he had in the last six-hundred years.

The cold water alleviated his aching hard-on but the desire to have her naked and under him was damn near unbearable. It wouldn't be long before the demon blood inside him reached boiling point and would demand he mate with or without her consent and to hell with the consequences. His self-control was dancing around the limits of no return. He yanked on jeans, leaving the top button undone, towel-dried his hair and pulled on the shirt he'd worn last night.

"Oh, you're awake and showered," she said as she peeked in the open door. "I've breakfast ready in the kitchen, if you're hungry."

"What I'm hungry for isn't in the kitchen." He lunged and swept her up in his arms, his mouth taking hers possessively while he eased down on the bed.

She giggled and tried to wriggle out of his grip. "You said we'd finish the conversation we started last night."

"You've taunted and teased me until my self-control is at the end of its tether. Which li'l witch is bad news for you." His hot breath caressed the hollow of her neck as he settled her in his lap and nipped at her fragrant flesh then soothed it with a warm wet kiss. He trailed his lips to the rise of her breast, tongue slipping inside the neckline of her low cut sweater and down between her soft mounds as his hand trailed to the waistband of her jeans.

With a flick of his thumb he had the top button of

her jeans undone and the zipper well on its way down, fingers exploring just inside her silky panties reaching for her warm, wet for him center. Gently spreading her thighs apart, he would have her now. His heart raced and breathing increased as if he was at the end of a long uphill sprint.

She shoved against him. "Wait, don't you want to know how Willow enlightened my world yesterday?"

"No," he said flatly, moving his other hand under her sweater, brushing her silky bra aside to cup her soft, firm breast and stroke her nipple with his thumb. Nostrils flaring, he breathed in her arousal as the haze of sexual desire enveloped him.

"No. No. This is not the way or the place I want our first time to be." She struggled against his iron grip. "Listen to me." She demanded. "I want it to be at your estate, after we've just been horseback riding. We'll go up to your bedroom, slowly undress each other. Then we'll step into your shower where I can run my hands over every inch of your gorgeous wet body. Making love should be about intimacy, knowing each other's body as well as your own. I want to lay naked on your king size bed as we enjoy each other until the wee hours of the morning, afternoon, or evening. Not in the apartment my brother protected with spells without my permission."

The panic pitch of her voice caught his attention. He pulled back. His smoldering gaze held hers, and he considered her words. She was consenting. Did she understand what her consent meant? He had to know. *This will be the last time you take me to the edge without gratification, li'l witch.* Lowering her feet to the floor, he growled, "Leave me alone for a few minutes.

I'll join you in the kitchen when I'm ready. Now get out of here before I change my mind."

The bedroom door flew open and she sprinted down the hallway to the kitchen

Bruce stood at the side of the bed, rubbing the back of his neck. *That witch will be the death of me, if I don't get control of myself. I am not some horny teenager.* He buttoned the top button of his jeans and pulled on a long sleeved t-shirt, breathing deeply he let it out slowly before he followed the scent of coffee down the hall. *What I really need is another cold shower.*

"Ok, so what information did you learn from Willow yesterday?" He shoved his hands in his pockets and paced around the kitchen.

Angie remained in her chair, nervously chewing on her bottom lip "Most of what you wanted to talk about. She thinks fate has determined that we should be together. Because of your birthright and position in the magic world, it's a big deal when you find your mate. Is she right?"

"She's on the right track." He nodded approvingly, grabbing a mug next to the coffee pot and pouring himself a cup. He closed his eyes, breathed in the delicious aroma and took a big gulp.

"Willow also said that once we make love, we are forever bound to each other, until death do us part, literally." She stared into the steaming mug of hot chocolate in her hands then took a sip and sat the mug back on the table.

"That's true, but with this commitment also comes responsibilities and dangers of being my mate. The choices I must make for the good of magic kind are not always popular or understood. My enemies will try to influence my decisions by threatening your well-being or continued existence."

Hands clasped in her lap, she stared down at them afraid he'd see the fear in her eyes if she looked up. Still she wanted to be with him, the connection between them soothed her even as he described what could happen.

"I've deliberately laid out the worse possibilities first, but there are benefits to being my mate as well. Those I can show you later," he purred suggestively, then winked. "Ok, enough talk. How about breakfast? I'm starving and you're due at work soon. Mind if I come with you to help out, so you can get out of there quickly. I have plans for this afternoon that I think you will enjoy."

Her chair scraped the floor as Angie stood up. "The apple cinnamon oatmeal is warming in the oven. It may not be as good as Megan's, but I like it." She crossed to the cupboard and took two glasses out, filling them with orange juice, then sitting them on the table next to the bowls.

Bruce opened the oven door and sniffed as he took the casserole dish out and sat it on the table. "Heavenly," he sighed. Taking a spoon from beside his bowl, he scooped up a bite and popped it in his mouth. "Mmmmm. Delicious," he purred his empty spoon hovering above the dish.

Angie quickly reached across the table and smacked his hand. "Don't put the spoon back in the casserole dish when you've had it in your mouth."

"Sorry," he murmured suppressing a grin, "it's wonderful. Could I have a piece of toast with the peanut butter concoction you fed me last night?"

She smiled reaching for the jar of peanut butter and bottle of honey. "Of course."

****

Once inside the back room of the shop, she handed him a clipboard with an inventory list. "I'll read off the item number as I unpack it and you mark it down as received. Then we'll compare the usual number we stock and I'll place an order for the items we are low on."

"I can do that." He took the clipboard and reached for a pen.

A tap on the front window made them both jump. Angie peered through the beaded curtain. Mrs. Staret stood outside the door with a plate of cookies. Angie unlocked the front door looking puzzled. "We aren't open on Sunday. Is there something I can do for you?"

"No dear, I always bring Willow cookies when she works on Sunday. Since you are here, I guess these are for you." She handed the cookies to Angie and looked around.

"Would you like to sit down for a bit? I'll get us a cup of hot cider to go with the cookies." Angie offered feeling Mrs. Staret's loneliness. "Is your daughter and her family out of town?"

"Yes, they took a trip to Colorado to see friends. They'll be back next week. But you are busy. I don't want to be a bother."

"Not a bother, sit down, I'll get the cider." She walked into the back where Bruce sat and said in a low voice, "Her family is out of town and she's lonely. I also suspect she saw your car out back." Angie got out mugs, heated the cider in the microwave, and put everything on a silver tray.

"I'll just finish this up, so you can place the order, and we can go, after your visit with Mrs. Staret," Bruce said.

"Thanks." Angie handed him a couple of cookies and a mug of hot cider. He stood and parted the crystal beads for her as she passed through to the front carrying the tray of cookies and mugs of hot cider.

"Oh, you're not alone." Mrs. Staret raised her eyebrows and clicked her tongue in disapproval.

"No, I'm not. Bruce is helping me with inventory." Angie put the tray down on a small table between two comfy chairs near the bookshelves.

Mrs. Staret walked to the table and paused as if trying to decide whether she wanted to sit. Finally, she settled into a chair, picked up a mug, and brought it to her lips. She took a sip and picked up a cookie. "I saw you two at the festival and fireworks the other night, you were with Willow and her young man." She took a bite and watched Angie decide on a cookie.

"Yes, wasn't it a beautiful night?" Angie took a bite of cookie and chewed thoughtfully.

"It was. Paul loved the Cherry Blossom Festival and fireworks. We never missed a year." Her eyes glistening, she looked down at the floor, then squared her shoulders and glanced toward the back room. "Paul was a wonderful man and didn't deserve what happened to him."

Unsure what to say, Angie nodded and said, "I am truly sorry for your loss."

Bruce stepped out of the back room. "Hello, Mrs. Staret, how nice to see you again."

"Good morning," she said curtly and put her half-eaten cookie back on her napkin.

Bruce cleared his throat. "Paul was a great man and an integral part of our team. I know you blame me for his death and feel you were kept in the dark about the circumstances. It wasn't intentional. I'd like to explain what really happened. Would you consider having dinner with Angie and me next Thursday evening? We'll pick you up around seven o'clock, or you can meet us at the restaurant of your choice. Later, we'll meet in my office, where we can speak freely without being over heard."

"I'll consider it, and let you know," she said icily as she sat her mug down on the tray and stood.

"Sure, just give me a call." He took out his business card, circled his cell number, and handed her the card. "You can reach me any time at that number."

She took the card and hesitated as if trying to decide what to do with it. Finally, she dropped it in the side pocket of her purse.

Bruce paused for a moment then said, "Or call Angie here at the shop." He smiled warmly and offered his hand to her.

She took his hand and shook it stiffly then backed away. "Good day to you both, I hope you enjoy your afternoon." She strode across the floor and waited for Angie to unlock the door, walking out without a backward glance.

"What was that all about?"

"Being a part of my life can be tedious, this is just an example of the things you'll encounter as my mate, food for thought before you make your final decision."

"Did you have something to do with Paul's death?" Angie asked.

"Not exactly, but he was following my

instructions," Bruce said tersely and ripped the order sheet from the clipboard handing it to Angie. "Let's get going."

She'd seen his eyes grow cold and his body stiffen before and knew the conversation was over. "Ok, let me get this order e-mailed off. Where are you taking me?" She asked cheerfully, hoping to brighten his mood as she confirmed the email and set the alarm.

"It's a secret, but I guarantee you'll enjoy yourself." He opened the car door and waited for her to get in and settled, the seatbelt secured. Then he walked around the vehicle got in and headed for the secret destination.

Bruce turned into the winding driveway of his estate and glanced over at her, surprised to see her anxiously picking at her finger nails. Remembering their morning conversation, he put a hand over the one she was picking at and smiled. "We are only going horseback riding for the afternoon. Jason already has Satan and Harbor saddled and waiting, probably not very patiently."

The look of delight spread over her face and sparkled in her eyes immediately. "Sorry I didn't…"

"I said there would be no pressure, as long as you don't tease me. I'll have you back home before dark."

He drove into the garage, cleared security, and descended into the underground corridor surfacing inside the stable compound.

"This place is amazing," she sighed. "Are there underground corridors to all the buildings on your property?"

"Yes. Look, Harbor is tossing her head toward you. She's impatient to be on her way." Satan pawed the ground impatiently as well.

They spent the afternoon riding the entire property, stopping only long enough to enjoy the snack Megan had packed for them. On the way back to the stable, Angie wasn't sure she would ever be ready to leave. It was so peaceful here. No wonder he called it his sanctuary.

"Do we have to go back tonight?" Angie asked batting her long eyelashes up at him. "Can't we leave really early on Tuesday morning?"

"Only if you promise to behave yourself and we sleep in separate rooms…all night."

"Agreed. Can we go riding again tomorrow?"

"Of course. Satan and Harbor would be very disappointed if we didn't."

****

Tuesday morning he dropped Angie off at the store shortly before dawn, left the SUV in the usual place, and walked to The Wycked Hair. Owen and Tobi were already at the salon, the aroma of fresh brewed coffee filled the air, and Tobi handed him a cup as he approached the front desk.

He smiled warmly. "Thank you Tobi. Glad you're back. Owen, come upstairs when you get a minute, I need to bring you up to speed on a few things. Arrange to have the private jet checked out and fueled. I'll need our pilot for Friday evening. It will be a late night so make sure he's aware and paid accordingly. Thanks."

Taking the steps two at a time without spilling his coffee, Bruce entered his office, flipped on the light then turned on the computer to address the waiting e-mails. He had a plan now and felt optimistic even though he knew it wouldn't be easy.

"Well, he's in a rare mood, guess I better see what went on while we were gone." Owen arranged for the jet and the pilot before ascending the stairs to Bruce's office.

"Keep busy while I was gone?" Owen inquired with a smirk, eyes bright with amusement.

"Nothing I couldn't handle. Make no mistake, I'm happy to lay it all back in your lap. Business at the salon went crazy. I helped for a couple of hours. Used Tobi's station, so if something is out of place, I'm to blame."

Owen's brows shot up and his eyes rounded feigning shock. Shaking his head in amazement, he said in an awed voice, "You serviced customers, with your own two hands? Will wonders never cease? Now wait just a minute, I bet you stopped time for a bit, worked your magic and released the time, didn't you?"

Bruce narrowed his eyes then grinned. "You know me better than that." The grin faded and his voice was matter of fact. "There were a couple of other issues that I took care of, but I need you to follow up. I'll handle Tristian. You call Bobby and get an update."

"On what?"

"A group of young changelings, demons, and a werewolf led by a rogue vampire, were apparently contracted to kill the front runner and independent candidate in an attempt to influence the outcome of the election. Rumors of intimidation at the polling places are also rampant."

"Do you know who put out the contract?" Owen asked as he walked around behind a chair, leaning his hands on the back and frowned. "Seems to be a lot of unaccounted activity recently."

"No I don't know who was responsible for the contract." Bruce paused. "Bobby would know more about that. The frontrunner was still in hiding last time I heard. The other one's missing, dead I imagine. I wonder if all this activity has anything to do with the individual that was rumored to have escaped the underworld recently?"

Shrugging his shoulders, Owen's eyes darkened in concern. "That's something we need to check on. Contacted the other Overlords yet? You sent Bobby and his team? Why not Tristian?"

Bruce took a sip of his coffee and frowned, it was cool already. "I sent e-mails the day we talked about it, they're working on it. Sending Tristian would have been a tangle, since I had to contact the Vampire Council. They decided to handle their own, so I sent Bobby for damage control and to get a handle on what was going on. He felt we needed to neutralize the whole group, so I sent Tristian in yesterday. I haven't heard back yet. The Council's assassin was in and out in a matter of hours leaving no trace. Tristian's done the same, I'm sure." Bruce sat his coffee mug down, picked up a pencil, and tapped it on the desk staring over Owen's head and out into the room.

"We'll probably hear from Tristian today."

Bruce nodded in agreement. "Need Bobby's reports on my desk before I leave town on Friday evening."

"I'll get right on it." Owen looked at the mug. "Want me to get Tobi up here with a fresh mug of hot coffee while I'm at it?"

Bruce shook his head and wrapped his hand around the mug. Steam immediately rose from the cup. He brought the mug to his lips, drinking the remainder, and then he continued. "Tristian has some personal business that needs his attention and he's taking some time off after this last assignment. When I talk to him, I'll see how he wants to handle confirmation and payment. The full written report can wait a couple of weeks, a verbal over the phone will do for now." Bruce stretched his long legs under the desk and leaned back in the chair.

"You don't want him around here do you? It's Angie isn't it?"

"That's my business. If I need your help, I'll let you know. Now that you're up to speed, did you and Tobi enjoy your time off?"

Owen raised his eyebrow at the sudden change of subject. "Yes, we did. Enjoyed the Cherry Blossom Festival and fireworks, then we spent the rest of the time at our cabin. Thanks."

"You bet." Bruce stood, his gaze met Owen's, then he walked across the room to the water cooler that had hot water on tap. He reached for a clean mug, glanced at the water cooler again, then pushed the intercom on the wall. "Hey, Tobi."

"Yeah?"

"Got any more fresh brewed Columbian?"

"Sure do. What's it worth to you?" Tobi said with a laugh.

"Give you a little time off and you get all cocky on me." Bruce snorted and looked down on the salon floor where Tobi stood hands on hips grinning up at him. She gave him a thumbs up, then picked up a mug and the coffee pot.

He cut his gaze back to Owen. "I want you to start training someone to cover for you and Tobi on occasion. We need to hire a couple more stylists too. Things are changing and you two may be traveling with me more often for a while."

"She's consented to be your mate," Owen muttered more to himself than to Bruce. "Shit."

"Owen," Bruce snarled, his amber eyes whirling orange. "You will keep your thoughts to yourself. Don't even share them with Tobi. Is that clear?"

"Crystal." Owen turned on his heel and strode to the door. "Watch your step. You're treading on dangerous ground that could get someone killed."

"Thanks. I'll keep that in mind." Bruce returned his attention to the laptop, pulled out the wireless keyboard, and replied to the emails that piled up in his inbox. He addressed the one from the Vampire Council first, noting a couple from other Overlords.

****

Willow came bouncing in shortly after Angie, closed the door and let her wings out, stretching them. "You're in early." She hugged her friend. "Well, did you?"

"If you don't stop asking me that, I'm going to seal your mouth shut." Angie's eyes flashed a familiar display of impatience.

"Oooh, testy this morning. I guess the answer's no, or you'd be in a much better mood."

"Wings feeling cramped from being tucked in, so Caleb won't know you're a faery?" Angie retaliated.

"I'm going to tell him and soon. Things are getting serious." Willow paused and sighed. "Angie, he wants me to move in with him."

Angie stood and hugged her friend. "That's great." She hesitated and held Willow at arm's length to get a good look at her. "Right?"

Willow sighed again, averting her eyes from Angie's direct stare. "Yes and no. I've got this nagging feeling he's not telling me something…something important."

Angie raised a brow. "Gee, now there's the pot calling the kettle black."

"Ok, you're right, but he disappears and says he's been at the gallery. Saturday evening the gallery called looking for him. He told me that was where he was going."

"Oh, that's bad. He's lying to you. Did you confront him?"

"Yes, he said they must have called after he left."

"Is that possible?" Angie asked

"Well, maybe." Willow admitted.

"Willow, time to be honest with him. Maybe he'll tell you what's going on, if anything. Usually, a guy doesn't ask you to move in with him, if he's hiding something. It doesn't give him any wiggle room."

"Bruce said he was going to meet with Caleb. Do you know if he has?" Willow asked.

"He didn't mention it. I imagine he'll be by here later this afternoon or evening. I'll ask him, or you can."

"You're a doll. Now spill, I want every little detail of your weekend."

****

Bruce stood up and rolled his shoulders, this whole business was wearing on him. *I need a diversion.* He pulled out his wallet and took a business card out of it. Turning it over and over, he finally reached for his cell phone. After a quick conversation, Bruce pulled on his leather jacket, walked downstairs and out into the parking lot.

****

A few minutes later the door to the gallery opened, and Caleb was waiting for him. They shook hands, Bruce looked for tell-tail signs of nervousness, he found none. "Thanks for meeting me."

"No problem. Glad to do it."

"My tastes are eclectic and the salon needs some new art work, so let me see what you have."

Caleb smiled and motioned to the area left of the lobby. "Follow me. My work is mostly landscapes, wildlife, or a combination. I've done some caricatures, but they don't seem very popular. I have a few at my place, if you're interested."

Bruce perused the exhibit and made a couple of purchases. "If you want to display any of these at the salon, some of the customers may be interested." He pointed to a couple others he found interesting. "I'll put them up in the reception area, with the filtration system they'll be safe from the chemicals and fumes common in a salon. Or I'd be happy to display flyers or business cards at the front desk."

"I would appreciate that. Do you want to take them with you or have the gallery deliver them?"

"Have the gallery deliver them. I'll tell Owen to expect the art. He will know where to put them." With business concluded, Bruce looked at the young man. "May I ask you a personal question?"

"I guess—no guarantee I'll answer it."

"Does Willow know?" He raised his brow and stared directly at Caleb.

"Know what?"

"That you are a satyr masquerading as a mortal," Bruce said flatly.

Taken by surprise, Caleb was speechless for a moment then stuttered, "I don't know what you are talking about."

"Ok, it's probably none of my business. But she is Angie's best friend and I wouldn't want to see Willow hurt. So if you don't tell her, I will." Bruce turned to leave then paused looking back over his shoulder at Caleb. "Son, believe me she won't care what you are, for some reason you've captured her heart. Do the right thing or risk losing her. The paintings will be delivered tomorrow morning?"

"Yes, I'll deliver them myself."

Bruce mentally ticked that uncomfortable task off his list. Now he'd stop by The Krystal Unicorn, and see if Mrs. Staret had called. He didn't expect her to, nor to accept his invitation this time, but she'd think about it and talk it over with her daughter when she returned. He hated loose ends, and Paul's wife was a loose end that he should have dealt with long ago. She deserved better and Paul would have expected better of him. It was a difficult situation at the time, but leaving her out of the loop seemed the best way to protect her and the daughter.

Chimes sounded as Bruce strolled through the door of Angie's shop. She was with a customer and Willow was ringing up one at the register, so he looked over the crystals in the glass case closest to the door and then leafed through a book on enchantments he found interesting.

Angie finished up with her customer then sidled up to Bruce whispering, "Is there something I can help you with?" She stood on tiptoes expectantly, face turned up toward him.

He slid an arm around her waist and pulled her closer. "Yes, but you can't do it here." His amber eyes sparkled with mischief as he kept his voice quiet. "I promise to make it up to you tomorrow night, when we're alone." Bruce waggled his eyebrows.

"Talk about teasing, you forbid me, and look at you," she murmured, and turned out of his grasp to put a respectable distance between them as new customers came through the door. Raising her voice, she said, "Follow me, the latest book in that series is still in a box in the back. It just arrived."

He returned the book to the shelf and followed her, holding the crystal beaded curtain open. "I just wanted to know if you'd heard from Mrs. Staret," he said in a low voice.

"I figured. She called to say she wanted to talk to her daughter first, so she declined the invitation this time, but would like to reschedule in a couple of weeks if that's OK. She said she'd be in touch."

"That's about what I expected. We'll reschedule in a couple of weeks when you're available. So it'll be just us tomorrow night, if you're still open for dinner."

"I am and looking forward to it." She batted her long blonde lashes and winked at him.

He turned her around so his back was facing the curtain and she was facing him and brushed his lips slowly over hers tracing her lips with his tongue. "Until tomorrow night."

"Wait, I need to ask you something, well really it's Willow's question, but she's busy. Have you had a chance to talk with Caleb?"

"As matter of fact I just left him at the gallery. I purchased a couple of his paintings for the salon and took a couple on assignment. Why?"

"Willow thinks he's hiding something and she's worried. He's asked her to move in with him, so things are moving fast and getting serious."

"He is hiding something, but he'll be talking with her real soon. Let's give them a chance to work it out."

"You're not going to tell me, are you?"

"Not right now, and I don't want you to say anything to her. If he hasn't talked to her by tomorrow night when I come to pick you up after work, I'll tell you both and he knows I will."

"Ok, but what am I going to tell her? I promised I'd ask you, if you came in."

"Tell her I'm working on it and that I should have something for her tomorrow night. Remember please be home before dark, unless you want to spend the night with me."

"I wish I could, but I promised Willow, we'd have a girl's night tonight. We'll lock up and be home before dark. Don't worry. Now I gotta get back to work."

On the way out of her shop, the phone vibrated in his pocket, he pulled it out and glanced at the screen, touched the answer button. "Tristian, everything ok?"

"It went as expected. The situation is neutralized, as well as all the participants. The frontrunner is out of hiding and declared the winner."

"Good job. The written report can wait a couple of weeks, enjoy your time off."

"About that, well, mind if I get personal for a moment?"

Bruce slowed as he arrived at the shop, but

remained outside the door to see how personal Tristian wanted to get. "That depends. Keep in mind I'm your friend but also your employer."

There was a moment's hesitation, his low voice sounding a bit awkward but steady. "Why haven't you chosen a wife, I guess a mate in your case?"

"That type of thing works differently for my kind. To answer your question without going into all that, I hadn't found the right one I want to spend eternity with. Once joined only death can separate us, so I want to make damn sure it's right."

"Ok, so answer me this. If you found her, being what you are and what the job entails, would you still take her as your mate? Would it be fair to subject her to all that?"

"It must be her choice, knowing exactly what could happen and accepting it without reservation. If she did, yes, I'd take a mate, if she was the one."

"Really. Course it's easy to say what'd you do hypothetically, huh?"

"Yes, I guess it is. Don't tell me a female has finally tamed you?"

"Not sure, but thanks for answering my questions." Tristian paused again and blew out a breath. "I guess there's one more thing. I need you to check out something one of the changelings said to me just before he died. Something about Rezar coming back and we're going to pay. That's impossible. Right?"

"If there's one thing I've learned, even the impossible is sometimes possible for the right price." Bruce paused for a beat. "I'll alert the other Overlords. Since we would be the targets, I want specific check-ins from you during your time off. If you fail to check-in, a team will be dispatched immediately to your last known location."

"Understood."

"Hold on, I'm nearly to my office where I can connect to a secure link and we'll set up the checkpoints."

"While you climb those stairs two at a time, you should know that Bobby and his team are damn good."

"I'm glad to hear that. I'll let them know you approve." He shut the door to his office, turned on the computer, and linked with his phone. Give me dates and times. We'll work around your schedule."

****

Wednesday evening Bruce dressed for dinner in a gray pinstriped Armani suit, light blue silk shirt, and light gray tie with matching blue stripes. He sprinted down the stairs, slowing to a walk, as he crossed the salon floor. Owen looked up from closing out the day's receipts and gave a low whistle. Tobi shoved at him, shaking her head in disapproval, and smiled at Bruce. The rest of the staff glanced up, looking from one to the other and grinned, quickly turning their attention to finishing up the afterhours duties.

"Who's the lucky woman tonight?" Owen called out across the room.

Bruce frowned, then smiled impishly. "No one you know."

"Like hell," Owen said.

Bruce strode out the door and down the street to The Krystal Unicorn. The sign said closed but the door was unlocked. Bruce crept in the door sideways avoiding the chimes and clicked the lock behind him.

Angie giggled, as she stood up holding the crystal

she'd retrieved from under the counter, her back to him. "Your magic signature is too strong and I recognized it before you opened the door." She turned and sucked in a breath. "And look at you." She fanned herself and pretended to swoon.

She stepped from behind the counter and it was his turn to be impressed, he let out a low appreciative whistle. Her dusty rose dress hugged all the right curves flaring slightly just below her hips and fell only a few more inches. Its low cut V-neck showed enough cleavage to be sexy but not trashy.

"Perfect," he murmured. "You look absolutely stunning."

Angie walked toward him, then stopped, and took a step back glanced toward the window and then pointed toward the beaded curtain. "Caleb came in a couple of hours ago, He looked like he'd lost his best friend, said he needed to talk to Willow alone. They went for a quick walk and have been back there ever since."

Bruce pulled the front window shade and stepped to her bringing his hand to her cheek trailing a finger down her neck, he caught her other hand, brought it to his lips, and nuzzled her palm. Then turned her hand over and placed his lips at her wrist where he could feel her thundering pulse. "Miss me?" he asked in a low seductive whisper that vibrated against her soft skin.

"Oh, yes," she breathed and stepped closer.

"Have fun with your girl's night in?" He dropped her hand and slowly wrapped his arm around her waist and pulled her to him."

She pushed at his arm. "What if they come out of the backroom and see you?"

A chuckle rumbled deep in his throat. "They

already know about us and I don't think either of them will tell anyone else."

"It's been very intense between them since they went back there."

"I'm not surprised, he's a satyr. Just guessing, but she probably told him her little secret too. Not that it will matter in the end to either of them after the shock wears off, but it may to their families."

"Really? A satyr? How'd I miss that? Caleb must be really good at masking his magic signature. Willow didn't catch it either, but she did know something was off." Angie shrugged then tilted her face up toward Bruce. "Could get interesting. Would you mind if they joined us for dinner tonight? I hate to leave Willow alone if things go bad between them."

"Not a problem. Probably best I'm not alone with you in that dress." A devilish look came into his eyes as he cupped her chin in his hand, letting the back of his hand caress the side of her neck and gently brush over the cleavage left bare by her neckline. Angie's heart fluttered at his touch.

She put her hand over his, stopping the downward movement. "They aren't dressed properly."

"A little magic will fix that, if they want to join us. It's not like we would be using it for selfish purposes and the amount to conjure up a couple of outfits, wouldn't stress us."

"Sure," Angie said hesitantly, she hated using magic for trivial things. It left her drained and feeling guilty. "Let's give them a couple more minutes, while I put the cash drawer in the safe, and then we'll ask them."

Willow and Caleb walked through the beaded

curtain, hand in hand. Willow' eyes rounded. "Wow don't you two look stunning."

"Thanks. Is everything all right?" She looked from Willow to Caleb and back worriedly.

"Yeah, we'll work it out. I'm going to leave most my stuff at our apartment, and just take a few things over to Caleb's. We're going to try living together."

"Well I hope it works out for both of you."

"Us too. Now our families' acceptance of the situation could be another thing entirely." Caleb winced then relaxed and put his arm around Willow caressing her lower back.

"Well, whatever happens, we'll face it together." Willow looked up at Caleb and smiled.

Noticing the intimate gesture, Angie smiled encouragingly. "It'll be fine once they get used to the idea. Hey, why don't you two join us for dinner?"

"We couldn't intrude, but thanks." Caleb said with a sigh glancing over at Willow.

"Sure we could." Willow peered at her friend. "But we're not dressed appropriately for where you two plan to go." She stared down at her bling jeans and sweater as well as Caleb's worn jeans and paint spattered t-shirt.

Bruce glanced at his watch then over to Angie. "Dinner reservations are in ninety minutes. Does that give you two enough time to change and meet us back here, or at the restaurant?"

"Willow, you could wear my black dress and silver heels that are in the garment bag in the bathroom." Angie winked and nodded toward the only bathroom in the shop.

"What garment, oh, ok." Willow patted Caleb's arm. "Be right back."

"Caleb, we keep a few sizes of suits at the salon in the event our clients need them. Want to take a look? Probably quicker than driving all the way home and back." Bruce motioned toward the door. "Angie, we'll be back."

"I guess that would be best. Since I'm not sure I'd have anything appropriate." Caleb followed him out of the shop and down the sidewalk.

Fifteen minutes later, Bruce opened the door to the Krystal Unicorn, Caleb walked behind him dressed in a black suit, European cut, frosty gray silk shirt and matching black and gray striped tie.

Bruce smiled at Caleb's round eyed expression when he caught sight of Willow stepping into the main room dressed in a snug black dress, and silver strap sandals with four-inch heels.

Willow did a little pirouette on tiptoes in front of Caleb and said, "I think we are ready to go."

They arrived at the restaurant five minutes early. Bruce gave his name to maître d who took them to a table in a quiet corner of the restaurant. The girls excused themselves and walked to the powder room. Bruce picked up a menu.

"How did you know about me?" Caleb asked staring boldly at Bruce.

He shrugged dismissively. "It doesn't matter how I knew, what does matter is that you be honest with each other, since you're moving toward a serious relationship."

The swaying of Angie's hips as she and Willow returned to the table, diverted Bruce's attention, and sent waves of lust straight to his groin. He shifted in the chair to relieve the growing ridge in his crotch.

Thankfully, the suit pant cut was looser than his jeans to avoid embarrassment as he stood and pulled her chair out for her. Caleb followed the example and held Willow's chair while she sat.

The dinner of lobster, scallops, and fresh baked bread was excellent and the conversation friendly and relaxed. Not exactly what Bruce had planned, but pleasant all the same.

Bruce dropped Caleb and Willow at the shop where they'd left Caleb's car in the parking lot, then drove Angie home.

"Want to stay here tonight?" Angie asked with a wide-eyed expression, batting her long thick blonde lashes. "I'll bet Willow won't be here."

"Certainly, but I won't." He leaned across the seat and whispered in a deep, deliberately seductive voice, "I'll pick you up Friday after work. We'll be spending the weekend and Monday at the estate. You'll also need formal wear for Friday night." His eyes shone with a glint of amusement as she frowned.

She regarded him with a speculative gaze. Before she could ask where he was taking her, his mouth moved over hers, devouring its softness.

Bruce pulled back, released her, and leaned back against his seat breathing rapidly. "I'll walk you to your apartment, check it out, but I won't be staying. You need to lock the door when I leave and be extra careful."

"Then why can't I go home with you?"

"Because you may be in more danger from me tonight than the demons at large." He grabbed her hand and pulled her toward the apartment, made sure it was safe and drove to his apartment to spend the night alone. *This whole business was going to change and soon.*

****

The digital clock on the wall read 4:15 a.m. in bright blue numbers. Unable to sleep, he flipped the comforter off, slid his feet to the cold floor, and glared out the window into the darkness. *I might as well get an early start so everything is done before we leave for our long weekend. Maybe Angie can sneak out of work early and we'll get dinner before the show.* Smiling, he rubbed his hand over his chin, stretched his arms out to his sides, and gave a jaw-popping yawn then reached for his pants.

The salon was quiet as Bruce stepped inside and turned the alarm off. Owen and Tobi weren't due in for a couple more hours, though he knew they arrived much earlier most days. He walked to the refreshment center without turning the lights on and started the coffee, then slouched in one of the chairs in the lounge area.

It had been just him, Owen, Tobi, and Ky when they started. His stature intimidated some of the early customers but his wizardry with the scissors put that to rest quickly. A good cut was the basis of a fantastic style. The Wycked Hair's reputation as a trendsetter in both nail and hairstyles kept the clientele coming back. He'd never felt it necessary to venture into the day spa business. Most days the salon had more business from DC's elite than it could handle efficiently. It was time to increase staff and add stations. Tasks Owen would handle, though he'd grumble about it. Bruce's lips twitched in amusement at the thought.

He needed to bring Owen into the loop regarding

Tristian's report and the comment by the changeling. It had been years since he sensed a serious threat. Guess that was about the time he quit looking for a fight and settled into his position as Overlord, having proved himself over a period of several years more than capable to take down any challengers.

Recently, he'd felt an inkling that something bad was coming, a sixth sense his mother had, and apparently passed on to him. At first, he thought it was just the anticipation of Tristian's reaction when he found out Angie had consented to being his mate, but now he knew it was more.

Keys jingled and the lock on the front door clicked. Still he sat silent. Owen noticed immediately the alarm was off and put his arm out to keep Tobi from entering further.

"The alarm's been deactivated." Tobi confirmed. "But I smell fresh coffee brewing. So either our intruder is a caffeine addict or Bruce is here."

"Correct on both counts." Bruce's deep voice rumbled through the salon. "Good morning."

"Right back at ya," Owen said cheerfully. "I'm glad you're here. You've got customers when we open this morning. They're scheduled for cuts. Knew you'd be leaving early, so I set their appointments first thing."

"You know I don't take customers anymore, besides I've got plenty of work to keep me busy upstairs." He frowned and shook his head. "Reschedule."

Ignoring him, Owen continued. "Apparently, they're friends of the woman whose hair you cut the other day while we were enjoying our time off. They were very insistent. I said Tobi was as good if not better than you, but they wouldn't be dissuaded. You always say give the customer what they want." A satisfied grin spread over his face. "So we did. Sorry boss."

"Like hell you are." Bruce considered protesting further, but thought better of it. Busy hands would make the day go faster and keep his mind off the growing feeling in his gut that trouble was brewing. "What time are the appointments?"

"Eight and nine."

"Good we've got time. Tristian picked up some information on the topic we were discussing before you left on your days off. Let Tobi finish here and join me upstairs." Bruce pivoted and climbed the stairs in his usual fashion.

Once in his office Bruce turned on the laptop. There were several urgent e-mails blinking from the Territory Overlords he'd sent inquires to after Tristian's report. Sitting in his chair, he opened the first. It confirmed rumors of like information, but no positive sightings...yet. The other e-mails contained similar communications.

"Owen, take a look at these e-mails, read the one I sent after first talking to Tristian." He spun the laptop around to face Owen, who sank into a seat across the desk. Getting up, Bruce shoved the chair back and paced back and forth stopping to look out the window, hands clasped behind his back. After several minutes, he walked back to the desk and settled in his chair.

Owen glanced at him over the edge of the laptop. "I had a bad feeling and even with all this you're still seeing Angie."

"That's my personal business."

"But you and Tristian have to put up a united front,

depend on each other to take this threat out. You can't do that with the situation you've got smoldering. Tristian is bound to find out, and when he does…"

"I am aware of that, and figure it will be sooner than later. Let me worry about my personal life, I have a plan."

Tobi's cheerful voice came over the intercom to Bruce's office. "Your eight o'clock client is here."

"I'll be right down." Bruce glanced up from the emails to glare at Owen. "No more customers without my consent. I don't have time for this right now."

"Understood. I wasn't aware the situation had escalated when I scheduled them."

"See what other information you can dig up, I don't care who you have to see or what you have to do, but get to the bottom of this." Bruce stalked out of the office and hit the stairs running. By the time he arrived on the salon floor, grabbed one of his smocks from the cabinet, and put it on, he was pleasant and prepared to deal with customers for the next couple of hours.

He finished up the first and she planned on waiting for her friend, so she checked into getting her nails done in the meantime. The second was Mrs. Staret's daughter, Jill.

"Bruce, how have you been?" She stepped forward and extended her hand.

"Good, and you?" Surprised by the friendly gesture, he clasped her hand.

"I understand you visited with my mother recently." Jill narrowed her eyes and scrutinized Bruce carefully.

"I did. Now that you're back, I hope you'll both accept my invitation for dinner and a private discussion."

"We intend to do just that in the near future, but first I want to finish researching information that came to my attention. I think you'll find it very interesting." She took her sweater off and eased into the chair. "I also wanted to let you know we learned you weren't entirely to blame for my father's death. Now, can you layer my hair as you did Amanda's last week?"

He was slow to answer as he considered all the information she had so easily laid out for him. Picking up the scissors and comb, he assessed her facial appearance. "Sure can, but your face is wider at the temples than your friends, and your eyes are bigger, so let's modify that cut a bit to enhance your features." *This is turning into a very interesting day.* He shook out the cape, slipped it around her shoulders, and began sculpting Jill's hair.

****

Bruce dressed for the evening and had just finished tying his tie when the intercom chirped. "The limo is here awaiting your instructions."

"I'll be right down." He sprinted down the stairs and strode across the salon floor; glancing back, he saw the smirk on Owens face. "Not one word, understand?"

"Yep."

Reaching into his pocket, he grabbed the keys to the SUV and tossed them to Owen. "You know what to do with these."

"Sure do."

"See you Tuesday sometime. If something breaks call me."

"Will do."

Bruce stepped out the salon door and into the

awaiting limo giving the driver directions to The Krystal Unicorn just a couple blocks down the street.

The limo stopped in front of The Krystal Unicorn, the chauffer stepped out and opened the door. Bruce emerged from the vehicle said something to the driver who closed the door behind him and stood beside the limo. Bruce glanced through the shop's window, Willow stood behind the counter staring at the limo, the corner of his mouth curved into a slight smile.

He sauntered in and snickered at Willow's wide-eyed expression. "Is my li'l witch around somewhere?"

Willow jerked her chin toward the storeroom. "Angie's changing. What if we'd had customers? So much for a low profile." She hissed.

"The time for remaining under the radar is almost over." He parted the crystal beads and walked to the back as he heard the bathroom door open. Bruce sucked in a breath as Angie emerged in a ruby silk gown that hugged all her curves, with a plunging neckline that stopped just short of the waistline, and slit up the right side of the dress to mid-thigh. The back was bare almost to her waist where black ribbons crisscrossed her delicate skin. She carried a black velvet cape with scalloped edges stitched in red over one arm. He blew out the breath in a whistle. "Wow. I feel like an awe struck teenager. You are breathtakingly beautiful." He loved the way her violet eyes sparkled with excitement.

****

Her heart pounded in her chest, partly because she'd not expected him to be standing there when she walked out the bathroom door, and partly because that's the effect he had on her. "A teenager? Huh, surprised you can remember back that far." She snickered as her gaze swept over him, so stunningly handsome in his black tux and tails, accented by a red silk shirt and black tie that her breath caught in her throat. The fit was perfect for his broad shoulders, long muscular legs, narrow hips and six pack abs. *He was one sexy package, and he was all hers.*

"You don't look bad yourself, the suit accents all the right parts, if you know what I mean." She raised one eyebrow and smiled seductively. "How did you know I was wearing red?"

"I didn't, red just happens to be one of my favorite colors."

The space between them disappeared as he took her in his arms, her soft curves molding to the contours of his muscular body. The caress of his lips on her mouth, trailing long the side of her neck and across the swells of her breasts set her entire body ablaze. "I think we better get going, or skip it and go directly to your estate."

"Oh, no, I intend to enjoy all the envious stares I'll get from the males in the audience and restaurants we patronize this evening."

"I don't believe she is going to be the only one attracting envious stares. You look hot!" Willow said, dramatically fanning herself as Bruce and Angie walked through the beaded curtain onto the showroom floor. "You two are going to make quite a stir where ever you go. So Prince Charming, are you taking her to the ball?"

"No. We're going to dinner in New York and then to attend a Broadway show."

"So you won't be back tonight? The limo is taking you to the airport." Willow said smugly.

"Actually, we'll be back early tomorrow morning. I have a private jet that will take us there and back. The limo service will pick us up again at the airport and take us to my car."

"Oh, I see." A look of disappointment passed over her features.

"No, you probably don't." He chuckled. "The apartment is all yours until sometime Tuesday when I bring her back." He reached over and encircled Angie's waist with one arm, pulling her close to him. Sliding a couple of fingers under the back of her dress, he played with the ribbons against her bare flesh.

She discreetly swiveled her hips against him, then turned her attention to Willow. "Oh, sorry. I forgot to tell you I'm spending the weekend with Bruce."

"That's OK. He knew what I was trying to find out. Caleb can spend the weekend at our apartment, since you'll be away. I want to get him away from his painting for a bit and just enjoy being together. He works all the time," she said with a frown.

"Then you need to distract him with your womanly wiles." Bruce suggested letting his gaze wander over Angie seductively.

"Feel free to borrow some of my things, if you want. I think we'll go shopping when I get back, at the little shop we found last month." She winked at Willow.

Willow looked perplexed and tilted her head up toward Angie. "What shop?" Then she took in a quick breath and the light dawned. "Oh, that shop. Perfect. That's exactly what I need."

Bruce opened the door for Angie and swept her off into the awaiting limo. Once inside, he put an arm around her shoulders tucking her against him. "Would you like something to drink, wine perhaps?"

"Is this yours?" She looked around at the white leather seats, plush light gray carpeting, small refrigerator, and LCD TV. There were even computer hookups, a printer, and a laptop. She opened the door to the little refrigerator and reached for a bottle of water

Bruce took out a couple of bottles of wine, turned them over to look at the label, returned one, popping the cork on the other. Crystal glasses sat in a glass case above the refrigerator and he reached for one, pouring a small amount of wine into it, took a sip, and carefully placed it in the recessed holder on the glass table between the seats. Then he turned his attention back to Angie.

"Yes, actually The Wycked Hair owns the limo as well as the jet we will be flying in. We have a couple limos, one for clients and I happen to favor this one." He leaned back against the seat and ran his finger slowly up and down her leg bared by the long slit up her dress.

The partition between them and driver slid down silently. "Are you ready to leave?"

"Yes."

The driver nodded slightly and the frosted window glided back into place.

"Can't you just port from one place to another?"

"Yes, I suppose I could, but traveling this way is so much more satisfying, especially with present company. Besides, you never know what obstacles or individuals you'll encounter when you port and then there's the wear and tear on the body when magic is involved."

"True, I hadn't considered that, especially at your

advanced age." She smothered a giggle.

"With age comes experience which you'll benefit from later." The corner of his mouth turned up into a sly smile.

They arrived at the airport and a pleasant looking young man dressed in a navy blue uniform waited for them. "Follow me sir. The plane is full of fuel and I checked her out myself. Enjoy your flight." He motioned them down a corridor to the plane.

"Who's that?" She whispered as they followed him.

"Sean, the mechanic. I trust him to keep my plane in tiptop shape until it's needed. He's been with me for years."

"Everyone has been with you for years."

"Well, not everyone." He grinned at her. "But most have. In my line of work, you must be able to trust those around you, or you don't last long. Either Owen or I handpick our employees for their abilities, knowledge of both worlds, and trustworthiness. We compensate them well, so they have no desire to leave or betray us."

Inside the plane Angie looked around, light beige carpeting complimented the deep maroon leather seats. There was a small stainless steel galley where a woman was preparing coffee on the right as they passed through. Everything gleamed. There were even fresh flowers in the crystal vases attached to the walls and conference table.

"Do you use this for business often?"

"More a few years ago when we were getting things established. With business running smoothly, it's mostly for entertainment of clients or for employee use when they have an emergency."

Arriving in New York's Kennedy International airport, there was a limo waiting to take them to the restaurant. The waiter showed them to a cozy corner table with a window overlooking the lake and held her seat for her as she sat down.

"Shall I order for both of us, or would you rather order your own?"

"Oh no, go ahead."

She enjoyed the food, especially the decadent chocolate dessert. Then it was time to return to the limo and off to the Broadway show Rock Ages."

"Where exactly are we going?"

"The Helen Hayes Theatre on West 51st Street. It reminds me of you in a way. It was built kind of as a rebellion against the commercial theater. The auditorium is small, just a little under three-hundred seats."

"How does that remind you of me?" She asked. "I wasn't even born yet."

"Rebellion, it's what you're all about." He smirked.

"I don't want to know what you're thinking. Do I?" Angie said with a pout.

"Probably not." Bruce had wanted to see Phantom, but thought Angie would enjoy the music video turned Broadway show channeling the hits of 1980 mega bands. Big hair, spandex, disguising make up, and mind-altering pharmaceuticals helped the mortal's fantasies come true. Or helped the non-magic community deal with the discovery that otherworldly beings existed.

During the 1980's, the Rock and Roll culture

mixed with magical creatures, their secrets were spilled at forbidden parties. Bruce made sure the magical offenders were rounded up and punished. But not before the secrets became lyrics and found their way into hit songs.

Bruce watched as Angie bounced on her seat to the rhythm while singing quietly the words to several songs. She giggled at the antics of the actors on stage and glanced seductively at Bruce during the more risqué scenes. An effect he'd considered possible when choosing the production.

"Did you enjoy the show?" He asked as they made their way to an exit.

"Oh, yes. It was entertaining and the songs were some of my favorites." The costumes, the sets, the production quality were simply amazing. I loved it, all of it." She threw up her arms and wound them around his neck planting a warm, affectionate kiss on his lips

By the time they were safely in the plane, Angie curled up against him with her head resting on his chest and his arms circled around her then drifted off to sleep.

Still asleep, he carried her easily from the plane to the limo and drew her onto his lap for the ride to Owen's house, where the Mercedes awaited them.

****

Angie awoke disorientated and alone in a large bed that was vaguely familiar. The sun streamed through the open curtains and she heard water running somewhere. A door opened and Bruce stood across the room from her, a towel wrapped around his waist and using a small towel rubbing his shoulder length chestnut hair. The blond highlights gleaming in the sun's rays.

As he walked toward her, he said in a deeply sensual voice, "Good morning sleeping beauty. I trust you slept well."

"The last thing I remember was getting into the plane in New York. Geez my brain is fuzzy."

"Let me clear it up for you." Sitting on the bed beside her, he leaned over kissed her nose, then her eyes and finally laid his mouth on hers with a tantalizingly tender kiss.

She quivered at the sweet taste of his lips and tenderness of his kiss. "We're at your estate aren't we?"

"Yes. Are you ready to get up and go for a ride? I believe Satan and Harbor are waiting for us."

"What time is it?"

"A little past noon. I'd hoped to take you for a sunrise ride, but I enjoyed watching you sleep too much to awaken you. Maybe tomorrow morning, when you are more rested."

Her red dress lay over a chair along with her shoes. "You undressed me?"

"Yes, and enjoyed every minute of it, though it was in the dark as I didn't want to turn on the light and awaken you." He trailed a finger along her jawline.

She shifted her head away. "You can see as well as I can in the dark, so don't try to say you didn't see anything." Feeling he'd taken advantage of her, the blood rose to her face along with a hint of temper. Unreasonable as she knew it was, she couldn't find her calm.

"I never said that…merely that I didn't want to awaken you. I left your underwear on against my better judgment." He shot her an irresistibly devastating grin.

"Ok, I can see I can't win." She sent him a look

meant to wither a man, pushed him aside, and threw back the covers since he'd already seen her in her underwear. Angie marched across the room, into the bathroom, still steamy from his bath, shut, and locked the door. He'd seen her in a tiny string bikini, which was less than underwear, but that was by her choice. This was something entirely different, or at least that was what she told herself, stepping into the shower.

The late night and a little too much wine left her irritable, maybe a little unreasonable. Really, he'd done nothing wrong. But did he have to be so arrogant, so smug, so confident, and controlling? She huffed out a breath, rinsed the shampoo from her hair, and stepped out of the shower. Steam thick as fog made it impossible to towel off or see in the mirror. She opened the door just a crack and peered out for moment.

A chuckle rose from his throat. He yanked on his jeans and sweatshirt, then pulled on his riding boots. "Breakfast is ready. I'll meet you down stairs in the kitchen. Megan gets testy, if we let her food get cold. I'll have her pack us a snack too, since I doubt we'll be back for a while."

****

"Good morning or I guess afternoon, Megan. What a glorious day." Angie greeted the housekeeper then slid into her chair tucking her foot under her and narrowing her eyes at Bruce.

"Yes it is. Now you two better eat quickly and get out there and enjoy it." Megan bustled around the kitchen pulling fresh baked cinnamon rolls from the oven and wrapping the sandwiches she fixed. She put a few rolls and the sandwiches in a backpack along with some fruit and chips. "Do you want wine with you or wait until you return and take it by the fire?"

"Four bottles of water will be fine. We'll have the wine tonight while we relax. Thanks." He turned and smiled fondly at his long time housekeeper.

"If you're lucky," Angie snarled sarcastically

His usual dark amber eyes flashed a quick fiery orange. "Megan would you leave us for minute or two?"

She raised her eyes brows and looked sternly from Angie to Bruce, but said nothing as she turned on her heel and left the room.

"You will never talk to me that way in front of my staff. If we are alone, you can say whatever you want to me, but I'll not have my staff involved in our personal life." His hands fisted on the table as he spoke. "You're angry because I took your lovely gown off and put you to bed in your underwear?" He snorted. "I didn't take advantage of you, though your body was more than willing after arousing both of us, maybe unintentionally or not as you curled in my lap on the ride from the airport to Owen's house."

Angie rolled her eyes and shifted in her chair waiting for him to finish.

"When I undressed you and laid you in my bed, I may have let my hands roam over your luscious breasts lightly so as not to wake you, even as you arched up against me. You've enjoyed my more intimate touches on several occasions and your underwear covered more than that bikini you chose the other night." He drew in a long breath and sighed. "Let's not ruin this day with a fight over such inconsequential actions. I'm sorry if you feel violated. You must know that wasn't my intention, only to appreciate as you've allowed before. I've not touched another woman or even thought about one since that day you blew me a kiss in the salon. This is uncharted territory for me."

Through gritted teeth, she sputtered. "Who do you think you are? Ordering me around, telling me what I can and can't do, what's acceptable and what's not, and how long you've been without. What the hell do I care? Screw the entire female population, if you feel the need." She shoved her chair back as she rose and strode out the door.

He sat his cup on the saucer with such force, the cup and saucer shattered as he rose from his chair to follow her. "For the love of…" he muttered trailing off. A slight breeze caressed his cheek, then a gentle hand gripped his shoulder. Bruce whirled around eyes blazing.

"Whoa there stud." Megan grinned, "Let her go, she needs to burn off some of that displaced anger. You might also consider what you're going to say before you say it. It just might keep you from digging a bigger hole." She shrugged.

His eyes met Megan with a glint of steel. She met his gaze with no intention of backing down. "She's spirited that one, not unlike your mother." Clicking her tongue, Megan shook her head laughing softly. "Your poor father was driven to distraction until he learned to handle her fire with restraint of his own. Something you'd do well to learn also."

How had he lost control of the situation, and in front of Megan? Most women were happy to share his bed. The sex was inconsequential as they were not his destined mate. He'd not even seen her temper coming. He shook his head tamping down his own. "Is everything packed and ready to go?"

"It is. Enjoy your day." Megan winked at him and busied herself cleaning up the kitchen.

****

Angie fled to the stable where Jason stood next to an open section of wall, waiting for them. She took a deep calming breath before engaging Jason.

With a raised brow he said, "Harbor and Satan are waiting in the pasture. Is the boss on his way?"

Remembering what Bruce said, she curtly replied. "He'll be along shortly. Harbor and I'll just get a head start."

Shrugging, Jason said doubtfully. "Harbor usually won't go anywhere without Satan, but you're free to give it a try. Just walk her around the indoor pasture area first."

Irritated that he still controlled her actions without even being there, she mustered up a pleasant voice and said. "Thanks, I'll do that." She walked to where Harbor waited and allowed her to nuzzle against her shoulder. Patting her neck, she swung up into the saddle and clicked her tongue to get Harbor moving.

Jason saw Bruce sauntering up the path and waited. "Boss, your woman requested to take Harbor without Satan. I suggested it wasn't a good idea but she's saddled up." He pointed to where Harbor and Angie were trotting out across the indoor pasture. Angie bent over the saddle giving Harbor's neck encouraging pats.

"That's fine. I'll take it from here." He whistled Satan back to the fence and grabbed his reins, stroking his neck. "It's all right boy, sometimes we need to give these girls a bit of space."

Satan nickered softly then snorted dancing

sideways. Harbor stopped and turned watching Satan.

Angie nudged her heels into Harbor's sides, tightened the reins on the left side to turn her head forward again. To Bruce's surprise, Harbor turned back around and began a slow walk toward the end of the pasture.

Bruce nodded toward Jason who was standing next to the control panel. Jason touched the button allowing the wall at the end of the pasture to open. Shaking his head, Jason muttered, "I hope you know what you're doing boss." Then shrugged and went back to his duties.

Harbor passed through the door and looked back, whinnied loudly and continued walking. Bruce knew she would not speed up her pace until Satan was at her side, regardless of what Angie tried. He gave her a bit more time, mounted Satan and followed, holding Satan to a walk as well, though he snorted and danced around threatening to rear up on his back legs.

"Take it easy boy." Bruce crooned patting the horse's neck, "We'll catch up with them soon enough. Angie's a little upset with me, so we'll just give her time to cool off."

Satan snorted, flattened his ears to his head, and again swung his head from side to side. "Let's do a couple laps around the pasture then we'll head outside." Bruce loosened the reins and touched his heels to Satan's sides.

Several laps later, Bruce allowed Satan to exit to the outside and gave him his head to find Harbor.

As they caught up to Harbor and Angie, Bruce said carefully. "Angie, I'm sorry, if I came off as tyrannical back there in the kitchen. It's just that my personal business can't be aired in front of the staff. That's how I run my homes and businesses. If you're to become part of my life, you need to understand that our privacy must be maintained."

"I'm not sure I want to be part of your life," Angie said testily.

Without missing a beat, Bruce countered. "That decision is entirely up to you. At least let me explain the reasoning behind my decision. If someone captured one of my staff or worse, they wouldn't be able to compromise us by giving personal information, like our weaknesses or what we disagree on. It is absolutely necessary that we present a united front at all times. That's one of those responsibilities I mentioned early on in our relationship. As for the other, I'm a very carnal creature and being without for any period of time is a big deal to me. Though it's my choice." He suspected the little game of sexual titillation they'd played over the last few weeks, was partly to blame for her temper as his simmered close to the surface as well.

Angie straightened in the saddle. "You are too much like Tristian. I spent most of my life under his thumb. I'll be damned if I am going to spend the rest of my life under yours. I understand presenting a united front. But…for our relationship to work, mutual respect in all areas of our lives is required. As for you and another woman—" Angie unclenched her fist and flicked her hand in a dismissive gesture. "I'll destroy her."

"That's fine, we'll have disagreements, and you can tell me whatever you feel, just not in front of the staff, not ever. As far as women, you are my mate. I've no interest in another."

"I got that."

"Great, then let's allow the horses to run for a bit, have a snack and head back to the house before dark." He nudged Satan into a canter then loosened the reins. Angie did the same.

They arrived back at the stables at dusk groomed the horses, and put them in their stall, where Jason had feed waiting for them.

Chapter Twelve

Bruce held the door open for Angie and followed her inside the house. The delicious aroma of pot roast, potatoes, and carrots wafted through the room combined with fresh baked rolls. His mouth watered. Angie went to the powder room and he washed up at the kitchen sink. With oven mitts, he took the roast out of the oven, sliced it, and put the meat on a platter. The rolls were in the warmer and he plopped them in a napkin-lined wicker basket, Megan had prepared. He put the basket and platter on the breakfast bar beside two place settings.

"Something smells awfully good," Angie said entering the kitchen.

He waved his arm with flourish toward the breakfast bar. "Dinner is served."

After dinner, Angie cleared and washed the dishes. Bruce took the wine out of the refrigerator, selected two wine glasses, and carried them into the living room where the fire crackled merrily.

He sat on the couch and patted the seat next to him. "Have a seat, we'll relax and enjoy the fire." He poured the wine and handed her a glass. The crystal tinkled as he tapped the rim of his glass to hers, and took a sip. She did the same then set her glass on the table as he continued to sip the amber liquid.

Settled next to him, her head on his warm chest,

her hand massaged the inside of his thigh. She slid her hand further up and began unbuttoning the shirt he'd traded for his sweatshirt earlier.

He watched her hand without comment, then set his glass on the table and brought his mouth down on hers hot and demanding. His hand gently outlined the circle of her breast over her sweater. Surprised at her instant arousal, he reveled in her eager response to his touch, When her fingers caressed his growing erection, his breath quickened and he let his legs fall open, leaving her more room for exploration.

"Angie," he murmured against the pulsing hollow of her throat then raised his head to look into the smoldering depths of her violet eyes. "I think we need to go upstairs, if you're sure you want to go where this is leading."

"I've never been more sure of anything in my life," she said, her breath coming in little gasps as his fingers danced between her legs.

The fire popped as he stood, and swept her into his arms and carried her upstairs to his, no, he corrected, their bed.

She wound her arms around him and buried her face in his neck breathing soft sensual kisses along his angular jaw line while he carried her up the stairs. She rubbed her cheek against his bare chest inhaling his scent. He felt her body quiver in anticipation and tightened his hold.

As her feet touched the floor, his large hand took her face and held it gently as his mouth covered hers hungrily, then his hands moved down her arms slowly. His muscles tingled as he slid his hands under her sweater, unfastening her bra and feeling the weight of firm round breasts spill into his hands. Gently he rubbed his thumbs over her nipples until they were hard little berries. Unable to wait any longer, he lifted the sweater over her head tossing it to the floor, baring her breasts to him.

She moaned and spread her legs. Rubbing against the hard ridge still confined in his jeans and arched her breasts toward him.

He took the soft mound in his mouth, and sucked while his tongue flicked over her nipple, then took it delicately between his teeth as the tip of his tongue continued to lick the tip of her nipple. His mouth moved to the other breast while caressing her nipple with his thumb to keep it hard and her aroused. He'd have her tonight, but not before, he had her begging. A sly smile turned the corner of his lips.

Angie pulled back, covering her breasts with her hands. "My turn," she purred and ripped opened the rest of his shirt, shoving it off his shoulders. Slender fingers spread out over his chest, letting her sharp finely manicured nails rake across his nipples and down his abs. She leaned over and soothed the scratches by licking them with her warm wet tongue. When she unbuttoned his jeans, he sucked in a breath. Her hand slid inside his silk briefs, wrapping her fingers around his thick length and brushing her thumb over the slick head. Easing down the zipper, she tugged his jeans over his hips. Her hands slid between his thighs and she cupped his balls massaging first one then the other. He moaned and thrust toward her. Completely naked to her, she slid further down his body, her intent clear.

Before she leaned over to take him in her mouth, he scooped her up in his arms. She squealed in protest as he carried her through the bedroom into the master bath. He turned on the shower and waited for it to fill the large marble area with steamy warmth. There were several adjustable spray heads in a variety of heights on one side of the marble wall. On the opposite wall, a bench ran the entire length of the shower. Built in dispensers labeled with a wide variety of shampoos, soap, body washes for male and female ran along another side next to a shelf that held additional supplies.

"You need a shower," he said in a low rumbling voice, unbuttoning her jeans, he put his bare foot between her thighs pushing her jeans to the floor. "Step out of those my li'l witch," he said seductively, guiding her into the water spray.

"You don't shower alone often do you?"

His gaze wandered over her lazily, lingering in some areas longer than others, considering her statement. "Have you forgotten that you are the only woman I've ever brought here? This is my sanctuary from the world. The dispensers were installed when my parents lived here. I filled them in anticipation of your stay."

"Oh, sorry, I remember you saying that," she murmured, slithering against him. Angie slid her soapy hands up his back, fingertips tracing the sinewy contours, kneading his tight ass and then she moved against his growing erection. With soapy hands, she gently caressed his length until he moaned thrusting forward. Moving out of the spray, she lifted her leg to wrap around his waist. He caught her leg, knelt down brought it to rest on his shoulder, ran his wet hands up her thighs, and spread her legs wide. His thumbs spread her petal soft lips as the tip of his tongue explored the folds around her sensitive clit then thrust his tongue deep into her over and over.

She screamed, arching against his magical mouth, fisted her hands in his hair as the first wave of pleasure crashed over her, even as he was untangling her fingers from his hair, and moving away. "Liked that did you, li'l witch?" He smiled wickedly running his tongue around his lips slowly as he straightened, his fingers still caressing her sensitive area, still sliding in and out building her pleasure.

She took that opportunity to slide down and flick her tongue over the head of his engorged cock. He involuntarily jerked toward her and she took more of him into her mouth. Groaning he ran his fingers through her wet hair, she relaxed her throat and pleasured him further enjoying his salty taste.

"That's enough, much more and I'll have nothing to offer you when I take you to bed." He turned off the shower and opened the door. She stepped out and he wrapped her in a warm towel. She scrambled up on the bed, snuggling into the warm towel that nearly engulfed her. She stilled as he lay at her side propped up on one elbow watching her, his arousal still very apparent. She tilted her head, one brow raised questioningly.

"I'm in no hurry. I intend to savor this night and remember it always. You are my mate. I love you and want to pleasure you in every way possible."

She opened the towel and rolled against him rubbing her bare breasts over his sculptured chest, her tiny foot resting on his hip, as he gathered her in the comfort of his arms. He shifted, her leg wrapped around his back and her body pressed forward seating his slick head where she was already hot, already wet, and ready for him.

"You are so beautiful," he murmured bringing her mouth to his, lips moving eagerly against hers.

Angie could hear the hum in his blood becoming louder. Soon there would be no holding back. His hands slid up her body cupping the underside of her breasts and he pressed himself between her legs.

As if by magic, she switched positions and straddled him, hovering over him allowing only the tip to penetrate her. His hips involuntarily thrust up and she moved slightly away, smiling enticingly. "Patience. We are savoring the moment we become one for eternity. Remember?" She leaned over allowing his lips to kiss a trail down her neck. His tongue reached her breasts exploring each nipple, a shudder of pleasure swept over her. Angie slowly lowered herself, taking him in as he stretched her until she thought he would split her, then he moved slowly, gently inside her thrusting deeper until she had taken all of him.

They took time to explore, to arouse, and to give each other pleasure even as her witch's blood sang for final consummation of their mating. Together they found the rhythm that bound their bodies. Angie moved against him until giant waves of pleasure pulsed through her and with a final thrust, he released inside her. She collapsed on top of him panting, as his own breathing was still ragged. He rolled her to the side and curved his body around her, holding her in the security of his arms.

Bodies still moist from lovemaking, she snuggled against him as their legs intertwined and they succumbed to sleep of sated lovers.

Chapter Thirteen

Far off in a mental fog, he heard his cell phone ringing. Not a familiar ring tone, he thought lazily in no hurry to break the spell they'd woven last night. Bruce reached his hand over to the nightstand feeling for his phone, still looking at the beautiful woman who lay curled against him. Her head nestled in the crook of his arm. His mate. His fingers feathered against her naked breast, then kneaded the firm flesh.

Angie blinked up at him sleepily. "Aren't you going to answer that?"

"Eventually." He rolled over and brushed his lips across hers. Then his brain clicked. That ring tone was his parents. Urgently he grabbed the phone, his voice still horse from sleep. "Father, what's wrong?" He started to get up and move out of Angie's hearing, then stopped. She was his mate, whatever the reason for his father's call was now her business as well as his.

"What a way to greet your father. If it had been an emergency, by the time you answered, it would have been too late." Andre chuckled. "Caught you in bed with a beautiful woman, huh?"

More relaxed because there was no discernible urgency in his father's voice, he bantered back. "As a matter of fact you have, but it's not what you think."

"Isn't it?" Amusement rang in his father's deep voice.

"No, it's not, all knowing one." Bruce said, aware the revelation would shock his arrogant father. "I've found my destined mate and last night was our first night together. We'll spend the weekend here at the estate and return to the city on Tuesday."

"You mean you consummated it last night, without telling us you'd found her? Do I have the right of it?"

"Yes. I wasn't ready to…or rather it's complicated."

Andre didn't bother to cover the receiver while he called out loudly, "Matiah, our son has taken a mate, finally."

Bruce couldn't make out his mother's barrage of questions in the background but heard his father's tolerant reply.

"I don't know, Matiah. Give me a moment, I need to discuss business with our son first, then I'll find out. Patience, darling."

A slow smile crossed Bruce's lips. *Now I know exactly what Megan meant.* "We've kept our relationship under the radar, because of one little problem." Bruce hesitated considering whether to tell his father the whole story, or wait. *Oh, hell, he'll get it out of me anyway, or mother will.* He blew out a breath. "She's the little sister of Tristian, my best enforcer, friend, and longtime associate which is complicating things." He paused again frowning.

His father, Andre, snorted. "If it's a problem, you didn't get his permission and he doesn't know. Tristian, he's a warlock and your paid assassin, right? A demon hunter, so to speak?"

"Yes."

"I don't imagine he wanted his little sister mated to

a demon. You know, he's going to be furious as hell, probably try to kill you."

"Yes."

"Then you better get it over with, because what I have to say is only going to complicate things further."

Bruce could hear his mother's voice in the background again, but unable to understand what she was saying. His father's side of the conversation came across loud and clear.

"Settle down, Matiah, Tristian probably won't be successful, but it's something Bruce will have to deal with. He made the decision to pursue her, without Tristian's knowledge. That's enough Matiah. We'll discuss this later."

Bruce knew that tone in his father's voice and his mother lost that battle. His lips twitched as he remembered being on that end of a discussion with his father a few times. "I hate to interrupt, but complicate what?"

"If Tristian doesn't kill you, I may. Your mother's upset and she'll be difficult as hell to deal with now until she sees you and your mate. What is her name?"

"Angelique Shandie."

"Her name is Angelique Shandie. Happy now?" His father relayed to his mother. "May I continue my conversation with your son?" There was a soft sound of ascent. "Now down to business. I've confirmed rumblings that have been circulating for some time. Apparently, you collared and spell bound a powerful demon known as Rezar, sent him back to the underworld. Correct?"

"Yes, I did, with Tristian and Paul's help. He and Farier set up a trap that nearly killed Tristian. Tristian took out Farier, but we had to hunt down Rezar after he went underground."

Andre took a deep breath and sighed heavily. "Well, he called in favors and found someone in the underworld to do a partial release of Tristian's spell and he's back, good news the collar is still in place. He's weak and hiding in the Far East trying to regain his strength. Word has it he's out for revenge. You and Tristian are his targets. He's brought reinforcements."

"Sounds about right. Paul died as a long-term result of injuries he sustained in that battle. Slow acting poison was responsible and unknown to us, until it was too late." Bruce bit his lip, attempting to tamp down the rage that tried to boil over each time he thought about Paul. *Rezar will get what's coming to him, I'll see to it.* "Paul left behind a mortal wife and half witch daughter that I believe inherited his abilities." Bruce ran his hand through his hair and sat down on the edge of the bed, taking Angie's hand in his. Eyes full of concern, she wrapped her other arm around his waist and pulled him tight against her.

"You should have killed him outright," Andre said flatly, allowing his irritation to radiate through the phone.

"I planned to but so many things went wrong in that battle that he escaped before I could finish. Not an excuse and like you say, bad decisions always come back to haunt you. I got it."

"Not an I told you so, it's serious concern. This guy's bad as they come."

"I am well aware of that. We'll have to take him out now while he's weak. I'll take my best men with me, do it on his turf, not mine."

"Exactly. If you don't mind a suggestion, bring Angie down here to stay with us. You know she'll be safe and you can devote your mind to the task at hand."

"Won't that compromise your cover?"

"Not a concern. A couple of other things. First, strengthen the bond between you and Angie before you return to work. Her strength and power as your mate will be of great benefit to you both. Then get this thing straightened out between you and Tristian. If you survive that, we need to talk."

"If?" Bruce snorted. "After the situation with Tristian is settled, Angie will be there with you. Wait, strengthen the bond?"

"That's why I want you to bring her to us. I'll explain when you get here. Probably should have told you years ago, but we figured you'd never take a mate. Just play with those females who attracted your interest. You do know that you and Angelique are part of each other now."

"Yes, I understand that."

"Now I have to go smooth over the situation you've caused with your mother. Talk to you some time Thursday evening. That should give you enough time to straighten things out with Tristian and get a plan together. I don't want my old position back, so you better make sure Tristian doesn't kill you. We'll prepare a comfortable place for Angelique."

Bruce snorted. "Talk to you soon, and thanks." He disconnected the call and looked at Angie.

"Trouble?"

"You could say that. We are going to have to face Tristian Tuesday afternoon or evening when we get back." He kissed the tip of her nose and brushed a strand of hair from her face as he explained the situation in detail and his plans to deal with it.

"So we need to return to DC now?" She asked trying to keep the disappointment out of her voice.

"No, our plans remain the same. This will wait until we return Tuesday afternoon. Right now, I have just taken the woman of my dreams as my mate. I intend to spend the next seventy-two hours showing her just how much I desire and care for her, in hopes she'll reciprocate." He held up his index finger. "Right after I make this phone call." He laid her back on the bed and slid between her legs, as he rested on his elbows he speed dialed Owen's number.

"What are you doing?" Angie squealed as he pinned her effortlessly to the bed with his aroused body and slid the fingers of his unoccupied hand between her legs stroking her.

"Clearing up one thing so we can enjoy each other without interruption for the next few days. Any objections?"

"None." She nipped at his neck with her teeth then soothed the bites with long wet licks of her tongue. Deliberately making it near impossible for him to concentrate on the phone call he was making.

"Ah, Owen, I need you to set up Tristian's report meeting for Tuesday night in my office after the salon is closed. The staff will need to clear out early. You'll be required to attend and I want Bobby's team to wait downstairs. The first order of business is I inform Tristian that I have taken his sister as my mate. Second order of business is that Rezar is back."

Owen cursed. "Tristian said he would be here when you arrived on Tuesday afternoon. I think he already knows about you and Angie. At least that you are seeing her."

"All the better. Now for the rest of my time off, I don't want any phone calls, unless the matter is so serious, you can't handle it. Understand?"

"Yep. Got it."

Bruce ended the phone call and turned all of his attention back to his sexy mate.

Chapter Fourteen

A feeling of dark foreboding, like storm clouds forming on the horizon before a violent storm, washed over Bruce as he maneuvered the SUV into the parking lot behind The Krystal Unicorn.

Tristian was already there and it wasn't to give his report. Bruce could feel the fury in Tristian's magic signature hanging in the air. A silver tipped arrow penetrated the windshield, split the arm securing the rearview mirror, and stuck in the headrest a quarter inch from Bruce's neck. Blue liquid oozed from the tip and a stream of red mist escaped from the other end of the arrow.

"Hold your breath and don't open the door or windows. The influx of fresh air will spread the poison." He hissed though his teeth not daring to take a breath.

Air pressure inside the vehicle changed, Angie's head felt like it was going to explode. *Bruce.* She whispered into his mind, a benefit of being mated.

I know, just a few seconds more, I've got it handled. His deep smooth voice floated reassuringly in her mind, as he reached over caressing her shoulder.

The pressure eased and the red mist sucked in on itself disappearing along with the oozing liquid. He pulled the arrow from the headrest, fingering the hole in the upholstery.

Through gritted teeth, Bruce growled. "His first mistake was that he missed me. His second deadly mistake was he risked your life. That is unforgivable." Those two things also told Bruce that Tristian wasn't thinking clearly, fury was coloring his judgment. That gave Bruce an edge, though the attack caught him off guard. He hadn't expected Tristian's attack to put his sister at risk.

The console between them lowered to seat level. He hoped to add fuel to the fury burning inside Tristian. Bruce put his arm around Angie's waist and pulled her against him, his lips pressed against hers then gently covered her mouth as his tongue traced the soft fullness of her lips. He drew back, touched his lips to hers again trailing them down to the pulsing hollow of her neck and whispered, "You're going into the shop now, Willow is waiting just on the other side of the door. Please stay there, you'll be able to remain in my mind just don't interfere. I need your presence there as a calming one. Willow can help you."

"I don't understand."

"I know. There wasn't time to explain how everything works and I'm not exactly sure myself. Only that I can feel you in my mind and I assume you can feel me in yours."

"Yes, it's a weird sensation," Angie said a tremor in her voice.

"We'll learn together to use it to our benefit, now is as good a time as any to practice."

She snorted, "Sure, our lives are on the line. No big deal." She threw up her hands.

"That's the spirit." He grinned raising his head and cupping her trembling chin in his steady hand, not taking his eyes off hers. "Believe me when I tell you, I won't kill your brother. Although he is making it damn difficult. Nor do I believe he will kill me. Though that is his intention, right now. So put those thoughts out of your mind, they won't help either of us."

The shop door opened a crack signaling Willow was ready. In a blur of movement, Angie was in his lap and they were out the passenger door. Willow reached out and grabbed Angie's arm as Bruce shoved her though the door, closing it tight, adding a spell to seal it.

Just as Bruce turned, Tristian appeared dagger in hand and sank it between Bruce's neck and shoulder. He fell against the wall of the building, sliding toward the ground and took a deep breath to control the pain. A white-hot electrical bolt surged from his upraised palm directly into the center of Tristian's chest as he advanced. Tristian stumbled backward, giving Bruce a split second to dislodge the dagger and pull it free. Blood flowed freely from his shoulder, across his chest and stomach.

Bruce staggered to his feet, hand held over his head dripping with his own blood and lunged for Tristian driving the dagger into the small of his back and jerking it upwards. Tristian let out an anguished scream and crumpled to the ground in a pool of spurting blood. He struggled to the side, took aim, and released a final sliver tipped arrow from his wrist gauntlet before collapsing. This one hit its mark.

Bruce howled tearing at his upper thigh, stumbling back against the car, he slumped to the ground. It was seconds before he was able to yank the knife from his belt and slash his thigh hoping to slow the progress of the poison, but the spreading blue cast to his skin told him it reached the femoral artery. His last thought was for his mate. *Angie, I will always love you*, floated through her already panicked mind forcing her into action.

Angie and Willow rounded the corner of the building just as Bruce crumpled to the ground, unconscious. Angie stepped over Tristian, quickly assessing his injuries as she moved and knelt down beside Bruce. "Don't you dare die on me. You promised," she screamed angrily. "Willow put pressure on Tristian's wound. Gotta stem the bleeding." Angie put her hands over Bruce's chest and groin. Closing her eyes, a violet glow emitted between her hands and the area of skin she laid them on. The flow of blood slowed and the blue tinge to his skin began to fade slowly as Angie diluted the poison with her own body.

A crack rippled through the air as Owen appeared at her side. "What the hell happened here?"

"Just what it looks like. Tristian attacked us. Go into the shop and get the jars in the healing herbs section behind the counter. Bring them here. Hurry."

He was back before she noticed he'd gone.

"Open the jar with the olive colored lid, it looks like dried vines, sprinkle it over his wound. Then take one of those gauze packets and hold it tight against Tristian's wound. Willow, faery dust over both of them, please."

Willow eyed Angie and looked back at Tristian, blood seeping between her fingers from the wound. Owen kneeled down and replaced Willow's hand holding pressure and the packet against Tristian's injury. Willow jumped up and spread her arms wide over her head, turning in a quick circle. Sparkling faery dust floated through the air settling on the men disappearing into their bodies.

"Owen can you move these two into the shop? Lay Bruce and Tristian side by side so I can get between them?" Angie asked.

With a wave of his blood stained hand, Owen transported them all to the back room. Angie's face drawn and white as a sheet, lay between them one hand on each chest, a very faint violet light glowed beneath each hand. She closed her eyes and let her body go limp, fatigue taking control.

After a few minutes, the violet glow was gone. Willow grabbed Angie's shoulder and shook her gently. "That's all you can do. Owen switch her to the couch, they can't draw off her energy any more, or it'll kill her." Willow shook out the blanket infused with healing herbs her mother had given her and placed it over Angie.

Parting the crystal-beaded curtain, Owen strode across the room to the front window, and flipped the sign to closed. He turned back to Willow. "We can't leave them here. You have to open for business tomorrow. No one can know about the dissention between Bruce and Tristian, nor that they're both badly injured."

Without hesitation Willow said, "If you'll help me with Bruce, I can get Angie in the car and take them to our apartment to recuperate. It's better if we do it without magic, there's been way too much used today. Good and evil. It will leave a strong signature for others to find."

"I agree, though the cleanup crew should be here

any minute to remove all evidence of the battle and magic. Tobi will be here shortly to stay with Tristian, while I drive all of you to your apartment. She'll also drop my car back there for your use and I'll take the SUV. It wouldn't be a good idea to advertise where Bruce is staying."

The door chimes sounded as Tobi hustled in, parting the beads and surveying the scene. "I was afraid something like this would happen. How can I help?" She met her husband's eyes and quirked a brow.

"We're going to take Tristian to our home until he is well enough to travel. There are also loose ends to tie up before he leaves. Angie and Bruce are going to the girls' apartment, Willow will watch over them there."

"And who will watch The Krystal Unicorn? It will need to be kept open if we are to keep up appearances," Tobi said her brow furrowed in concern.

Willow said over her shoulder as she reached for Angie, "We have a part-time girl, Autumn. She helps out on Saturdays. I'll call her and see if she can come in tomorrow, after that Angie will be able to care for Bruce, and I'll run the shop."

Tobi nodded. "I can stop in and check on her tomorrow, we have a full crew at the salon and I have a light customer load."

Owen helped Willow load Angie in the car and then started back to the shop for Bruce. "When Angie wakes up have her call me. Bruce called a mandatory meeting for tonight, stating he had important information to share."

A wry smile tugged at Willow's lips. "He's not going to be sharing much for a few days. That poison causes severe muscle aches and fatigue for days in the most powerful of magic beings." Willow frowned and shook her head.

"I know that." Owen said curtly. "But I want to see if Angie knows what's up, so I can be prepared if necessary. Bruce indicated it was urgent business. He requested security back up to be on standby. So I need to tell them something."

"Understood. She'll call you as soon as she's able. I promise."

****

Angie awoke with Willow hovering over her. "Thank the stars you are awake. Owen has been driving me crazy wanting to talk with you or Bruce."

"How long have I been out?" Angie blinked her eyes and tried to focus on what Willow was saying.

"Eighteen hours, give or take." Willow fisted her hands on her hips and studied Angie. "You look much better, your color is back and eyes bright."

Angie struggled to sit up and rubbed her eyes, memories of recent events flooded back, making her head pound. "Have you been giving Bruce the pain killers and muscle healing herbs?"

"Of course. He's healing quickly, but you know how long recovery will be, even for him."

"I know, but trying to keep him down once he wakes up will be a formidable task."

Willow shrugged. "Hey, that's your problem. Right now, I need to get back to the shop, and you better call Owen. Something about an urgent meeting on Tuesday that didn't happen because of our little incident."

"Oh shit, he doesn't know."

"Can you hold off heading to the shop? I think you'll want to hear what I have to say to Owen."

At her friend's worried expression and serious tone, Willow sat down on the bed and handed Bruce's cell phone to Angie. "Don't overdo it yet, or you'll be flat on your back again." Willow drew her own cellphone from her pocket. "I'll just call Autumn and see if she can cover today. We are going to owe her a bonus for being at our beck and call lately."

Angie called Owen's private number and filled him in on all the details Andre, Bruce's father, had told him. Willow's interested expression turned to horror as Angie laid out the details over the phone.

Willow tapped in Autumn's number into phone and put the phone to her ear.

When Angie brought Owen up to speed, he said, "So after nearly killing each other, Bruce and Tristian have to work together to save each other. I'd better have a sit down talk with Tristian before we put those two together again." Owen paused. "Angie, Tristian is asking for you."

"He should have thought of me, before he attacked. Again, taking matters into his own hands, without consulting me." Fury still swirled in her voice. "I'll call him later. Don't want to say something I'll regret. How is he doing?"

"He is doing better, his balance is off, and the muscles in his back are slow to heal. It's going to be a while before he's battle ready. How about Bruce?"

Angie frowned and looked over at Bruce. "Hard to tell, we've kept him sedated so he'll heal faster, you may want to do the same to Tristian. Even twenty-four hours will make a big difference. I'll send Willow with the herbs. The lasting effects of the poison on Bruce's muscles will be with him for a few days after he's up and around and will be painful."

"Tristian has been asking for someone named Hannah? He hasn't had contact with anyone yet."

"As far as Hannah—I don't know anyone by that name, though Bruce did mention giving him some time off to get his personal affairs in order." Angie paused wrinkling her forehead. "You don't suppose a woman finally tamed him, do you?"

On a half laugh, Owen said, "It happens to the best of us. If that's the case, he's probably in big trouble with her too. I'll try to find out more, and then make a decision. As far as this situation with Rezar, I don't think we can wait for Bruce to come around. I'll e-mail the Far-East Overlord under Bruce's e-mail and see if there is anything new. A couple of our best teams are in town due to the scheduled meeting, I'm going to bring them up to speed and start working on a strategy."

"Sounds good." Angie paused for a moment then said into the phone, "Owen, Bruce is lucky to have you."

"I know, been telling him that for years. I'll be in touch."

Angie's forehead creased as she thought of her brothers actions. "Owen, can I ask you one more thing?"

"Sure."

"What's going to happen to Tristian? He tried to kill an Overlord, his employer."

Silence stretched for a beat or two, then Owen cleared his throat. "That will be up to Bruce. Under normal circumstances, we don't tolerate that type of behavior, especially over a woman. No offense."

"None taken." Ending the call, she turned her

attention back to a groggy Bruce. She leaned over him. "How do you feel?"

"Like hell. How long have I been here?" He struggled to open his eyes, and move his limbs.

"A couple of days. I hope you don't mind, I filled Owen in on the highlights of the situation. He's anxious to talk to you as soon as you feel able. It was more important to get your body healed so we sedated you. I knew if we didn't, you'd try to work through it, and that's impossible with that type of poison in your system. Still you will feel muscle aches, and severe fatigue for a few more days."

He frowned but took her hand and brought it to his lips. "Welcome to my world. Now hand me the phone so I can call Owen." He reached for the cell phone and checked the recent calls. It listed one missed call and a message waiting. He checked the number. "Shit. I must have missed my father's call."

"You did. I returned it and gave him a vague description of what happened. You'll need to fill him in."

"You're one efficient li'l witch. Handling this business like you're born to it."

"If I believe you and your destiny theory, I guess I am." She leaned down and brushed a kiss over his forehead.

"Oh, that's not enough for what I've been through." He reached under her sweater and caressed the bare skin of her back until he reached her bra, unfastening it he cupped the firm breasts he was so fond of and rolled her nipple between his thumb and index finger until it was hard then switched to the other. He sighed and his arm dropped too fatigued to engage in his favorite activity. Still he gathered her into him enjoying the warmth and curve of her body spooned against him.

The phone on the bed beeped, he picked it up and looked at the screen. "It's Owen, I've got to take this, and then we'll take up right where we left off."

Angie smiled. "I'll hold you to it."

Bruce put the phone to his ear. "Owen. Fill me in."

"Hey, boss. I was expecting Angie to answer. She's been taking care of business while you've been incapacitated. It's good to hear your voice, you sound great."

"That's what mates are for." He smiled wide at Angie lying beside him, tightening his arm around her as she started to get up. "We're not through," he whispered as he brushed his lips over her temple.

"What, I didn't quite catch all of that." Owen chuckled. "Sounds like you were a bit distracted."

"I said, you got it all handled?"

"Mostly. I briefed Bobby's team and sent them home, but on alert. Did the same to Paul's old team, Rubin is turning into a competent leader. He's not Paul, but damn close and he has the men's respect. That's something."

"How much did you tell them?"

"Everything Angie relayed that Andre told you. Nothing about the skirmish between you and Tristian. Figured you'd want to handle that yourself."

"Smart man. No one questioned why he wasn't there?"

"No. I said you'd given Tristian time off before I started the briefing. If they detected his signature, no one said anything."

"Is he able to take a meeting?"

Owen paused. "He's up and walking but still has balance issues due to the damaged back muscles but that's improving faster now with the herbal pack Angie sent over. His stamina is lacking but that too is coming along rapidly. Don't you think both of you could use a couple more days rest?"

"No, and don't question my decisions."

"Of course not, when and what time do you want me to set up the meeting?"

"Tonight, nine o'clock. The staff should be done and cleared out by then, right?"

"Tobi has the late appointment it's only a cut at seven, so no worries."

"Great. Tobi can stay. In fact ask her to join us."

"You got it. Now get some rest. I'll see you this evening." Owen disconnected the call before Bruce could reprimand him again for telling him what to do.

****

At eighty-thirty, Bruce held the door for Angie as she strolled into the Wycked Hair. He shut the door and joined her. Tobi smiled in greeting as Bruce continued toward the stairs.

"Tristian should arrive with Owen shortly. He spent the afternoon with Tristian since I had customers. Want me to brew a fresh pot of coffee and bring it up?" Toni wiped her hands on a towel and folded her smock, laying it on the back of the chair.

"That'll be great." Bruce called over his shoulder climbing the stairs slowly and one at a time.

"I'll help you, Tobi." Angie volunteered, as she watched Bruce attempt the stairs under his own power. He nodded and she returned to the salon floor.

Waiting until Bruce was out of sight and the squeak of his office chair sounded in the quiet salon, Tobi hugged Angie. "How are you?"

"A little shell shocked, I guess. But even with all that's gone on he's the best thing that ever happened to me." Angie sighed and followed Tobi to the refreshment center.

Tobi reached up in the cupboard for the cups and looked over her shoulder at Angie. "No regrets?"

"Absolutely not. I just hope Tristian comes around sooner than later. But well, he's stubborn and in a lot of trouble. I don't mind telling you that's got me worried."

Tobi nodded in agreement. "Bruce is a fair man and knows he's partly responsible for making the situation what it is. Though I can't honestly see what he could have done differently, other than ignore you, and we all knew that wasn't going to happen. There was no way Tristian would accept a demon in the family, gracefully."

"Yes, but if any one's to blame, it's me. I started it then…well…the rest is history."

Tobi got the can of coffee off the shelf as Angie reached for the filters. "No, you two were destined to be together, you can't fight against fate. You are so good for him."

"Yeah, but not so good for Tristian," Angie said with a sigh as she scooped the coffee into the filter and closed the lid. "If I'd had just a little more time…" Angie trailed off.

"He'll come around. You know he has a woman in his life now, right?"

"No, I didn't." Angie's eyes rounded in surprise. "When did this happen?"

"Not sure, recently to be sure. So whether or not he will admit it, he knows how you and Bruce feel. I gotta believe he will accept Bruce as your mate, not that he has any choice." Tobi brushed her bangs out of her eyes and tucked strands of auburn hair behind her ear." He knows how this all works, even if he didn't tell you." Tobi said.

"One can only hope."

"Just ask him about Hannah, that's her name." After washing her hands, Tobi dried them on a paper towel, and poured the water into the coffee maker. She got down a tray and Angie set mugs on it.

"I'm going to take this up." Angie glanced up at the glass office, chewing on her bottom lip as she watched Bruce slowly lean back in his chair.

"Go ahead," Tobi said. "I'll be up with the coffee as soon as it's done. Owen and Tristian should be here by then."

Angie turned back to Tobi. "I think I'd rather have hot chocolate, don't really care for coffee."

Tobi handed her an empty mug. "There's a hot tap on the water dispensers in Bruce's office. He also has packets of the hot chocolate you like. So you can make a cup up there."

"He does? Ok."

"That man's besotted with you and has been since the day you breezed in here and turned those violet eyes on him." She chuckled and shook her head. "How's he doing?"

"He needs a few more days of rest to be one hundred percent, but he's ok. The demon blood seems to rebuild faster with the healing herbs. I think he'll breathe easier once this is all behind him. I know I sure will." Angie flashed a smile though her heart wasn't in it. She climbed the stairs with the tray of mugs and knocked on the framework of the open door.

Bruce looked up, the frown fading from his face as the corners of his mouth curved up in a slow, easy, and devastating smile. "You don't have to knock, just come in."

"I didn't want to interrupt, if you were busy." She sat the tray and mugs on the table in front of the sofa.

"Never too busy for you, my li'l witch."

Angie smiled. She liked the way he called her his li'l witch. "It's rumored that you keep packets of the hot chocolate I like up here. She held out her mug.

"The rumors would be true." He pointed to the cabinet against the wall. "There's a hot tap on the water cooler."

She fixed a cup of hot chocolate, sprinkled a few marshmallows on top, and sat on the sofa stirring the smooth dark liquid just as they heard footsteps on the stairs.

"Showtime."

Angie stared down at the mug in her hands watching the marshmallows melt into creamy white swirls in the steaming hot chocolate then turned her eyes to him. "You're not going to have him killed are you?"

A laugh rumbled up from his chest, his eyes filled with amusement. "I'm not an ogre. I'm a demon with a heart. So, no, my li'l witch, nothing like that." He made a bad mistake and put you in mortal danger, for that he'll be punished."

"But what about trying to kill you, an Overlord?"

"Well there is that, but I never considered myself

any different with or without the title. Since only five of us know about his error in judgment, I think we can be creative with the punishment. Don't worry about it. Right now we have greater things to worry about, and I am going to need Tristian's as well as others help if we are to win this battle. There can't be any discord between Tristian and I."

Owen knocked on the open door and waited.

"What is it with everyone knocking on the frame of my open door? If I didn't want anyone in here, I'd close the damn thing. Now, come on in."

Owen flashed a grin, which faded quickly when he signaled Tristian to enter the room. His gait was unsteady as he took small steps and his hands remained at his sides. When he entered the room, his eyes shot daggers as they met Bruce's, yet when they swept to Angie, they filled with such sorrow she had to look away.

Tobi sat on the sofa by Angie and Owen escorted Tristian to the front of Bruce's desk, where he left him standing and took a seat off to his left.

"Owen, the magic shackles aren't necessary, he can't use magic in here and I am not afraid to take him on hand to hand. Let the man sit down. I think we've done enough damage to each other and the woman we both love. Don't you?" He looked over at Tristian whose eyes still raged, but he said nothing.

Bruce took a deep breath and blew it out. He needed to settle this with Tristian alone. "Tobi, Owen, and Angie give us a minute. Close the door behind you."

Angie stood and walked behind Bruce's chair putting her hands on his shoulders. "I'm not going anywhere. When you two finish, I have some things I'd like to say that's probably best heard by only the three of us."

Owen shook his head. "I don't think it's advisable to leave you two in the same room, yet." He shot a warning glance at Bruce.

"As I told you before, don't question my decisions. If I want your opinion, I'll ask for it." Bruce snapped.

"Yes sir." Owen turned motioned for Tobi to come with him and strode out the door closing it a bit harder than necessary.

"As for you," he said in a stern voice tilting his head back so his eyes met Angie's. "You can stay only because I love looking at you." He grinned up at her. Then turned his attention to Tristian, the grin faded, replaced by a look of displeasure and annoyance.

Tristian stood poised to leap over the desk. In a split second, they collided in midair as Bruce knocked him to the floor; the breath whooshed out of Tristian on impact. Bruce held Tristian's shoulders to the floor with his hands and a knee put slight pressure to his injured back. Tristian let out a low moan his body jerking.

The office door opened a crack. Owen looked in just as Angie came around the side of the desk. But Bruce shook his head. Frowning, she returned to stand behind his chair and Owen closed the door again.

"Now we can talk this way, or I can let you up and we can talk like civilized people. Which way do you want it?"

"Fuck you." Tristian spat into the carpeting.

"That is not an option. Guess we start out like this. I regret that I didn't come to you when this all started with Angie. Though I believe, the outcome would have been the same, if I had. The facts are, after being fully informed of what being my mate entailed, Angie agreed wholeheartedly to be my mate without reservations, which as you know is for eternity. We consummated our relationship over the weekend."

Tristian's body slumped to the floor, as if everything he'd been fighting for was gone.

"She's my destined mate, Tristian. I've waited over five hundred years for her. We both felt it at our first meeting, though Willow had to explain the situation to her, since you failed to teach her the ways of our world."

Bruce you need to let him up, his body is still much more fragile than yours. You damaged his back severely, and as you said yourself, you need him. Her voice resounded in Bruce's mind.

I know and I'll help him over to the chair in a moment. He answered in kind and smiled turning back to Tristian. "I'm going to help you up and over to the lounge chair. It would be advisable if you didn't fight me, as we need each other more than you know." He gently rolled Tristian to his back, assisted him to his feet, and settled him in the chair.

Tristian slumped in the chair, his eyes staring at the floor.

With one of the healing herb packs she'd pulled out of her bag in her hand, Angie went to her brother. She gently placed it at the small of his back and leaned him against it. "Idiot!" Then she returned to Bruce and slid one under his shirt.

He frowned at her but left the packet in place. "I'll cut to the chase. Rezar is back and sworn revenge on the two of us. This has been confirmed by a very reliable source."

Tristian winced as he tried to sit up straight and turn his full attention to Bruce. "Shit. How is that possible?"

"I don't know. But he must have paid someone handsomely to reverse the spell, and apparently, it only partially worked. He was able to return to this world, but he is weak, laying low to build his strength and still wears the collar so he can't wield magic. That will be to our benefit."

"Do you know where he is?"

"I've not been able to confirm it yet. Reports have him in the Far East. I'm waiting for confirmation before our plans are set in stone. We need to attack while he is weak and on his turf, even though he has reinforcements." Bruce stroked his chin with his thumb and forefinger thoughtfully. "Should have surprise on our side. I don't want to wait for him to get this far."

"I agree." Tristian said with very little of the anger he'd displayed earlier.

"The major problem that I see in all of this is the dispute between you and me. Trust is a big issue right now, for both of us. We can't win this battle if we don't have each other's back. You are the best at what you do and though we'll have several teams with us, it will come down to you and I and trusting each other."

Tristian was silent for a while, then blew out a breath. "I don't see how we can overcome that obstacle." Tristian crossed his arms across his chest, wincing slightly.

Bruce got up and moved to look out the windows, his arms behind his back, fists clenching an unclenching.

Angie walked over to the lounger, sat on the arm and reached behind her brother's neck rubbing at the stress knots. "Tristian, you and Bruce have trusted each other for years. We have done nothing wrong. I am of legal age and wanted what Bruce offered more than anything in my entire life. I have no regrets, only that it hurt and angered you. Can you honestly say that if we'd come to you sooner and told you what we intended, that you could have acted any differently?"

Resting back against the chair, he shook his head slowly. "No, I can't. I would never allow you to tie yourself to a demon. You don't know what they are capable of. He's only told you what he wanted you to know. Shown you what he wants you to see. I could tell you tales that would give you nightmares for the rest of your life."

"Tristian, he only confirmed what Willow already told me. Something you should have done long ago. As far as his vicious side, I saw that in the parking lot behind my shop. I realize he was holding back because he'd promised me that he wouldn't kill you."

Tristian sputtered. "I make my living destroying demonkind."

Angie grabbed his chin and forced him to look at her. "Listen to me. His promise was the only reason you got the opportunity to poison him, otherwise you'd be dead and he'd be unscathed."

Tristian jerked his chin out of her hand, his mouth set in a hard line, eyes blazing. She shifted on the chair arm so she could look him square in the face, eyes slitted. "Speaking of what some people are capable of, shall we discuss what you do for a living?"

His eyes cooled and he looked at the floor refusing

to meet Angie's eyes. "It's a necessary evil."

"So I've been told. Now before you say anything else stupid. Let me make my position perfectly clear. Knowing what being Bruce's mate entailed, I agreed to it completely, without being under the influence of magic. No way are you going to lay any blame on Bruce. Is this all clear to you?"

Tristian nodded.

"Good. I consented to be his mate because he is everything I could ever want in a man. So you are going to have to accept him and our relationship on those terms. Come on Tristian," she said soothingly, "you've been my rock since I was twelve. Let Bruce take some of that burden from your shoulders."

His hand on the other chair arm, Tristian pushed himself up and grabbed for her wrist. "You've never been a burden, and you're not his wife. You're only his mate, he didn't ask you to be his wife and acknowledge that important tradition in the world I raised you. Did he?"

She slipped neatly out of his grasp and walked toward Bruce. "No he didn't. But we've had precious little time together since that night and it doesn't matter how you define our relationship, it's forever. You know, 'til death do us part."

His fist hit the chair arm as he threw himself back against the chair in frustration. "It matters to me and would matter greatly to our parents." There he'd said it, what was bothering him the most, the fear that Bruce was just using her as a toy and would discard her as he had all the others only this time it would end in her death. It didn't make any sense, that ceremony, the little piece of paper, the promises given. Vows taken didn't guarantee happily ever after, but in the world he'd built for her, he'd hoped it would work. She shattered that hope by giving herself to, of all things, a demon. How was he going to reconcile that?

Bruce turned to reach out to Angie encircling his arm around her waist pulling her tight against him. "Tristian, I understand how you feel."

"How could you?" Tristian swore.

"But you know that when a mate is taken in my world, it's for eternity, only death severs that bond. Why would I bind myself to a woman, if I didn't intend it to be forever? I've had any woman I wanted most of my life, yet never took any of them as a mate, because I believe in destiny. I wasn't going to tie myself to just any woman no matter how beautiful or how talented in bed she was, when the one woman meant for me was out there somewhere. Now that I have found her, I will cherish her for eternity. All the women I've had pale in comparison to Angie. If she wants to be my wife, I'll happily marry her, but not for you. It's been her decision all along and will remain so. As I am sure you know she has no trouble stating her mind." He leaned over and nuzzled her neck then released her and paced back to the desk, shoving his hands in his pockets.

A slight smile formed on Tristian's lips as he nodded in agreement.

"Now you have less than twenty-four hours to decide whether you can accept Angie's decision to be my mate and rebuild the trust we've enjoyed throughout our working relationship. I truly hope you can, because it's going to take our combined knowledge and cunning to triumph Rezar, if the rumors are true."

"What about Angie? You know he'll come after

her first, if he is aware that you've taken a mate."

"Or your sister, someone he already knows exists. She and Willow will leave for a safe house soon, where they'll stay until this is over. Believe me there is no safer place on earth than where I am going to take them."

"What makes you so sure?"

The emotional roller coaster of the last hour or so had taken its toll. Bruce felt achy, his self-control was wearing thin, Angie was right he needed to rest. Leaning back against the chair he chose to ignore Tristian's question and said gruffly. "You're free to go. Although, you may want to consider a safe place for your woman, Hannah." He closed his eyes. "Owen, Tobi please step inside and join us."

Quietly the office door opened, Owen and Tobi slipped inside taking a seat on the sofa.

"You mean I can go home?" Smirking, Tristian jerked his chin up at Bruce, his brow raised incredulously.

"I never intended to hold you against your will, only make sure you healed. Your attack on Angie and I will be dealt with later."

"Angie walked to her brother and put her hand on his back. You're healing nicely, but far from battle ready." She'd heard Bruce use that term and thought it fit. "It would be better for you to stay with Owen and Tobi a few more days, rather than tax your body by traveling too soon." She glanced over at Owen. "If they are willing to put up with you for a while longer."

Owen looked at Tobi who nodded. "Not been a problem so far."

"If you are concerned for Hannah, have her come

here." Angie suggested.

"That's a great idea. You two can stay at my apartment in the city. A state of the art security system surrounds the facility."

"And where will you stay?" Tristian narrowed his eyes as he assessed Bruce's offer.

"I have other homes, and I've grown fond of Angie's place." He smiled over at her, knowing she didn't like his apartment and figured they'd stay at her place or drive to the estate.

Bruce took out an iridescent disk from his locked desk drawer. "This is a visitor's pass to my apartment." He tossed it to Owen. "I'll stop by there tonight and sign you, Tristian, and a guest as resident visitors. Owen, you'll have the authority to provide information on the guest."

Owen caught the disk and turned it over in his hand. "I'll take care of it. Where will I be able to reach you, should a problem arise?"

"See that it doesn't. My cell phone will be on, I may not answer right away, since I want all communications secure, but it won't be long. Starting now, I want a rotating eight then twelve hour check in for Ruben, Tristian, and Bobby. They'll report to you." He studied Owen's face and body language to make sure there were no objections he wasn't voicing. "On the opposite intervals, you'll report to me. If any check-ins are missed by any one, the rest will immediately travel here." He raised both arms from the chair where they rested and pointed his index fingers to the floor of the office.

"What if it's just a screw up, forgot?" Owen rubbed his chin thoughtfully raising a brow while looking from Bruce to Tristian.

"Then he'll have several pissed off individuals to answer to. The chain of command shall remain as always, me, Owen, Tristian, Bobby, and now Ruben. If anyone is missing or killed the next in line will take command without question. Mission is first, next of kin way later. Find the missing, then the bodies." Head leaned back against his chair, Bruce pressed thumb and forefinger against his closed eyes. The weariness and muscle aches were closing in again, he couldn't afford to let it show. Taking a deep breath, he let it out and sat up straight, giving each individual in the room a calculating stare with piercing dark amber eyes.

'If Tristian determines he can't work for me, cut him loose to handle his own protection and affairs. Then locate a trusted replacement from our ranks and change everything we discussed here today except completion of the mission. This time Rezar's neutralization will be permanent and his dust scattered over earth, sea, and between."

"Now." He motioned Angie to him as he leaned back against his chair, and reached up for her hand, using her healing essence to bolster his physical and emotional well-being as energy flowed between them. "Any questions?"

Silence filled the office as they looked from one to another shaking their heads.

Tristian's jaw clenched, the vein at his temple bulged as he watched the interaction between his sister and her demon mate. "I'm in 'til the end as I've always been."

"Great. I've your oath on Angie's life that you'll have my back as I will have yours, should it be necessary?"

Without hesitation, he swore. "Yes, damn it. She's made her choice, I don't like it, but she's tied herself to you for eternity. I feel betrayed by both of you, but I'll learn to live with it. As far as you and me, it's business as usual."

Bruce arched a brow wondering at Tristian's quick change of heart. "You sure?"

"Yes." Tristian said matter-of-factly.

The worst of the meeting finished, Bruce squeezed Angie's hand. *Later my li'l witch.* He spoke in her mind.

Promises, promises. Her lips curved into a slight smile as she turned to face him.

He stood feeling stronger. "We are done. Tristian if you choose to travel…"

"I'm not." Tristian interrupted pushing himself out of the lounger, he extended his hand, Bruce clasped it firmly.

Hoping to ease Tristian's mind, Bruce reiterated his stance once more. "I'll be good to her, you've my word. There'll be no other. You've my word on that also. Just as you've found happiness with your woman, I have with mine."

"Yeah, but acceptance…" He trailed off. "Thanks for the use of your apartment. I'll call Hannah tonight. I guess Owen and Tobi will have a house guest at least one more night, if they've no objections."

"We'll get you set up in the apartment tomorrow." Owen stood rolling his shoulders then reached down helping Tobi to her feet. "You're welcome to stay with us. Let's go, I'm beat, and you look like hell."

"Owen, send the jet for Hannah, if she's amenable

and Tristian agrees," Bruce said.

"I'll see to it, boss,"

Bruce followed them to the door." See you tomorrow. Owen there'll be additional changes on the salon's expansion. We'll discuss them when I arrive in the morning. Good night." He closed the door behind them and turned to Angie, drawing her to him, he laid his cheek on top her head, breathing in her wonderful scent as she curved into him. "We need to talk about The Krystal Unicorn and your extended absence."

Her body stiffened and she tried to pull away. "I'm not going anywhere."

"Yes, you are. It won't be safe for you here while we hunt down Rezar." He held her tight while she wriggled against him making it difficult to keep his mind on the discussion. "My parents want you to stay in the cottage on their property, until I get back. Willow should go with you too."

"I don't know your parents. And I've made a place for myself here. I'm not leaving, neither is Willow. She won't leave Caleb. Our business is doing very well. I can't just up and leave. You should know that better than anyone else."

He grasped her shoulders, held her out at arm's length as he tamped down his temper. "Yes, you can and will. I can't do what I need to do in battle and worry about your safety too. It would give the enemy an advantage and I don't have a death wish. After six hundred years, I just found you. I want to spend the rest of my life enjoying what we have together."

His words stilled her for a moment, then she tilted her head and peered up at him. "Ok, so if I agree, what do you propose to do about The Krystal Unicorn?

We've worked too hard to just walk away."

"Walking away is not an option for you. I understand that. After the expansion of the salon, I'll have approximately two thousand square feet of unused space at the end of the building. You could relocate your shop there. It would have outside access to the street and a door into the salon. That way while you and Willow are gone, Tobi could help out your part-time person in the shop for a few weeks, until you return."

"Have you discussed this with Tobi?"

"Not yet, but I know her well, she'll be happy to help. I'm going to talk with Owen tomorrow morning and get his input. I wanted to discuss it with you first. You and Willow are welcome to sit in. In fact you two could see the space and decide how you want it designed to fit your business."

Angie chewed on her bottom lip then sighed. "What about the current lease, it's not up for another couple of months."

"Owen helped negotiate that lease. I think we can work something out, besides we have time." Let's go have a look. I can show you where the separation wall will be, if it's not up yet."

She nodded and drew out a little bottle out of her pocket. "You need to drink this before you expend any more energy."

"What is it?" Bruce asked suspiciously.

"An herbal potion I prepared to help you heal and keep up your strength. Now drink it."

"Ok." He took the bottle and downed the liquid. "Happy now?"

He took her hand in his entwining their fingers as they descended the stairs together. At the bottom, he flipped on the lights and pointed to the construction area cordoned off with large sheets of plastic from floor to ceiling. "Through here." He parted the plastic, holding it open for her.

A thin layer of white dust floated in the air when the plastic was disturbed and landed lightly on the flat surfaces. The tile was down, the stations set up; chairs covered with more plastic were arranged in each station. Rolls of wallpaper sheathed in plastic sleeves leaned against the wall.

"This way." He stood in an arched doorway cut into the unfinished wall. They walked through another archway into the dark area. A white blue ball of light appeared at his fingertips, he tossed it into the air where it floated illuminating the area in a soft blue hue.

Angie arched her brows. "Just gotta bend the rules."

Bruce shrugged. "You know what they say, meant to be broken. Anyway, there's no electric run in here yet, don't want you stumbling over anything, so I'd say it was a necessity."

"You're just showing off. Need I remind you again, I can see as well as you can in the dark."

"It's romantic though, isn't it? He leaned over and nuzzled her neck.

The area was huge compared to their current shop down the street. Plenty of room for a storeroom, a larger shop with full-mirrored wall, separate section for herbs, potions and ingredients and maybe a small sitting room surrounded by bookcases. The possibilities were endless.

"What's this going to cost per month? It's nearly twice as big as our current space."

"You'll have to talk with Owen, I own the buildings, he handles the salon finances and paperwork. I believe we can work out a deal that is acceptable to all parties. After all you are…"

"Don't say it. It's so cliché." She stifled a giggle wrinkling her nose and grimaced.

"Sleeping with the boss." He winked as his eyes sparkled with mischief. "Believe me there is nothing cliché about our relationship." He pulled her to him and took her mouth with his, penetrating her lips with his tongue exploring her softness and savoring her flavor. "Mmm…so sweet," he murmured.

She curved her body into him running her hands over his firm butt she found so enticing. She slithered against him until she felt his excitement. "I think we better get a room."

"Got one."

"One with a bed."

He pressed her up against the wall, leaned over and gently put his hand behind her knee and lifted her leg spreading her so he could slide between, pressing his length against her. He could smell her arousal as he moved his hand further up her thigh to the crotch of her panties. She was wet and ready for him.

She unbuttoned his pants and slid her hand inside gripping his thick, pulsating shaft straining for release. Her thumb slipped over the slick head as she moved her hand up and down the length. He jerked forward involuntarily and moaned, "That feels so good."

"Not here," she murmured. "Someone might come in."

He raised his head looking toward the salon. He could see the steady red light through the plastic indicating the alarm was on. "No one can come in without us knowing." He slid a finger under her panties and into the heat. "Besides it adds to the excitement, don't you think?" he whispered, a wicked glint in his eye as the corners of his mouth turned up in a naughty grin.

She bucked against his hand breath ragged. "Please not here. I want to enjoy you. Not like teenagers afraid of getting caught."

In a husky, seductive voice he said, "Sometimes the reward is worth the risk."

"Not this time." She tried to wriggle away succeeding only in more stimulating contact with his clever fingers. "Ooh this is so unfair."

"Who told you life was fair?" Chuckling quietly, he slid another finger into her tight channel, caressing her soft folds and teasing the sweet spot inside her. She moaned and arched against his hand more urgently.

Shifting he leaned his shoulder against the wall, freeing his hand braced against the partition and just above her shoulder.

Her eyes flew open as she panted, "Don't you dare conjure a bed here."

"Then it's the floor." He started to lower her down. It wasn't going to be slow and sweet like the first time, he needed her hard, fast, and waiting wasn't an option. He swept her up into his arms and took the stairs one at a time carrying her to his office. The door locked, he shrugged out of his shirt and touched a panel on the wall. With a creaking sound, the leather couch folded out into a bed and soft strains of classical music filled the room.

"This better?" he growled sitting on the side of the

bed with her in his lap. He pulled her sweater over her head, flicked open the clasp on her lacy bra and took her soft rounded breasts into his mouth sucking as he caught her nipples between his teeth, circled his tongue around the tips, taking his time and sucking gently.

"It is." She moaned aloud as he lay her down.

Instinctively, her body arched toward him feeling his erection pressed against her, the hardness electrified her.

Barely able to control the raw animalist power and demon desire that coiled through his body, he kicked off his pants. He gathered her skirt above her hips, and ripped off her matching lacy panties, spreading her legs wide. "You're absolutely beautiful," he panted as he slid between them. She was his mate and he'd possess her without caution.

She gasped as he lowered his body over hers, felt her breasts crush against the hardness of his chest, and quivered at his touch. She wrapped her legs around him as he thrust deeply into her. His tormented groan encouraging her to tighten her legs, taking more and more of him deeper inside until she'd taken his entire length. The rhythmic slap of naked flesh against naked flesh was the only sound until the organism ripped through her. He thrust violently into her, filling her once more.

Normally, he kept a leash on his dominant male demonic nature. Tonight, she'd snapped that tether and took all he had to offer and reveled in it. The electrifying thrill of it sent shivers down his spine. Both sated, they lay motionless savoring the feeling of their fire, passion and finally contentment.

"We can't stay here," she murmured, her head

cradled in his shoulder with his arm wrapped around her.

"Sure we can," he replied sleepily. "I locked the door, we won't be bothered."

"But they'll know we…"

"Spent the night here, together. I don't think that is a news flash. Everyone knows I've taken you as my mate and with the carnal nature of a demon, I will continue to do so as often as possible. Now can we get some sleep, or." His hand slid between her legs caressing her swollen lips and teasing her still damp entrance. "Would you rather test my stamina?"

She reached for him stroking his semi erect cock. "Hmmm, let me think about it."

****

They got up before dawn and drove to her apartment, showered and changed, then sat in the kitchen at the breakfast table, sipping coffee and hot chocolate. Willow walked into the room, rubbing her eyes and yawning widely. "You guys are up early, since you didn't get in before two this morning."

"Keeping tabs on us?" Bruce said with a broad grin.

"Well no, not exactly. Caleb didn't leave until around two. So I was still up, kinda."

"Sure you were and I don't want to know about it." Angie held up her hand and rolled her eyes giving Willow a knowing smile.

"We do have some things to discuss with you, have a seat," Bruce said. "Angie made enough hot chocolate for you or there's coffee in the pot."

"Oh, sounds serious." Willow said flippantly then poured herself a mug of hot chocolate, tossed a few marshmallows in, and sat at the table pushing the marshmallows down into the hot chocolate only to have them bounce back on top. Her eyes blinked slowly as she yawned again. "Getting too old to keep these kinds of hours." Grinning she looked from Angie to Bruce, then her grin faded quickly. "Is something wrong?"

"Sort of, well we think so."

"Stop trying to sugarcoat it, Angie." Bruce launched into the whole story leaving nothing out, ending with Willow and Angie would need to relocate to a safe place until it was over.

Willow's eyes went wide in horror as she blew out a breath. "And you expect me to just disappear without telling Caleb? No way. What about The Krystal Unicorn, we are having a fantastic first year." She crossed her arms across her chest, set her jaw, and leaned back against the chair shaking her head vigorously. "This can't be happening."

Angie took a sip of her hot chocolate, looking over the rim of her mug at Willow, giving her time to digest what they'd just told her. "I understand how you feel, but the fewer people that know the better."

"He can be trusted." Willow insisted warming her cold hands on the warm mug of hot chocolate, she'd yet to taste.

Patiently Bruce explained. "It's not a matter of trust. If you tell him, you're putting him in danger. They could use him as a pawn to get to you and Angie and then me. This will be a battle of mental strategy as well as magical abilities, physical strength, and dominance. I don't intend to leave anything or anyone behind that could be used against me or divide my attention."

"What about Owen, Tobi, and the salon?"

"They've been through this before and are prepared. Since we are still gathering intel, you've a bit of time."

"But aren't Owen and Tobi a direct line to you?"

"No." He didn't elaborate, the less she knew the safer she'd be.

Chapter Fifteen

The Lear jet landed on a private runway at Faa'a International Airport in Papeete, Tahiti, where a sleek white limo waited. Bruce tucked Angie's hand in the crook of his arm as they descended the stairs from the plane to the tarmac. The driver, a pleasant looking muscular man stood beside the open door, Bruce nodded to him as they entered the limo and he closed the door behind them.

Settling in the driver's seat the man turned the key and the engine purred to life. The limo left the airport via a private road and turned onto what looked like a main road. "The smoke glass partition between them faded away. Nice to see you my lord, you're looking well."

"Thanks Joab. How's Lin, still keeping you in line?" Bruce said warmly.

Joab glanced backward with an appreciative smile. "Yes sir."

"Cut the crap, it's Bruce and you know it." He put his arm around Angie. "This is Angie Shandie, she's my mate."

"So it's true." His eyes met hers in the rear view mirror and he nodded. "Nice to meet you, Ms. Shandie." He returned his attention to the road. "Andre and Matiah are looking forward to meeting you." Smiling he said under his breath, "They didn't think there was a woman alive that could tame him."

Unsure of whether he was talking to her or to himself she decided to set the record straight. "Well, I don't know about that Joab, but we seem to be able to handle each other well enough so far." She giggled as Bruce's hand slipped down to tickle her ribs.

"Yes ma'am." With that, the partition between them reappeared.

The limo took a wide curve and appeared to drive right into the side of a mountain. Before Angie could catch her breath, the vehicle plunged into darkness. Panic rose in her throat, she opened her mouth to scream just as Bruce leaned over and kissed her lips whispering, "It's all right, just the magic boundary to my parents place. We'll be on the other side in a moment." As the words left his mouth, the darkness faded into a thick mist surrounding the limo. The vehicle continued on and the mist lightened then finally disappeared altogether, replaced by lush green foliage as far as the eye could see.

A bluish-gray and rose stone villa with a decorative gated courtyard sat nestled in the center of the greenery. Waterfalls cascaded down the towering cliffs behind the villa creating a mist that floated above and behind the structure. The driver pulled the limo into a circular driveway stopping at the multihued stone path that meandered through the open decorative wrought iron gate and across the courtyard. Several panels of stained glass depicting a large golden dragon frolicking with a variety of faeries, wood nymphs, and water sprites adorned the arched front door.

Angie was still coming to terms with the whole situation when the limo door opened. Bruce slid out and reached for her hand to assist her from the vehicle. She turned toward the villa door just as it opened. A tall muscular man with silver streaked sable hair stepped out, an older version of Bruce, and beside him, the most beautiful woman Angie had ever seen. She had light reddish blonde hair that hung in graceful curves over her shoulders, slight build and bright blue eyes that sparkled when she smiled.

Rooted to the spot, Angie couldn't take another step as fear and anxiety gripped her. Then his mother turned slightly to speak to his father and the tips of frosty white wings feathered with charcoal at the edges were just disappearing into her back, she shrugged her shoulders, like Willow did as her wings retracted. But Willow's wings were nothing like these.

Angie's eyes rounded in utter astonishment as a soft gasp escaped her lips. "Oh my stars, your mother—she's an angel!" she said louder than intended. Immediately her cheeks flushed and she lowered her lashes in an attempt to hide her embarrassment."

"She is." He sprinted up the path dragging Angie behind him. "Relax, li'l witch they're looking forward to meeting you."

Composure restored, Angie planted both feet on the path, yanking him to a skidding stop. "Quit dragging me you big demon," she said with a grin. "What do I call them? Lord and Lady, by their names or what?" she whispered a slight quiver in her voice.

His dark amber eyes glittered with amusement. "Don't use Lord or Lady unless you want to set my Father off. Address them as Andre, Matiah, or Mother and Father. Whatever feels right, believe me you can do no wrong in their eyes, they are thrilled to meet you."

"What if they don't like me?" She gripped his large bronze hand in her two small creamy white ones while searching his eyes for reassurance.

He encircled his arms around her drawing her against his warm chest. "They already love you, because I do. You can't do anything to change that, so relax."

The color rose in her cheeks as surprise spread across her face, she quickly willed both away. This whole situation set butterflies loose in her stomach and her heart pounding. She drew in a deep breath, released it slowly caressing his cheek with her hand, then let her arm fall to her side.

"Ready?" He guided her hand around his waist as he rested his other hand at the small of her back eventually moving it to just above her hip. "Let's not keep them waiting any longer." Smiling he brushed his lips across her still blushing cheek.

Andre leaned toward his mate and whispered. "She's nervous, he's lovingly reassured her, who knew our arrogant son could display such tenderness?"

"I don't need a play by play, I can see with my own eyes," Matiah chided Andre. "He's always had that in him and just chooses to exhibit the arrogance he learned from you."

His father snorted then pretended to sneeze. *Like father, like son, huh?*

"Exactly." She tilted her smiling face up toward him.

Seizing the opportunity, he swept her off her feet with his arm curved around her waist, lifted her to him, then his lips were warm and sweet on hers. "That's not all I taught him," he murmured against her lips.

Loosening his hold, she slid down his taut body landing lightly on her feet. She turned only to be caught in her son's embrace. He whirled her around and kissed her cheeks setting her down; he patted her back whispering, "You didn't get them tucked in time." Then with a raised brow, he said, "Arrogant? Have you forgotten I have preternatural hearing and I suspect Angie does also."

She shrugged and kissed his cheek. "I don't try to hide anything, especially from family."

Bruce grinned and smothering a laugh said, "So we saw."

Angie stood beside Bruce extending a hand to Andre who took it pressing a kiss to her palm then turned it over and did the same to the back of her hand. "Welcome to the family," he said in a deep smooth voice not unlike his son's and tugged her into a strong embrace.

"Thank you," she said quietly as Andre released her.

"My daughter." Matiah said lovingly, stepping to Angie drawing her into a warm embrace. "I didn't think this day would ever come."

Andre reached for Matiah's hand gesturing toward the door. "Let's all go inside, get you two settled, and then enjoy a glass of wine out back on the veranda, where you can watch the falls." He winked at Angie, noticing her interest in the waterfalls.

"That would be wonderful," she said eagerly her hand held tightly in Bruce's.

Andre led them across the entryway tiled in white marble veined with turquoise to the rich wood floors of the living area. "We took the liberty of renovating your living space in the right wing of the house, once you told us the exciting news." Andre said over his shoulder to Bruce. "We didn't think she'd appreciate your bachelor pad paintings of naked women and various other items from your conquests."

Bruce grinned looking at his father. "I imagine you're right, she wouldn't appreciate it. We'll just go on up and get settled. Meet you on the veranda in about thirty minutes."

Andre raised a brow and looked from his son to Angie, nodding. "No hurry, take your time." The corners of his mouth turned up in a knowing smile.

Shoving an elbow in his side, Matiah gave him a mild rebuke. "Don't start." She smiled over at Angie. "Join us when you're ready." She took Andre's hand and led him through the room and out the double glass doors.

"Lead the way." Angie entwined her fingers with Bruce's as her eyes wandered over the walls where a variety of watercolor paintings hung. The furniture was European, the wood polished to a gleam. A fireplace took up one entire wall, Angie's violet eyes widened beneath raised brows. "A fire place in a tropical climate?"

Bruce shrugged. "My mother is a hopeless romantic. She'll turn the air conditioner up just so she can coax my father into building a fire and they can cuddle together in front of it." He touched the small of her back and guided her to the right. "This way."

Torch shaped wall sconces flickered as they walked down the hall. Bruce opened an ornately carved wooden double door. Angie stepped into a sitting room where Polynesian art hung tastefully on the walls. Two white leather chairs separated by a frosted glass table with scalloped edges faced a maroon fabric love seat settled against the wall. A large orchid plant with deep purple flowers sat in the center of the table. Angie ran her fingers lightly over the smooth scalloped edges of the table as she admired the orchid. It was one of her favorite flowers, though she'd never been able to grow them herself.

Bruce brushed past her through the arched doorway into the bedroom. She followed and found the room definitely masculine, a massive king size bed dominated the center of the room. Its four posters speared toward the mirrored ceiling.

A slow seductive smile curved his lips as his warm amber eyes glanced around the room. "Well at least they left the ceiling intact. It always was my favorite part of this room." Angie stirred his blood like no other as he imagined watching the mirrored images of their naked entwined bodies on the bed. His eyes burned with lust as they slid over her.

"Oh, no you don't. I want to freshen up and join your parents on the veranda. We can indulge our fantasies tonight," she purred glancing up at the ceiling, and then stepping to him, she brushed her hand inside his partially unbuttoned shirt.

He caught her wrist, pulling her to him curving his body against hers and laid his lips on hers warm and possessively. "Tease," he hissed then sighed motioning toward the other end of the room. "Follow that curved marble wall, it opens into the bathroom. I imagine my mother made sure everything you need is there."

He stepped out the glass doors onto the small balcony that faced the white sandy beach. Several ocean birds screeched then swooped above and dived into the frothy waves. The light wind tousled his shoulder length hair as the cool ocean breeze, heavy with brine, wafted into their suite. Hip propped against the railing, he turned to gaze at Angie.

She watched him a moment longer then followed the curved wall, letting her fingers glide along the smooth surface. It opened up to a large room with marble walls. Angie stood in awe as she spun around taking it all in. On one side of the room, several water nozzles, set at different heights, imbedded into the wall and the floor sloped to a small drain in the corner of floor.

On the other, double sinks set in a white marble counter top with veins of gold running through it, heated matching tile floor and a tub big enough for both of them. A crystal vase with fresh bird of paradise blooms sat between the sinks. The mirror above the vanity reflected the rows of crystal jars filled with creams and lotions along with bottles of shampoos, liquid and bar soaps.

Yes, his mother had thought of everything and I can't wait to try it all, she thought, picking up a lilac colored jar and sniffing. A pleasant floral fragrance wafted in the air before she replaced the lid. She splashed water on her face and washed her hands before dipping her fingers into another jar of cream that smelled of orange blossoms, smoothing it over her hands. She ran a brush though her hair and deemed herself presentable. The large diamond paned window above the tub looked out at the waterfalls. She stood mesmerized watching the water crashing to the rocks below. There were bright orange birds of paradise growing between the moss-covered rocks and lush green foliage surrounding the area. Tall trees grew beside the falls creating the effect of a mini rain forest.

"Beautiful, isn't it?" Bruce stood behind her, reaching out he ran his hands down her arms gently then turned her toward him. "Let's join them, before I do something neither of us will regret." He let his hand slide to her lower back and guided her out of the bathroom and toward the door.

"That was quick," his father said with a grin as they walked through the door and out onto the veranda.

"Andre, I'm warning you. Now quit with the innuendos, you're making Angie uncomfortable."

"What? I just meant."

"We know exactly what you meant. Now stop it."

"Angie didn't want to keep you waiting, so I'm forced to wait until later." Bruce chuckled and kissed her cheek.

Matiah blew out a breath and shrugged her shoulders. "These two have always been incorrigible. I guess we'll just have to live with it." She leaned back against the chair, her wings unfurled on either side of the chair, the feathers ruffled by the light breeze. "Have a seat." She gestured toward the double swing next to them as she handed Bruce and Angie a glass of wine.

"This is absolutely spectacular, it takes my breath away." Angie stood, her hands on the railing watching the falls for a moment then crossed the veranda and sat on the swing next to Bruce who put his arm around her shoulder. "Willow would love it."

"Your friend isn't joining us?" Andre frowned and glanced from Angie to Bruce.

"No, she decided to go to ground with her soon to

be mate. She's probably in Ireland by now, her family came from there generations ago, and she'll be safe inside the faerie mounds beneath the hills in Ireland. Caleb will be welcomed there as well, I hope." Angie chewed on her lip worrying about her friend.

"I see." Andre swirled his wine around in the glass, then took a sip.

Those two words seemed to convey an understanding beyond explanation, Angie thought, as she wished fervently her friend had accompanied her here.

Bruce gave her shoulder a reassuring squeeze. "She'll be fine. This whole business should only take a couple of weeks." He raised his glass toward his father and nodded. "With the information that you provided." Then he took a sip of the wine.

"If there is a problem, we'll intervene and make sure she is brought here safely with her mate, Andre said

"No, I won't have your life complicated any more than we have already. Mother blessed this place with angel magic when you retired to assure a safe haven for you both. I won't endanger that."

"Son, relax. The magic here is strong. And just so you know my magic had a hand in it too," Andre said dryly. "We can provide protection for your mate and if necessary her lifelong friend and her partner without endangering our existence." Andre leaned back against his chair and smiled at his mate. "It took centuries for Matiah's people to accept that she'd chosen to spend her life with a demon. They even went so far as to blacken her wings when she ignored their ultimatum and chose to stay with me. Your birth is what finally brought them around. Now all that is left of that terrible time in our lives is the dark fringe of feathers on her wings. Which I think is very becoming." He ran his hand lightly over the charcoal fringe and brushed his hand over Matiah's face lovingly.

"I am well aware of that but Willow won't come without Caleb, therein lays the problem."

"It won't be a problem, if an intervention becomes necessary. That will mean that things have gone terribly wrong and Caleb's joining her here will be the least of our problems."

"True."

"For tonight, let's put the reason that brought you here aside. Your mother and I want to get to know the wonderful woman who has brought out the best in you. The changes we see are monumental."

"Oh give it a rest. I wasn't that bad." Bruce rolled his eyes even as the blood rushed to his face.

"Need I remind you how things were left the last time you were here."

"No. You don't," he said fiercely. Then shifted his gaze to Angie's questioning one. "Last time I was here, I'd just won Territory Overlord at the cost of many good friends and allies lives. I spent over a year proving my right to rule and fighting many vicious and bloody battles. All he said was congratulations. It seemed cold and calculating at the time, I guess I was looking for comfort. I didn't find it here."

"How long ago was that?" Angie asked.

"Longer than it should have been."

"And now?" Andre inquired.

"Now I understand that there is a price for the freedom we enjoy. Not everyone will obey the rules we live by. There is always someone waiting to take advantage of a moment of weakness. They have to be dealt with swiftly and permanently."

"Or you have the situation we are currently dealing with." Andre added with a stern glance.

"Let's not go into that. If I'd had the opportunity to finish the job, I would have. Paul's poisoning and eventual death then Tristian's near death shook my focus. We had no reason to expect an ambush, though I know to expect the unexpected. I'm not perfect and won't be caught off guard again." He viciously slammed his wine glass on the table where it shattered. Bruce pushed up from the swing and strode off the veranda toward the falls.

"Still a sore point," Andre said calmly watching his son.

Angie got up slowly glancing at his parents, then toward the falls. She walked toward the steps and turned at Andre's voice.

"Let him go girl. He'll walk it off and be better for it." Andre commanded.

Matiah glanced at Angie and back to Andre with fire in her eyes. "Andre, stay out of it, you don't know your son as well as you think you do."

Angie stopped for a moment and looked over her shoulder at them then calmly said, "We'll be back later, don't wait up for us." She continued down the steps and then sprinted toward Bruce. He'd stopped in front of the falls, standing in the mist, fists clenched at his side.

Angie came up behind him and put her arms around his waist, laying her cheek on his back, listening to his heart thunder. She thought she felt him relax against her and then he jerked forward.

"He had no right to bring that up again." His hands fisted now on the rock he leaned against and turned his head toward her, his eyes whirling orange.

"No, he didn't but don't you think Rezar will do worse, if its psychological games he intends to play? You said a clear head and calm demeanor would finish this." Looking up at him with an arched brow, she said softly. "I think your Father was testing you, not taunting you." She moved her hands up his sides and around his shoulders, standing on tiptoes she pulled herself up to his neck to nuzzle and breath a warm affectionate kiss there. She felt his shoulders shudder then relax as he leaned his head against hers.

Bruce turned in her arms and wrapped his around her. They stood there silently for quite a while listening to their synchronized heart beats against the roar of the waterfall.

We are truly one, she thought, in more ways than she could have imagined when she agreed to be his mate. She considered her brother's troubling words regarding their parent's disappointment with him in allowing her to become involved with a demon. Tristian was wrong. She was sure of it and had only to look at Bruce's mother, an angel to confirm her feelings. That explained a lot about the man she'd come to know. Bruce's touch as he lightly brushed the damp hair from her eyes brought her back to the present.

"You ok?" His eyes clouded with concern as he leaned down eye level with her. "Seemed to be lost in your thoughts."

"I'm fine, just thinking about my brother's reaction if he knew your mother was an angel." She patted his check and smiled mischievously. "You know that explains a lot of what puzzled me about you."

"Really? But that's something he'll never know. I keep my family information heavily guarded." He ran his fingers through his damp hair and rubbed the back of his neck wondering if she truly understood the price she could pay for being his mate.

"I understand, but it's fun to imagine the look on his face after all the things that he said to you, to us." She nodded toward the house. "Your parents are still on the veranda, want to return or walk down to the beach?" Angie murmured against his neck.

He glanced up at the house and decided to return. "Let's see if we can salvage this evening. We'll take a walk later."

"Sounds like a plan." She kissed the tip of his nose and followed him up the path.

Away from the roar of the waterfalls, Bruce heard the murmurer of his parent's voices.

****

"Shit Matiah, did you see that. She walked right up and put her arms around him. He didn't flinch or push her away. His temper under control already."

"You don't know him anymore. He's finally found his mate and they love each other. She brings out the best in him, he's learned to appreciate and enjoy that. Sort of like someone else I know." Matiah turned her eyes lovingly toward her husband and sighed. "Remember."

"I do. It seems to me it was years before we settled into our relationship as they have in a few months."

"He's as much like me as he is like you allowing him to compromise and show his true feelings, to her anyway. It also appears she's a fiery sort and won't back down from him."

"You didn't back down from me on very many occasions," he said with a smile as he put his hand over hers entwining their fingers.

She looked down at their hands and out to the falls where Angie and Bruce were walking toward them. "Looks like you haven't ruined the evening after all."

"Me, I was just trying to…"

"I know." She patted his hand with her other one. "Just try being supportive, that's what he needs right now. Not the hell on wheels demon, making him tough enough to survive. He's got that part."

Sauntering up the steps like nothing happened, Bruce waited for Angie to sit on the swing and slid in beside her as he cocked a brow and looked over at his parents. "Now tell me, how have you and mother been spending your time?"

Andre and Matiah looked at each other and smiled then Andre winked at her. "Enjoying each other in every way possible."

"Should have known better than to ask." Bruce shook his head and reached for the bottle of wine refilling his replacement glass and Angie's.

Andre picked up his own wine and took a drink. "Seriously, we also enjoy the company of old and trusted friends that visit on occasion. That's how I came upon the information I called you about."

"So you aren't completely retired." Bruce swirled the amber liquid, watched the sun's rays sparkle through the crystal and across the surface of the wine before he took a sip then set the glass on the table. Angie pulled her legs up under her and cuddled into his side as he leaned back against the swing putting it in motion.

"Yes and no. We can't sit idly by when that kind of information comes our way."

"I understand."

"How about Tristian? Still mortal enemies?" Andre asked as a chuckle rose in his throat and he shook his head. "Only you would find yourself in such a situation over a female."

"Not just any female, my one and only forever." He smiled at Angie, putting his arm around her pulling her tighter against him. "As far as Tristian is concerned, we'll be ok. The dynamics have changed substantially, we are family now, and he's got to come to terms with it. As far as work, I'd still trust him with my life."

"Glad to hear it. That was a tough situation, no matter whose prospective you were looking from." He crossed his foot over his other knee and relaxed against the chair, still holding Matiah's hand.

"Angie, I want to hear what attracted you to him." Matiah asked. "Since we missed the courtship, will you tell us all about it?"

"Sure. He tried to ignore me, but I won." She laughed and poked Bruce in the ribs. "People told me he was evil and not to mess with him, but I saw through that façade and decided he was worth the effort. Something about him just kept drawing me in. Then he tried to scare me off, with his big bad demonic routine. That didn't work either. I just felt, as he later admitted he did, we belonged together. I don't mind telling you the sensation that runs between us is the strangest thing I've ever felt."

Matiah smiled. "I know exactly what you mean."

"So you've seen him change, physically?" Andre

asked refilling his wine glass.

"What. Change how?" Angie's brows flew up and her eyes widened as she turned to look at Bruce.

"Just can't keep your nose out of my business, can you?" Bruce heaved a heavy sigh. "No she hasn't seen me change, but she will before I leave here. Unlike you, I rarely take on physical demon characteristics of dark red skin and black symbols etched across my body. My cover has always required human form, so it's more natural to me. Even if I lose control of my emotions, I'm still able to stay in human form. Which is more than I can say for you."

"In your father's defense, he's pure demon, born to a mated pair of demons. You on the other hand have a balancing set of DNA. So as to speak." Her lips curved slowly in an affectionate smile and she patted Andre's fisted hand "I don't know if you would be able to change completely, due to my angel blood."

"Oh, so when you get angry, the whirling orange eyes are part of a shifting from human to demon?" Angie hadn't thought about the possibility of him changing, physically. Now she wondered exactly what that entailed and if he made the change completely from human to demon would it bother her. She decided that discussion could wait until later. Nothing he could do would change how she felt about him. Besides, she always had a weakness for the bad boys.

"You've brought up a good point, mother, I don't look like him even when I loose complete control. My transformation resembles a bad sunburn with much lighter etched symbols and only on my upper arms, shoulders and a few scattered across my chest. There isn't much of a scaly texture to my skin either, like I remember on him."

"You two do realize I'm sitting right here," Andre grumbled.

"Of course, dear, how could we ever forget?" Matiah smiled, poking her husband in the ribs.

The glass doors to the veranda opened quietly and a petite Tahitian woman with waist length black hair, dressed in a white starched apron over a red flowered dress stood silently. Andre acknowledged her with a nod.

"My lord, dinner is prepared and set out in the formal dining room, unless you would rather eat out here?"

Andre paused for a moment and glanced toward Matiah. "The dining room will be fine. We will be in shortly. Thank you Maeva."

"As you wish," Maeva said and backed through the glass doors, which closed silently behind her. Once inside the house, she turned and disappeared down the hallway.

Andre rose from his seat and stepped toward the doors. "Shall we?" He held a door open as Matiah brushed past him, caressing the small of his back gently with her hand, a twinkle in her eye. Bruce and Angie followed his mother through the door and down the long hallway.

Bruce smiled when Angie gasped as he entered the large dining room at her side. An oval glass table with beveled scalloped edges engraved with small flowers and oak accents occupied the middle of the room. A huge oak cabinet stood against the wall closest to the table filled with several styles of fine china place settings and exquisite crystal stemware. White china plates with a tiny rose bud pattern sat on multi-colored crocheted placemats next to matching napkins. Crystal water and wine glasses sparkled in the candle light next to the place settings. Heated dishes of lobster and tuna sat in the middle of the table beside a bowl of yams, a platter of sliced fresh pineapple, and a basket of freshly baked bread. Small crystal bowls of melted butter and silverware also sat next to each plate.

Bruce pulled out a chair for Angie as his father did the same for Matiah. When they were all seated, Andre pointed to the carafes of wine at each end of the table. "I didn't know if you would prefer a rich white wine or a fruity red since both can be delicious with tuna and my lovely angel prefers a white with her lobster." Andre winked at Matiah. "So I selected one of each for your pleasure." He motioned Maeva over to the table. "Just let her know your preferences and she will serve you."

Angie sat with her hands in her lap and watched as Maeva, knowing Matiah's preferences, took her plate, placed a succulent lobster tail, one small yam, a slice of pineapple along with a piece of bread on it and returned the plate to its original position.

Maeva turned to Angie reaching for her plate. "My lady, what may I get for you?"

Angie smiled up at the woman. "First of all it's just Angie, and I would love a piece of tuna, a couple of slices of pineapple, and a piece of bread. Is that tuna prepared with ginger?" Angie breathed in the savory aroma.

"Yes." Maeva smiled. "It's the best way. The pineapple is from the valleys of Moorea, they are small but very sweet."

"You'll really miss their fresh picked flavor when you return home," Matiah said as she licked her lips. "Nothing quite like it."

Maeva filled Andre and Bruce's plates as instructed and quiet descended on the room as the couples consumed the deliciously prepared food. Angie reached over once and forked a piece of the lobster from Bruce's plate, dipped it in her melted butter and popped it in her mouth.

She closed her eyes. "Mmmm this is good."

Angie opened her eyes and looked at Bruce from under her long lashes. "Sorry, I just wanted a taste," she whispered and smiled over at his parents, who were grinning at them.

Tane, Maeva's golden haired husband with just a bit of gray at the temples cleared the table. Maeva brought out a tray with colorful fruit tarts on it. She placed a tart and clean spoon at each place and stepped back.

Matiah picked up her spoon and pointed at the dessert. "This is Maeva's famous Vanilla Tart with fruit and sweet wine glaze. It is fantastic." Matiah scooped up a spoonful of tart slid the spoon in her mouth and closed her eyes, slowly pulling the spoon from her lips. "Nothing like it," She whispered chewing slowly.

Angie scooped up a spoonful and tasted the sweet concoction. "Mmm, this is wonderful."

"Eighty percent of Tahitian vanilla is grown on Taha'a, an island not far from here," Andre said proudly.

"You have really embraced the Tahitian way of life," Bruce teased.

"We enjoy the islands." Andre grinned. "Shall we

return to the veranda and enjoy a relaxing glass of wine?"

Bruce refilled the wine glasses and they all strolled out to the veranda. Bruce and Angie stood at the railing sipping their wine and once again taking in the breathtaking view. Andre and Matiah settled into the wicker loveseat facing the waterfalls.

Angie finished her wine and padded over to swing to sit down followed by Bruce. It was a companionable silence as they watched the shadows grow longer and the sun disappear behind the trees.

"I think we'll call it a night, I promised to take Angie down the torch lit path for a walk on the beach."

"Thank you so much for dinner," Angie said. "Everything tasted wonderful."

"Yes. Enjoy yourselves. We'll see you in the morning." They rose and started into the house, Andre's arm around Matiah's waist sliding slowly to the curve of her ass.

Angie quietly giggled watching them. "Now I see where you get it."

"I told you demons have a carnal nature and it doesn't diminish with age." He stood and brushed the wrinkles out of his pants, then offered his hand to help her out of the swing still in motion. "You ready for a walk on the beach or do you want to change your shoes?"

"No, I'm ready." She kicked her shoes off before taking his hand. "I want to walk barefoot on the beach." Wriggling her toes, she reached for his hand and leaned out of the swing, bumping lightly against his chest as she stood regaining her balance. "Oops, a little off balance." She took a step back, surveying the light blue linen shirt that he wore open to mid-chest level, decided that wouldn't do and began unbuttoning the remaining ones.

He watched her amusement lighting her violet eyes. "Right here?"

She looked up at him bewildered at first, then tossed her head, her long golden hair fanning out around her shoulders and down her back. "No, I just want to enjoy that muscular bronze chest while we walk."

"Ok," he said slowly, raising a brow and a mischievous smile curving his lips. "There's much more to see, if you like."

"Oh, is there?" Smiling seductively, her eyes wandered over his entire body lingering longer in one area than in others. "I think we'll save that for later." She turned heading toward the beach, then stopped staring out at the water. "Is that a yacht floating out there?"

"Yes. It belongs to my parents." His hand slid around her waist settling at the small of her back as he guided her toward the path. The torches flamed high radiating heat in a wide swath as the couple passed by, the shadows danced over their faces and across the windswept sand. Bruce's shirt bellowed out behind him as they walked along the path. He stopped to roll his pant legs above the knee before following her into the surf. But he wasn't opposed to skinny-dipping in the warm waters of the cove. In fact, he intended to encourage it, to see and feel her warm fragrant flesh beneath his hands. He went hard at the thought.

The warm sand under her feet and squished between her toes made Angie smile. It had been too long since she'd enjoyed such simple pleasures. For the next few days, she would indulge herself in many more fun activities with Bruce by her side and commit them to memory for darker days she feared loomed ahead. *Enough with the depressing thoughts*, she told herself and ran into the warm surf, glad she'd changed her slacks for shorts when she'd freshened up.

Bruce took off his shirt and pants and left them folded on the sand to join her in the surf. Catching her by the waist, he whirled her around just above the water. "How about a midnight swim?" he murmured suggestively against her ear, floating backward into deeper water he drew her body over his, nuzzling her neck, he bit lightly and soothed with the flick of his tongue.

"But your parents." Angie twisted trying to look back toward the house but had to wrap her legs around him for balance, feeling his erection, a hungry desire spiraled though her.

"They are otherwise occupied by now," he whispered as he peeled the wet blouse off her shoulders and took her taut nipples into the warmth of his mouth. She arched against him tightening her legs bringing him where she wanted him most.

"Li'l witch, let's take off those shorts so we can both enjoy where this is leading."

She loosened her legs, gripping his shoulders; she floated over him while he removed the offending clothing.

He tossed her wet clothes to the shore and floated her out to deeper water. In the warmth of the tropical water, she wrapped her legs around his hips again and welcomed him, one thrust and pleasure radiated through her as she felt him pulsate inside her.

****

Sated and sleepy they wound their way up the moon lit path to the little veranda just outside their room. He opened the sliding glass door and scooped her into his arms. She encircled her arms around his neck and rested her head on his shoulder breathing in his musky scent as he carried her into the shower. With gentle caressing hands, they rinsed the sand and salt water from each other's bodies then stumbled into bed.

****

A terrifying scream roused Bruce out of a sound sleep, to find Angie writhing, damp with sweat next to him. Sitting up he curled her onto his lap and held her tight against his chest, cheek resting against her hair. Still the screams escalated. He rocked back and forth crooning, "Angie, it's all right, you're safe, it's just a nightmare. Bruce shook her lightly and murmured, "Wake up sweetheart."

Matiah and Andre burst through the door. "What's wrong?" Andre asked urgently.

"It's just a nightmare, she has always had them, but this is the first time in a long while and I can't seem to awaken her." He drew back from her and shook her again by the shoulders, his voice louder. "Angie, wake up, it's ok. Only a nightmare."

The screams finally became whimpers and her eyes opened slowly. She grabbed hold of Bruce, her nails digging in and holding tight, sobbing.

Matiah laid a hand on Bruce's shoulder, reaching behind him to draw up the blanket around their naked bodies. "She'll be more comfortable this way." Taking a corner of the sheet, she knelt down and wiped tears from Angie's face, then looked up at Bruce. "Have you considered she may be a precog?"

"Yes, we've discussed that. She doesn't think she has the sight, though her mother did."

Breath ragged, Angie buried her face in Bruce's warm chest. "It was terrible. His body was twisted and thin. His face, it was horribly scarred. He yanked at a shiny metallic collar locked on his neck. I could see his decaying teeth as he screamed revenge would be his against you and Tristian. The whole time he laughed manically. His eyes were crazy wild." A shiver of fear shot up her spine as she turned her face to Bruce and fought for composure.

She drew in a long breath and let it out slowly as their eyes met. "The man was covered in sweat and violent tremors racked his entire body. When the tremors slowed, I think he held up something. It looked like airline tickets, but it was hard to tell. I've never had such a vivid nightmare."

Bruce brushed the damp strands of hair from her eyes and cradled her close against his chest, turning his eyes clouded with worry, toward his parents.

Matiah nodded confirming his fear as she sat on the side of the bed.

Chapter Sixteen

Bruce sat on the couch in the room just off the bedroom, his arms around Angie as she snuggled into him, both wrapped in robes. Matiah knocked lightly on the door then pushed it open a crack. "Thought you might need something in your bellies."

"Come in," Bruce said

She pushed the door open wider, the breeze from an overhead fan ruffling her wing feathers lightly and motioned her husband inside the room.

Andre brought in a tray of iced tea, chilled water, juices, and a pitcher of iced-cold milk to go with the plate of double chocolate fudge cookies, one of Bruce's favorites. He put the tray down on the glass table between them. "We'll see you in the morning."

"Thanks. Good night," Bruce said.

After the door closed, Angie shivered, blinking her eyes slowly, then straightened against Bruce. The signs were all there, she had inherited her mother's gift. The vivid scene that played out in her dream left her shaken, but the realization of her talent was a kind of relief. After all she'd come from a long line of witches with the ability, but it manifested itself differently in each person.

She'd long ago decided the talent had skipped a generation, and was ok with that, never considering the role her nightmares must have played in her ability. *Did*

Tristian know? She shook her head as if to shove the remaining questions to the back of her mind, so she could deal with the situation at hand.

"If that was the future I saw, you can't leave me behind. You have a much better chance of taking Rezar out with my help."

"Absolutely not," he said in a flat tone that left room for no argument.

Ignoring his gruff response, Angie continued. "Is there any way we can confirm his movement, or location?"

"Possibly, but I'll not put you in danger. If you are a precog or seer of some type, your abilities are too new to control. Depending on them would be foolish."

"Not if you are willing to help me get a handle on them." She stifled a yawn. Despite the terrifying nightmare that spiked her adrenalin, now her body was exhausted. Perhaps she should try to go back to sleep and maybe learn more about where Rezar was located or where he was headed. Could she control her ability? If not, convincing Bruce to let her help would take all the energy she could muster, so it would be to her benefit to get some rest.

"There's a couple more hours before dawn, do you want to go back to bed and try to get some more sleep? You're worn out." He looked closely at her still ashen face, as her eyes blinked slowly.

She nodded and curled warmly against him drifting off to sleep. Bruce lay awake strategizing and deciding how to confirm Rezar's whereabouts and possible relocation. By Angie's description he still wasn't anywhere near a hundred percent, giving the advantage, if there was one in this situation to Bruce and his teams, if they moved quickly enough.

****

Slivers of rich golden sunlight spread over the bright red and black patterned comforter. Bruce opened his eyes and sighed watching his li'l witch still sleeping peacefully, her head on his shoulder, his arm wrapped possessively around her.

He shifted slightly to lay the other arm over her. She opened her eyes and blinked sleepily. Nuzzling against him, she placed her warm moist lips to his neck kissing him lovingly. "Good morning," she murmured against his neck.

"And good morning or more appropriately afternoon to you." He rolled her against him and brushed a gentle kiss across her forehead, trailing his lips across her cheek he took her mouth with his. She deepened the kiss lingering and savoring every moment.

He drew back searching her face. "No more nightmares?"

"No. I'm sorry I upset everyone last night with another nightmare."

"I think we both know last night's dream was more than just one of your nightmares. You've inherited your mother's abilities, whether you want to admit it or not. I think you've always had those abilities. I also believe Tristian downplayed them and made you believe they were just regular nightmares caused by your parent's deaths."

"Probably." Sitting up she swung her legs over the side of the bed reaching for her robe folded neatly on the nightstand. "I don't mind having the abilities so much, if they will help keep you safe," she said over her shoulder as she padded to toward the bathroom.

"The only safe you'll be involved in is your own and right here," Bruce said dismissively yawning widely and stretching his arms over his head. He rolled to his side and slid out of bed.

She stopped and turned to look at him, her violet eyes glittering with determination. "You are not leaving me behind to wait, wonder, and worry, when I can help."

"Again, I repeat, absolutely not," he roared, temper flaring. "I can't do my job and worry about you too. You'll stay here where I know you're safe."

"I can take care of myself."

Bruce snorted. "You've been protected all your life from this world. Sure, in your world, you're a powerful witch, but in mine, you're completely unarmed. Never had to be vicious, never faced a kill or be killed situation. Never saw your best friends and allies die protecting you and what you stood for. No. You're not going. End of discussion." His words were clipped, and nostrils flared as he shook his head angrily. Orange whirled in his dark amber eyes and under his skin, dark runes appeared as barely visible scales formed across his upper body.

Prepared to stand her ground, she fisted her hands on hips, feet planted firmly and shoulders flung back. "You can't tell me what to do."

"I can and I will." He took a deep breath, blew it out slowly, and attempted to rein in his temper as it vibrated through him. "But first I'll ask you to respect my decisions since I've just a bit more experience in these matters than you."

Wanting to slam his fist into something, anything,

he yanked on his jeans instead and strode out the sliding glass door, it shattered as he slammed it shut. "Shit." Glaring angrily he watched the shards of glass skitter across the floor. He raised his hands up palms out; a blue mist engulfed the fragments transforming them into a sheet of glass and back into the door. One hand on the veranda railing, he vaulted over landing on the lush grass below and sprinted toward the path leading to the beach. He needed to find some objectivity where Angie was concerned.

****

She watched him disappear down the path then flopped in a chair, propped her bare feet on the edge of the glass table and laid her head against the back of the chair. Pressing her fingers against her eyelids, she felt the anger ebb away. *Why can't I see at will what is going to happen, like my mother could? Random nightmares that's all I have and not even concurrent ones.* She pounded her fist into the pillow beside her. *Was he right? Would I be a liability rather than an asset? No, I can't believe that. I'll find a way to help keep him safe. I can't lose him now.*

A soft knock sounded at the door. "Angie may I come in?" Matiah's comforting voice inquired from the other side of the door.

"Of course."

Matiah pushed the door opened and rolled a stainless steel cart with white enameled side panels and hand painted flowers into the room. The top of the cart contained a basket of sweet coconut bread, an iced bowl of fresh fruit, and couple bowls of dry cereal. An iced bucket contained a carafe of fresh squeezed orange juice and one with ice-cold milk. The warmer below the first shelf contained sweet rolls and a small plate of scrambled eggs.

"Thought you might be hungry after the night you had." Matiah reached down to the third shelf in the cart and brought out two glasses and filled them with orange juice, handing one to Angie.

"You would be right, I'm starved. That's quite the set up," Angie said nodding to the cart. She took the plate of eggs and added a piece of the coconut bread. Taking a bite of the bread, she moaned. "Mmm this is fantastic. Did Maeva make this?"

"Yes, we are quite lucky to have Maeva. She is a very talented chef." Matiah said smiling.

"And Maeva is married to Tane?"

"She is. Tane is the younger brother of Bruce's housekeeper, Megan. I assume you've met Megan."

"Oh, yes many times, she is wonderful. It amazes me how with just a few words she can tame Bruce." Angie grimaced, hoping she hadn't been out of line with that last statement.

Matiah threw her head back and roared with laughter until tears streaked down her face. "That's one of the reasons we allowed Megan to remain with the estate when we retired. Though she was like family to us, we all agreed she would be best suited to stay with Bruce and run his household. He can be a bit difficult from time to time." She rolled her eyes and wiped the tears away with the back of her hand taking in a deep breath. "Tane was married and living in Tahiti at the time we retired and were a wonderful fit for us. They take care of everything."

"So is Maeva a magical…?" Angie began.

"Oh, no. She is just a very intuitive mortal. The

Tahitians seem to be born with the gift, not to mention she is extremely talented in the kitchen. Tane enjoys getting his hands dirty and really has a way with plants and flowers. The landscaping has never looked better. He helps Maeva with the household chores too, so it's like family around here and that's the way Andre likes it. He's not a very trusting soul," Matiah said.

****

White capped waves crashed on the shore as Bruce waded out into the surf. Dark clouds gathered just beyond the protected cove. Bright white lightning slashed through the air electrifying it. The hair on the back of Bruce's neck stood up and a shiver ran down his spine.

The gleaming blue and silver yacht that stretched over seventy feet was moored in the middle of the cove last night was gone. *Father must have moved it in advance of the storm.* Buried deep in his thoughts, Bruce jerked involuntarily as a hand gripped his shoulder. He'd felt his father's presence earlier but ignored it preoccupied with his own problems.

"We moved the Seraphim to safer waters. Hell of a gale moving in, the sky will soon be black as your mood." Andre chuckled. "Woman troubles?"

"You could say that." Bruce picked up a rock and flung it violently into the churning ocean.

"It appears you've found a fiery, opinionated, and stubborn woman, who's fiercely protective and loyal to a fault." Andre paused nodding. "I like your choice, son. Shares the traits of another woman I've known for centuries." A laugh rumbled deep in his chest. "But your li'l witch can also be of great assistance to you, if you let her.

"Not you too!" Fury sparked in Bruce's eyes as he whirled around to face his father.

"Oh give it a rest and follow me. Show you what I mean. By the way, her intelligence and passion will keep life interesting for centuries. I know whereof I speak." Andre winked and slapped his son on the back as he turned and headed toward the falls.

"Good to know." Scowling, Bruce shoved his hands in the pockets of his soaked jeans and walked alongside his father.

Andre sidled between the falls and rock wall, a portion of which disappeared at their arrival, giving way to a narrow tunnel lit with flaming torches set in polished brass hangers. They entered the damp corridor. Several yards inside, Andre ran his hand along a solid rock ledge. It fell away to reveal a room banked by state of the art computers and monitors, in the center of the room stood a six-foot wide flat screen monitor.

"Good morning, Alish," Andre said as a pair of large luminous sapphire eyes blinked at them from the screen.

"Good morning, Andre. Who's the handsome young man you've brought with you?"

"My son." He smiled broadly turning to whisper to Bruce. "A woman who knows her place even if she's Artificial Intelligence."

Bruce watched the screen blinking in disbelief. "So this is how you spend your retirement?"

"Yes. Wanted to keep a finger on the pulse of our world. At first, I thought you might need my help, but it soon became apparent you were capable of handling things on your own. So your mother and I just watched with pride as you grew into a respected and powerful leader."

"So what does it show you?" Bruce wondered aloud, his eyes bright with interest as they darted from screen to screen and finally back to the center screen.

"She will show us any place you've been. Track down any place or person I want to keep tabs on. Alish, show us The Wycked Hair."

The luminous almond eyes faded in a swirl of sapphire as the main floor of the salon swam into view. Tobi appeared on screen, bright pink streaks in her auburn hair that matched her smock. She was putting a client under the dryer with foil folded over sections of hair. Owen smiled as he talked on the phone scheduling another customer into the computer. The view panned to the construction area, the plastic sheets replaced by a gold cord strung between silver toned poles. A sign delicately painted in warm rich hues stood in front of the rope announcing the opening of the newly expanded area and addition of The Krystal Unicorn next Saturday.

Irritated that his father had been spying on him for possibly years, he shoved that thought away for now, intrigued by the whole system and its usefulness in the current situation. "Find Angie," Bruce commanded experimentally. The salon slowly faded from view as Angie appeared sitting with her feet still resting on the table chatting and giggling with his mother. Amazed he turned to Andre. "How is this possible?"

"That's a bit of magic." Andre jerked his chin toward the screen. "The rest is lot of computer savvy and connection to world wide security cameras."

"You have security cameras in our bedroom?" Bruce roared.

"Definitely, not. Only the sitting room, wanted to keep an eye on the workers while they remodeled your living area. We deactivated the camera before your arrival, but I guess Tane didn't have a chance to remove it. The device apparently reactivated at your request to locate Angie. I'll have Tane remove it immediately." Andre narrowed his eyes examining Bruce's tanned upper body. "Have you blood bonded with her?"

"W—what… No. That's a barbaric practice and I have no intention of subjecting Angie to that." But hadn't he fought against doing just that as he took her to his bed that first night, desire so strong, so primal that his demon nearly broke free. At the last minute, he gained some semblance of control and reined it in concentrating on her pleasure as well as his own.

His father arched a brow and the corners of his lips turned up slowly. "Don't you? Not even in the throes of taking her as your mate? What about her?"

"What do you mean what about her? Don't be so cryptic, just spit it out." Disgusted, he shook his head. "Never mind, it's none of your business anyway." He flexed his hands and rolled his massive shoulders deflecting the tension that was threatening to overpower his good judgment, again.

"She can remain here and track your progress with Alish. Personal communications over long distances will be an issue without a blood bond," Andre said matter-of-factly and began walking toward the door.

"Since I took Angie as my mate, we are in each other's minds. Are you telling me there is a limit to that ability?"

"Yes, over short distances it's great, but over longer distances it's unreliable without a blood bond."

Bruce raised his scarred hand rubbing his jaw with the roughened pads of his thumb and forefinger. "Ah, so there's more to the blood bond than barbaric ritual."

"Yes." One corner of Andre's mouth curled up in a slight grin.

"You and Mother?"

Andre's eyes sparkled at the chance to make Bruce uncomfortable. "Of course. At our first…"

"That's enough. Don't need the details." Bruce winced slowly shaking his head.

Trepidation showed over Bruce's face, Andre steered the discussion another way. He shrugged. "Maybe you're right. Let's join the women and discuss keeping Angie safe while she assists you in neutralizing Rezar forever."

"She can't be involved."

"So you've said. I'm not sure she agrees with you."

"Shit," Bruce muttered under his breath, *this doesn't bode well at all.* He scanned the room and jerked his chin up. "Secure?"

"None better."

Bruce slid the lock across his cell phone screen and touched #1—auto-dialing Owen.

"Bout time you checked in."

"Yeah—well, I've been busy. Mobilize the teams and have them stand by. We're going after the bastard within seventy-two hours. He'll probably be on U.S. soil by then."

"You got it. Assembly point?"

"Not sure yet, I'll call you back in a couple of hours."

"Wait Bruce, we talking about Rezar? So you know his location? His condition? How many are we looking at?"

"Don't have all the answers yet, but Angie may."

"Great. What? How? Angie? Are you both coming back?"

"No. Anything I should know?" Bruce asked.

"Nope, everything here is running smooth and on schedule. We're really busy." Owen paused a moment. "Only…"

"What?"

"A couple of new customers. Came in a few hours apart. I got a weird feeling about them. Nothing I can put a finger on."

"Tobi, she feel the same?"

"Yeah. Both asked for you specifically, as if you were in the habit of working the floor on a daily basis."

"And."

"Said you weren't taking appointments this week, you were meeting with suppliers. They acted almost irritated then did an about face and booked with Tobi, but neither showed."

"Human or other?"

"Not sure, but probably other category. Definitely female, but masked their signatures. Since so many do the first time they come in here, I didn't think much about it until they didn't show a couple of hours ago. I was just getting ready to call you."

"Don't like the sound of that. Did the surveillance camera catch them?"

"Maybe. I was about to check the feed on the computer when you called. Let me finish and get right back to you?"

"Do that." Bruce touched the screen of his phone and ended the call. "I need to wait here for a bit, if you don't mind."

"Alish, should be able to access the video right now. She could directly pull it off the hard drive." Andre nodded toward the video swirling into view.

Bruce could see the individuals standing on the counter as he waited for Owen to return to the phone.

"Yep, got em on video," Owen confirmed smugly.

"I can see them and I don't recognize either one," Bruce said slowly.

"But...how did you? That was fast." Owen finally said.

"Father has very sophisticated computer equipment. We'll update ours when I get back," Bruce said matter-of-factly and rubbed his chin considering the situation. "I don't like it. Station security indiscreetly at the entrances and exits of the salon. Have security teams patrol the perimeter. The teams are to report anything unusual to you immediately. Keep me in the loop."

"Of course." Owen frowned and looked at his watch. "I'll have security in place within thirty minutes."

Chapter Seventeen

The morning hadn't gone as she wanted. However, with him it rarely did. Their fiery tempers, strong will, and passionate desires created chaos as often as not. A wry grin spread across her face as she considered, *I wouldn't have it any other way.* Matiah's soft chuckle brought Angie's thoughts back to the present.

"His father was the same, stubborn, proud, and determined. Not to mention much more controlling than…" She broke off mid-sentence.

Bruce pushed open the door to their rooms and leaned his wide shoulder and tall tanned body against the door jam. "We aren't breaking up this little female meeting of the minds, are we?" The corner of his mouth kicked up in a devilish grin that was sexy as hell.

Excitement rippled through Angie reminding her exactly what she was dealing with. Angel, demon, lover, mate, he was the best she'd ever had and didn't intend to give him up. Ever. "Not at all. We were just discussing a few ways to correct the many irritating faults in the male species," Angie said, voice sweet as sugar. She dropped her feet from the table to the floor, angled her face toward him, and batted her long eyelashes.

He glared at her for a moment, then looked around the room and his gaze locked on the cart his mother brought in earlier for Angie. Coconut bread in a woven basket and fresh fruit in an iced bowl remained on the top of the cart, fragrant sweet rolls in the warmer below the top shelf. "Well I see you didn't invite us for breakfast."

"You were more than welcome but your timing wasn't good," Angie said a wicked grin spreading across her face.

Andre shoved Bruce aside and strode into the room. "Ladies, sorry to interrupt but we'd like to show you something." Before he motioned them out the door, he reached for a slice of coconut bread and poured himself a glass of orange juice, just as Bruce grabbed a sweet roll and took the glass of orange juice offered by Angie. Matiah, Angie, and Bruce trooped out the door. Andre stepped up behind Bruce and whispered, "Pick your battles son. This is one you won't win." He nodded toward Angie. "She's strong willed and as protective of you as you are of her. There's middle ground here, find it."

Jaw clinched and hands fisted in his pockets, Bruce opened his mouth prepared with a sharp retort, but thought better of it and followed the others back to the room behind the falls. He thought about his father's words. He disliked being told what to do but damn he hated it when his father was right. Andre's smooth baritone voice reiterated the same information to the women that he'd given Bruce in private a short while ago. Bruce relaxed and began to consider the alternatives available to him that would still keep Angie safe, but involved.

His phone buzzed in his pocket, he checked the screen before putting the phone to his ear. "Owen, what you got?"

"We showed the video to the staff and Riki thought she'd seen each one on separate occasions walking in front of the salon, didn't think much of it at the time. But now…"

"Upload the video to my phone. I'll take a closer look."

****

Catching Angie's hand, Bruce closed the door to their rooms with his foot and murmured, "Can we reach a compromise, considering what you've just seen?" Brushing her hair aside, His thumbs massaged in tiny circles at the base of her neck easing the knots there then moving over her soft shoulders using his entire hand to sooth away the tightness he felt there. After a few moments, he moved his hands slowly down her arms to encircle her small waist and bent to nuzzle her neck flicking his tongue at the delicately pulsing vein. *The desire is definitely there, but am I ready to go through with it?*

"Maybe." She tilted her head hesitantly and lowered her shoulder to allow him access.

"What are you doing?" He grasped her shoulders and pushed her away just enough to look at her face.

Staring into his eyes, she raised her hand to his cheek caressing it. "Making it easier to do what you need to do. I'm not going to let you track down Rezar without giving you every weapon available to win."

"How? How did you know?" Releasing her, he turned and paced to the sliding glass doors, putting his hands on the metal frame he leaned against it watching the sea birds swoop and dive into the ocean for their dinner.

"I don't see the big deal. "She shrugged and

stepped toward him. "Your mother explained the bite merely creates a blood bond between us so we can communicate telepathically over great distances."

"And can act as a locater beacon both ways. So you're willing?" Amazed he twisted to look at her over his shoulder.

"Of course. I could see the desire in your eyes when you almost marked me at the estate, that first time. It scared me then, but now, I've learned what it means to be the mate of an Overlord." Pausing she said softly, "You didn't tell me that a demon taking a witch as a mate was forbidden."

"What does it matter? Anyway, that was long ago. Things have changed."

"Not so much, according to your mother." Angie pressed.

"And she would know, since a demon taking an angel for a mate was so accepted." He snorted, staring at the wall as if he could find his mother and pin her with his stare. "She should stay out of my affairs."

Ignoring his last statement, Angie continued calmly. "No, she said the situation made it much harder for your father, but like you he was stubborn and did as he saw fit."

"Some things are worth the trouble. You and I were meant to be together, we feel the connection, the fact that you're a witch just makes it that much more interesting." Determination glittered in his eyes as he turned to embrace her. "There's been enough talk." With that, he took her mouth with his and lifted her easily into his arms carrying her to their bed.

A muffled scream woke Bruce out of a sound sleep, he watched Angie struggle for a moment then still, she moaned softly, then silence. He tried to awaken her without success, she went limp, the edges of her body blurred and she didn't respond to his efforts.

Chapter Eighteen

Angie awoke to a feeling of nothingness. Muted sounds penetrated her mind. She sensed there were others in close proximity. Movement from the adjoining room vibrated through the walls and floor. Something was very wrong. Opening her eyes warily she took in her surroundings, she wasn't in Tahiti and Bruce was nowhere to be seen. She was floating in some kind of bubble. There was no one around, so she moved over a bit to reach out and touch the crystal-clear substance. As she pushed her hand through it, an excruciating pain shot up her arm. Yanking her hand back inside the bubble she let out a silent breath of relief as the pain subsided.

Footsteps vibrated just outside the door, she closed her eyes and returned to the floating position she'd been in when she awoke only with her back to them. She could see what was going on in the reflection of the bubble.

"She still out," a gruff male voice announced from just to her left.

"Are you sure you didn't kill her when you captured her? A damaged witch ain't gonna do me any good, no matter who she is."

This strained wavering voice she recognized from her nightmares. Was she still dreaming?

"You didn't give me much time to weave the damn

spell. I guess something could have gone wrong and suspended her between this world and the dream world. But that's highly unlikely." The man scrubbed his hands over his weary face and ran his fingers through his short black hair. Eyes hollow and cheek bones sharp, he looked as if he'd not eaten or slept enough to fuel his once strong muscular build.

"Can't we reach in and shake her or bring her around somehow. She looks normal enough, but that's only her spirit?"

"Absolutely not. That would kill her. You damage that phosphorescent bubble she is contained in and her spirit, which is what you captured, will die immediately, whether it looks normal or not. I told you that when you demanded she be snatched from the dream world and brought here. This was a bad idea." He shook his head, shoulders slumped.

"I didn't ask for your opinion. You are to serve as my spell caster until I decide your debt is paid. Need I remind you of our agreement or whose lives hang in the balance?"

"It didn't include this. You can't just take someone out of the dream world without consequences. The rest of her body is somewhere and you can bet someone is looking for her."

"She shouldn't have been seeking me. Besides, I didn't capture her. You did. So the consequences will be yours to pay." He snorted and drew in a raspy breath. "We are so close now, I can smell their fear."

His breath rattled in and out reminding her of the night wind rustling through dead leaves. She bit back the fear that was clawing inside her. This wasn't the time to lose control. If she wanted to survive this, she had to be strong and think.

Bruce's image swam into her mind along with his deep voice tinged with worry. *Angie where are you? Can you hear me?* Was this an illusion used by her captures, her mind playing games, or real? It didn't matter, she couldn't respond, not until she figured out what the hell was going on. Her intense fear melted into a simmering anger, which didn't help matters at all, angry outbursts always led to bad decisions and regret.

The raspy voice commanded vehemently, "Confirm who she is so I can decide how to use her for our benefit. And, I am tired of all your excuses."

Suddenly she felt heat and electricity snap across the room. A scream resonated through the air then a heavy thud and silence. The door slammed and the raspy voice cursed loudly from farther away.

Remaining still she listened for movement for several minutes, then opened one eye The short once stocky wizard lay sprawled on the floor about six feet from her. His breathing was labored; his face blackened and eyes swollen shut. The collar of his shirt was singed and whiffs of black smoke curled around his neck. The smell of scorched flesh made bile rise in her throat, she closed her eye and turned slowly so her back was again toward the door. The reflection on the bubble of what was happening behind her was distorted, but better than nothing.

The doorknob turned and the door creaked opened. "Malic, won't you ever learn?" A sympathetic voice said softly. "John, give me a hand, we need some medical magic here and quickly." Shoes scuffed the floor and she heard a low moan as they drug the wizard out of the room, closing the door with a bang.

Silence fell over the area again and icy fingers of panic gripped her. The only way out of here was her mind connection to Bruce she had to risk it. *I'm here and alive but a prisoner. Don't respond...yet.*

Bruce's voice slid carefully into her mind wary of detection. *We're looking. Any idea where or who?*

She breathed a sigh of relief thankful for the blood bond. *Stateside, I think. It's him. I'm sure of it. Someone's coming.*

Footsteps hesitated outside the door. A sliver of light crossed the room as the door opened silently and closed with a quiet click. A male voice whispered, "If you can hear me, don't acknowledge it. Your only chance for survival is to remain unresponsive. We're just outside D.C., set for attack as soon as the Overlord shows up at his salon. The warriors have gathered, so it's only a matter of time. Tell him to stay away and to scatter his legion before it's too late. Rezar has stolen…" His voice faltered a moment. "Someone's coming. I won't get another chance to talk to you, so I hope…this is enough."

Her nostrils flared as the scent of magic filled the room dissolving the stench of burnt flesh and wood.

"No change in the witch." The same voice stated flatly as the door closed again.

Rezar burst through the door. "She's no good to me this way." Grabbing a fist full of the protective globe, a turquoise light gathered at the point of impact and shot a bolt of white-hot electrical current through the air. "Shit." Propelled backward, he crashed against the wall and slid to the floor, his up turned palms singed and wisps of gray smoke curling from the blackened holes in the heels of his charred shoes.

The bubble bounced lightly around the room, leaving blue phosphorescent smudges in its wake, forcing Angie to return her body to a horizontal position inside the bubble without rupturing the sphere. The globe came to rest against the wall opposite Rezar. Angie lay motionless inside the orb.

In the reflection, she watched Rezar's eyes narrow and lips contort into a nasty sneer as he got unsteadily to his feet.

He watched her closely. The slow rise and fall of her chest indicated she was still alive, if barely. Or maybe she was just pretending. He couldn't tell with her back to him. "So…you are our exalted Overlord's flavor of the month and Tristian's sister to boot." Laughing maniacally, he rubbed his hands together, leaning back against the wall for support. "What a find!"

He turned toward the door and snarled. "Get Malic in here. I want to find out what she knows without killing her…yet. For that, I want an audience, her brother and our exalted Overlord will do nicely." Rezar staggered through the door, leaving it wide open.

Angie turned slowly opening one eye to glance through the door into the adjoining room. A well-worn wooden table and chairs sat directly across from the open door. The wooden floor creaked as the men moved around the room.

In the far corner, a long handled, double-sided axe leaned against the wall. Gold metallic ropes wound around the shiny silver blade securing it to the ebony handle. Rubies, emeralds, diamonds and sapphires inset on the upper portion of the handle winked in the fire light. She'd seen that Labrys before, but couldn't recall where, or to whom it belonged, certainly not this rag tag group of creatures. The aura of power it gave off just sitting there worried her. Who could wield such a weapon?

Chapter Nineteen

Bruce paced across the room. "Why can't we see her on your almighty screen?"

"Because only her essence or spirit has been stolen, her body remains here," Matiah said in a soothing voice.

Andre nodded solemnly. "The jet is fueled and waiting on the air strip should we need it. But you, my son, must stay behind with Angie."

His mother nodded in agreement with her husband.

"Like hell," Bruce said furiously, his hands balled into fists at his side. He took two steps forward and carefully shoved his father aside.

Andre stepped back in front of Bruce. "Son, you don't want to do this. Control your temper and think. You'll need to bring her spirit and soul back to her body once she is released from the dream world Rezar has captured her in. If she gets lost between the worlds, she is lost to you forever." Andre stood between Bruce and the door.

Bruce turned on his heel and paced the room like a caged animal. "Ok, ok." He took a deep breath and tried to settle himself and formulate a plan. "Tristian, should have a team assembled ready to go by now."

"Good choice," Andre agreed. "His blood connection to her and magic abilities in addition to his assassin training will serve him well. But he is also a target…"

"I'll suggest he send his team in first." Bruce drew in another breath and ran his fingers through his hair. "He is the expert in these types of situations, the best of the best, so I'll have to leave the plan execution up to him." Bruce shook his head, uncomfortable with leaving his mate's life in someone else's hands, even her brother's. "I hate not being there. I'll remind him what's at stake." Bruce pulled his cell phone out of his pocket and touched in the number two, speed dial for Tristian.

Tristian picked up on the first ring. "We moving out?"

"Yes." That one short word said it all. Bruce filled him in on the recent events and warned him failure was not an option.

"Don't tell me how to do my job," Tristian growled. "We'll get her back safe and sound. You have contact with her?"

"Yes."

Andre watched his son. A rough road to getting there, but he was a great leader, even facing one of the worst trials of his life. Matiah's eyes glistened as she looked from father to son, finally putting aside their differences, when it counted. She lowered her eyes and turned to look out the window. They had created an extraordinary individual, in spite of her banishment and dire heavenly predictions. Smiling, she lifted her eyes to the heavens and sighed. "They were all wrong," she said quietly.

****

Stefan, the Vampire Council's assassin, peered in the dirt-streaked window, his dark eyes searching the dimly lit room, *there it is,* he willed his body to relax, he'd found it, finally. In the far corner leaning against the cracked plaster wall was the Harbinger Labrys of Power stolen from the Vampire Council's chamber a few months ago. Ordered to find and retrieve the Harbinger at all costs, Stefan Talltree, the council's enforcer, followed whispered leads from fearful informants in dark alleys for the better part of a month. They recounted encounters with a once high-ranking demon in the service of the underworld's guardian now looking for vengeance on those deemed responsible for his fall from power. Word on the street was that the demon was insane, caused by his attempted escape from the collar that imprisoned him and his return to the mortal world. All of Stefan's investigations led to this isolated cabin in the backwoods of Cherryfield, Maine.

Stefan checked other windows for changes in inhabitants from his previous surveillance. The cell phone vibrated against his thigh. *Shit.* In a whisper of movement, he positioned himself a mile away from the cabin and yanked the phone out of his pocket. "Your timing sucks."

"Mind your insolence, Stefan." A commanding female voice chided.

"Sorry Lady Rose. What can I do for you? I've found the Harbinger."

"Then retrieval is imminent?"

"Yeah, but there is a problem."

"Then solve it and return with the Labrys."

"It's not that easy. The renegade band of creatures led by a demon they call Rezar has an innocent. There is a ghostlike woman captured in a phosphorescent bubble floating in one of the rooms. If I take down the group, chances are she'll be killed."

"Really? Now that's fortuitous."

"It is?" Stefan said incredulously, his brow creasing. Lady Rose could be ruthless when the circumstances warranted, but as a rule, she was a fair individual and rarely allowed harm to come to an innocent.

A soft laugh came through the receiver, then Lady Rose cleared her throat. "I mean, the reason I called, was a request received from Lord Bruce, his mate was snatched, and he's looking for information leading to her whereabouts. Since you've covered a lot of ground recently, the council thought you might be in a position to help. And we were right. You may have found her. Is this innocent small, with long golden hair and violet eyes?"

"Petite with long blond hair, yes, but her eyes were closed, I can't confirm the color. So what do you want me to do?"

"Send me your location. Can you sit tight until I contact Bruce?"

"Yeah, I can hold off, it doesn't appear they are going anywhere soon. If things change, I'll improvise. They won't leave with the Harbinger, regardless. Find out how soon the Overlord's force can mobilize and get here."

"Certainly. Good work, Stefan."

"Thank you, my lady." He touched the screen and disconnected the call, shaking his head. *More complications, just what I need.* The tall blades of grass near the cabin's foundation swayed in the light breeze as twilight descended. Stefan crept closer rounding the corner and stood next to the window where he'd first seen the filmy figure captured in the bubble. This time he paid closer attention, she was small and lithe with miles of blonde hair streaming down her back. As he peered in at her, she opened large violet eyes and stared at him for a moment. He backed out of her line of vision and away from the cabin.

Phone in hand, he crouched down in the underbrush and touched the screen to redial the last number. "It's her," he whispered into the phone. "I'm positive. Those haunting violet eyes are unmistakable and the magic signature is barely discernible, but one of a witch."

"Good job, Stefan. I'll be in touch."

The phone call disconnected, Stefan sat back on his heels to wait.

Suddenly the cabin door banged open, illuminating a wide arc in the darkness. A body sailed out the door and landed with a thud on the damp forest floor. The male lay motionless on the ground within fifteen feet of Stefan. Nostrils flared as he sniffed the air. *Vampire and demon.*

A rail thin demon with an uneven gate walked over and viciously kicked the body. "You lied. You can't wield the magic of the axe any more than I can." Light flooding from the open door glinted off the silver collar encircling the demon's neck as he shuffled back inside, slamming the door with a loud bang. The body twitched and a low moan carried back to Stefan's ears.

Chapter Twenty

"I can't sit here and do nothing," Bruce said loudly, frustration seeping into the deep timber of his voice. His large hand wrapped protectively around her tiny limp one. His cell phone vibrated on the dresser, skittering across the surface announcing a new e-mail. Long sweaty fingers grasped the phone and touched the lit screen. He scrolled down and highlighted the e-mail from Lady Rose. Heart thundering in his chest, he read the message. Bruce bent over and brushed his lips lightly over the knuckles of Angie's hand then released it and strode through the bedroom door, closing it softly behind him.

The hallway was empty. Bruce ran his fingers through his hair for what seemed like the hundredth time as he hurried down the hallway in search of his parents. Seeing their silhouettes against the rising full moon, he shouted. "I received an e-mail. Lady Rose thinks her enforcer has found Angie. We need to leave right away."

With a rustle of wings, his mother met him in the entrance to the veranda. "No my son, your father is right. You must stay with Angie and help bring her spirit back to her body. We can't afford to lose her between. Let her brother go, his magic will be able to release the spell...safely."

"Where is she?" Andre asked urgently as he came

to a quick halt behind Matiah.

"Held captive at an isolated cabin in the forest just outside Cherryfield, Maine. Several weeks ago, the vampire council sent their enforcer in search of a stolen weapon, which is in Rezar's possession and Angie is sequestered in a room in that cabin. Bruce handed the phone to Andre so he could read the e-mail for himself.

"Have you called Tristian?" Andre asked.

"Not yet, I just got the e-mail." Bruce touched the screen, shifted from e-mail to phone, and said, "Call Tristian." He raised the phone to his ear and waited impatiently.

Tristian answered on the first ring. "We're ready. Owen said your jet is fueled and the pilot is awaiting instructions on the runway. Where are we going?"

"I just received an e-mail from Lady Rose, it includes the coordinates. I'm sending it to you now. The council's enforcer, Stefan, is waiting your arrival. Apparently, Rezar has something that belongs to the Vampire Council and they are anxious to get it back. Stefan's orders are to terminate the thieves and return with the weapon. Angie is captive in the cabin."

"Rezar stole the council's Harbinger? He's got bigger balls than I thought or that collar fried any brain cells he had left. No one can wield that Labrys but a vampire of true blood. What a fool. Fortunate for us, Stefan will insist on terminating Rezar, so I can turn my full attention to releasing Angie. It'll be fine." Tristian assured Bruce. "You're going to wait there to help her across, aren't you?" Tristian said, more of a statement than a question.

"Yes," Bruce bit out, knowing his place was here with Angie, but wishing he could get his hands on the demon that snatched her.

A gentle hand rested on his shoulder, his mother spoke softly in her melodic soprano voice. "Son, revenge is not something you need to exact. He will get what's coming to him by the vampire council's assassin. Stefan was trained by the most ruthless assassin the vampire realm has ever known."

Bruce patted his mother's hand and nodded hoping she was right, before turning his attention back to Tristian. "When you get the coordinates, head out and keep me in the loop."

"Just got em. Already assembled the teams, we'll leave now. I'll be in touch." Tristian broke the connection.

Bruce dropped the phone into his pocket, slid a sidelong glance at his parents, and stalked back to Angie. His mother followed silently in his wake, his father spoke softly into his cell phone a short distance behind her.

****

Outside the cabin, Stefan waited, watched until he sensed Tristian's men encircle the perimeter giving wide berth to the structure. Tristian touched in the phone number provided by Lady Rose and waited.

"Stefan." The assassin grunted into the phone.

"We're set. My team has the place surrounded, magic barriers are up, and I'm just outside the bedroom where you saw Angie. There is nowhere for Rezar and his men to go once you storm the front of the house. On your signal, I'll enter Angie's room at the same time you enter through the front. Correct?"

"Yeah."

'Sure you don't want some of my men to back you

up?"

"No, they'll just get in the way. Rezar's men will flee. They aren't loyal to him. That's where your men will come in. Terminate the enemy as they scatter. I don't want anyone to escape, take no prisoners. Got it?"

"Got it."

"Then GO." Stefan said tossing the phone in the bushes outside the cabin door. He kicked the door open and had the Harbinger in his hand before anyone in the room realized he was there. From the corner of his eye, he saw Rezar do a belly slide across the floor toward Angie's holding place. Two werewolves dove for the window, a vampire ran for the door behind Stefan, and various leather-winged demons flew toward the fireplace. The black handle felt warm in his palm as he swung the doubled bladed axe taking aim for Rezar. Bursts of blue electrical current flowed from the head of the axe as its golden glow of protection surrounded Stefan.

Its shining silver blade sliced through the bodies it connected with, Stefan cut a wide swath through the room then bringing the axe full arc, terminating any remaining creatures cowering in the corners. Blood curdling screams filled the crisp night air, blood spatter covered the walls and pooled next to detached body parts of the offending werewolves and vampires. Ash rained down from the ceiling from the incinerated demons who attempted escape. With satisfaction, Stefan rested the Harbinger on his shoulder and nodded. He strode across the bloodstained floor and pushed open the door to the room that held Angie.

Tristian stood transfixed, eyes closed, leaning against the wall of the empty room. The warlock who stood guard over Angie splayed in the middle of the floor. The rise and fall of his chest told Stefan he was still alive. The phosphorescent bubble was gone so too was the ghostly woman it detained. Rezar was nowhere to be found.

Stefan stepped over the warlock and nudged Tristian with his elbow. "Everything all right in here?" He moved the Harbinger from his shoulder and took aim at the warlock on the floor.

Tristian's eyes still glazed, but his hand flew out to block Stefan's arm. "No don't, not yet." Suddenly, Tristian's face contorted and he screamed. "Noooooo, Bruce watch out."

Stefan crouched as he whirled around on his heels, the axe stretched out in front of him. There was no one there except the warlock on the floor. Stefan looked back to Tristian, the vacant look in Tristian's eyes telling Stefan that Tristian's mind wasn't in this room.

****

At the same time Stefan busted through the front door, Tristian had materialized inside the room, raised his hand to the warlock guarding Angie.

Don't hurt him, Angie's voice pleaded inside Tristian's mind, *if not for him, I wouldn't be alive.*

Tristian muttered words under his breath, palm still facing the guard as he slumped to the floor. *He's not dead just incapacitated for now. I'll deal with him later.* Tristian's words drifted through her mind. "Now for you, you gave us quite a scare, but I think I can return you to your worried demon." Tristian sneered, determined not to show his true feelings. "I need you to concentrate on Bruce, your room in Tahiti and don't let anything break your concentration."

Tristian raised his voice in chant and a smoked filled layer surrounded the bubble. "You realize I've never done anything like this before," he said gruffly to Angie.

She nodded, her violet eyes watching him intently. *You can do it. You have always taken care of me, even when it wasn't easy.* Angie smiled. *I love you, big brother.*

No, you don't, or you wouldn't have given yourself to a demon and not just any demon, a Territory Overlord, and my boss. Nor would you be in this mess.

Tristian's disgruntled voice faded from her mind. *You know as well as I do that it was meant to be. Now get on with it. Stefan can't hold them off forever.* Angie closed her eyes following Tristian's instructions.

Tristian cursed, then held his palms flat to the outside protective shield he'd created and murmured several words in cadence, pushed his hands through the first barrier and through the bubble taking hold of the essence of Angie with both hands at her waist and shoved. The bubble closed in around her. As she faded, a gnarled hand caught hold of the blue phosphorescence tail attached to her filmy dress and before Tristian could reach him, they were gone.

"Noooooo, Bruce watch out." Tristian bellowed.

Rezar latched on to Angie's essence in an attempt to follow her into the dream realm, thereby escaping Stefan and Tristian. The failed attempt dumped Rezar unceremoniously at Bruce's feet as Angie seamlessly returned to her body.

Rezar first to react drove his dagger deep into Bruce's thigh, twisting the dagger against bone as Rezar tried to right himself.

Blood poured down Bruce's leg. Unconcerned he watched Angie's violet eyes flutter open and lock on his. "Welcome home, my li'l witch. Never taking his eyes from hers, he shoved the barefoot of his good leg into Rezar's ribcage, sending a surge of energy through Rezar temporarily immobilizing him. "Rest now, my love," he said quietly to Angie suppressing a groan as the pain surged through his thigh and down his leg, he wiggled his toes to make sure nerves, tendons, and muscles were still intact. *Yep, all good there.*

Bruce wrapped his hand around the dagger, sucked in a breath and wrenched it out of his leg, blood poured from the wound, streamed down his leg and pooled on the floor. With unbridled rage, he thrust the dagger now pulsing with his powerful magic directly into Rezar's heart. His blood-curdling scream filled the room. Angie's brow creased as she shifted in the bed. Silence settled in the room as a puff of gray smoke rose from where Rezar fell, a pile of ash all that remained. The silver collar glinted in the room's soft light as it spun on its edge and came to rest on the floor encircling the ash next to Bruce's bare foot.

Andre rushed into the room with Matiah close on his heels. He grasped her arm and whispered, "Wait until he settles or asks for your help in healing the wound. He's a warrior and has been through a lot worse."

"Not in my home." Matiah protested and wrenched free of his hold.

Bruce felt his mother's presence. When his weary gaze locked on hers, she glided slowly toward him and he nodded. She ripped open his pants leg around the wound and laid her hand gently over the area. A subtle lilac glow emanated from her hand as the wound closed and new pink skin appeared. Bruce watched his mom glance from the dark liquid congealing on the floor to the red spatter on the bedding, the corners of her mouth twitching in an attempt to conceal a grin. "You'll have to clean up this mess," she chided gently patting his shoulder, "when your witch awakens, which should be soon."

Bruce raised an eyebrow, staring at his mother. "I'll get right on that." He remained on the edge of the bed, his fingertips lightly caressing Angie's forehead.

Angie slowly opened her eyes again, blinking at the bright sunlight streaming through the window and tried to focus on the individuals surrounding her bed.

"Welcome back li'l witch." Bruce leaned over, kissed her lightly, and released a sigh of relief along with his parents.

Angie smiled up at Bruce. Glanced at Andre and Matiah, and then looked around the room. "I'm happy to be back," she said slowly. "That was quite a trip." She blinked several times, took a deep breath pulling herself into a sitting position and leaning back against the headboard, she wrinkled her nose. "I need a shower and change of clothes. It smells like fire and brimstone in here." She glanced at the floor, her heart raced as she fought back a wave of panic. "I hope that's not yours," she said as nonchalantly as possible while inclining her head toward the pool of blood.

"Unfortunately, my love, it is but nothing to worry about. I'll clean it up while you shower."

The others laughed. Bruce lifted her out of the bed, ambled to the other side, and let her stretch her legs until her bare feet touched the floor and she steadied herself. He dropped to one knee and took a little red velvet box out of the nightstand. With his thumb he flipped open the lid revealing a ring set with a sparkling marquee cut emerald nestled between two blue diamonds in platinum . "Angie, would you do me the honor of becoming my wife?"

Andre's forehead creased in puzzlement as a single tear rolled down Matiah's cheek, which she quickly wiped away.

"Of course. But you don't..." Angie started.

"I do. Your beliefs and traditions are as important as mine. Together, no one will put asunder." He slipped the ring on the ring finger of her left hand and brought her hand up to his warm lips.

Epilogue

Willow squealed as Angie pushed her way through the heavy glass door to the Krystal Unicorn, followed closely by Bruce. The chilly wind whirled around the room as Willow came from behind the counter to envelope Angie in a hug. "I've missed you. Don't you ever do anything like that again."

"I'll do my best," Angie said unable to stifle a giggle at Willow's reaction. "Now, if you'll just loosen your arms as well as your wings, maybe I could breathe." Angie made exaggerated gasps for air, pulling at Willows arms.

Willow grinned and released Angie, then whirled around to face Bruce. "And you," Willow said taking a step forward, poking her finger in Bruce's broad chest. "You were supposed to keep her safe, all powerful one," she sneered.

"Watch it Faery," Bruce warned in a low growl flicking her finger away from him. "And you might want to pull in your wings before those watching discover they aren't fake." He jerked his chin toward the customers milling around just outside the interior shop door shared with the salon's waiting area.

Several pairs of gossamer wings hung just inside the showroom window that faced the salon. They were a popular item and tough to keep in stock. Willow glanced at the wings in the window and dipped slightly behind Angie while tucking in her own.

Angie looked around the shop. "This place is absolutely magical, what a wonderful job you've done. I love the cozy overstuffed chairs near the bookshelves, and the mirrored tiles etched with unicorns on the wall behind the counter, where'd you find those? The ivy twined sparingly over the tiles is a really nice touch, not to mention how much bigger it makes the shop look." Angie continued turning in a three hundred and sixty-degree circle taking in all the changes. "I like the light green carpeting and the pale yellow walls. Flowering vines climbing the corners of the room is a nice touch." She sniffed the air and sighed. "I love the aroma of the scented candles."

Willow shrugged. "I wish I could take credit for it all, but Tobi found the tiles and did a lot of the decorating and arranging before I returned. But the pastel colored faery wind chimes and the Irish crystal snowflakes hanging from the ceiling are my additions. Brought them back from Ireland. Don't you just love em?"

Angie nodded and reached up to touch a low hanging snowflake. It spun in the sunlight casting rainbows across the room.

Still tweaking her shoulders a bit, Willow straightened. "If we order in bulk, we can get a much better price on the snow flakes. I know a guy." Willow's voice trailed off as she noticed the sparkling gem on Angie's left hand. "What is that?" She asked raising a brow, her ice blue eyes sparkling as she grabbed hold of Angie's hand.

"Just what it looks like. An engagement ring." Angie couldn't keep the bright smile from her lips.

"So…your demon Lord bowed to your brother's pressure?" Willow smirked. "Not a good example for our powerful Overlord to set." She cut her eyes, filled with mischief, to Bruce.

"You're digging yourself a hole, that I won't be able to rescue you from," Angie warned laughing. "You know better than that. No, Bruce asked me to marry me because he loves me and…"

Willow interrupted, "And wants to make sure you belong to him in every way possible."

"Oh, you're impossible. Just maybe he respects my traditions as well as his own." Angie reached for Willow, grasping hold of her wrist. "I believe you have some explaining to do yourself." Angie's eyes twinkled as she lifted Willow's hand up so Tobi and Owen, peering in from the Salon, Bruce and a few good customers crowded around could see the rock on Willow's finger.

Willow's cheeks blushed crimson and she smiled wide, jerking her hand out of Angie's grip. "Yes, I've news of my own. Caleb asked me to marry him and I agreed. Our families are not really on board with it yet, but they will get used to it." Willow paused chewing on her bottom lip. "I hope."

"Of course they will," Angie assured her friend then pursed her lips and considered. "Willow, I wonder what your families would think of…"

Bruce nudged Angie and peered over her head toward the outside salon door just as Mrs. Staret swept in with her daughter, Jill. The older woman paused for a moment scanning the salon before she caught sight of Bruce and Angie among their little throng of friends. Mrs. Staret walked purposefully toward them.

Uh oh. Bruce's words wafted through Angie's thoughts. *This can't be good.* He wrapped his arm around Angie's waist protectively, angling her body slightly behind him.

Mrs. Staret gave Willow a quick smile and stepped toward Bruce her hand extended.

"Good afternoon, Mrs. Staret," Bruce said graciously, dropping his arm from Angie's waist and moving closer to the older woman, he clasped her hand in both of his. "To what do we owe this pleasure?"

She glanced toward Jill who was now standing beside her mother and said, "My daughter and I are ready to take you up on your offer, if it's still available."

Never missing a beat, Bruce smiled broadly. "Of course." His arm returned to Angie's waist and drew her next to him. "We'd be happy to have you join us for dinner. Just so happens we are free this evening. Will that work? "

Somewhat taken a back, Mrs. Staret's eyes went wide for a moment. "Why, yes, I believe it would," she said as her daughter nodded in agrecmcnt.

"Good, would you like us to pick the two of you up, or would you rather meet us at Anthony's around 7:30 this evening? Italian all right?" Bruce paused and shifted his attention to Jill. "Would you like your husband to join us?"

"No," Jill said firmly. "He isn't aware…uh…the less he knows about this situation the better." She shifted from one foot to the other uncomfortably.

"As you wish, but it's been my experience secrets between couples usually lead to trouble," Bruce said.

Mrs. Staret cleared her throat. "Yes, Anthony's is

one of our favorite restaurants and we'll meet you there." Mrs. Staret and her daughter gave a curt nod and walked back through the salon and out the same door they'd entered.

"That was interesting," Angie mused, wondering if their meeting would set things to right, or if Mrs. Staret had an ulterior motive.

"I think she just wants closure. I will certainly be glad to put that particular situation behind me. But it bothers me that Jill's husband is being left out of the loop."

"Oh powerful one, it's none of your business." Angie crooned and patted Bruce's arm.

Willow lowered her voice so only the three of them could hear and said, "No, Bruce is right. Jill's husband, Seth, doesn't know the family secret. Mrs. Staret says two of their three children inherited the abilities and it won't be long before he figures it out, then all hell will break loose. At least that's what Mrs. Staret thinks."

"Still none of our business," Angie said sweetly.

"Unless Seth freaks out when he finds out and endangers the rest of us," Bruce said gravely. "It has happened."

"Oh, I didn't think about that. Maybe we can carefully address the situation at dinner," Angie suggested.

Bruce surveyed the salon; each stylist was with a customer and a few still in the waiting area. Perfect. Tobi turned toward them smiling and gave a quick wave. "That's enough business talk, aren't we celebrating the grand reopening of The Krystal Unicorn?"

"Just one more thing. Angie, what were you

wondering about my family before we were interrupted?" Willow asked.

Angie opened her mouth about to speak, then caught movement out of the corner of her eye and looked toward The Krystal Unicorn's entrance off the street. *Now what.*

The shop's door chimes sounded as Tristian strode in then held the door for a pleasant looking young woman with bright blue eyes and dark red hair that curled just above her collar. He reached down and caught her hand in his as they approached the group. Tristian's usual somber expression brightened considerably as the woman smiled shyly up at him, then switched her gaze to the group. Her glance swept quickly over Bruce and lingered on Angie for a moment then returned to Tristian.

He wrapped an arm around Angie's neck and pulled her to him kissing her cheek. "Morning sis."

"Oh, Tristian you came to the grand re-opening of the Krystal Unicorn. How thoughtful," Angie said.

"Of course. But I'd also like you to meet Hannah Shaughnessy." Tristian slid his arm around Hannah's waist and arranged her slightly in front of him. "Hannah, this is my sister, Angie, who chose to tie herself for eternity to the cause of all our trouble—" He lowered his voice. "The Western Hemisphere's Territory Overlord." Tristian bent over at the waist in an exaggerated bow toward Bruce, then quickly took a couple steps backward tugging Hannah along with him. "And my boss of many years. We were even friends until he took up with my sister. Now…well as you know we are working on it."

"Nice to see you too, Tristian," Bruce said

cheerfully. "And a boss that has made you a very wealthy man, let's not forget that."

Ignoring Bruce, Angie reached for Hannah and gave her a quick hug. "Hello, Hannah. It's wonderful to finally meet the woman who tamed my brother. And believe me, I know that's no small feat." She winked at Hannah and grinned.

"Oh, I wouldn't say that." The blood rushed to Hannah's cheeks and she took a sudden interest in her shoes.

"Oh, I would and he's a better man for it." Angie batted her eyes at her brother and smirked, just daring him to retort.

Tristian's blue-gray eyes blazed but he said nothing.

Hannah looked back at Angie then over to Tristian a puzzled look on her face.

"Bruce leaned forward, careful not to intimidate Hannah. "I would be the trouble to which Tristian is referring. I'm Bruce. It's a pleasure to meet you Ms. Shaughnessy." He offered his hand to Hannah who took it tentatively.

"Please, just Hannah," she said with a nervous smile.

"Hannah, are you enjoying your visit to our historic city?"

"I am now," she said with a slight grimace. "I'm kinda new to this type of intrigue. But now that it's safe…"

"Oh…it's never…" Bruce began.

Frowning, Tristian interrupted and waved his hand toward Willow. "Hannah this is Angie's life-long friend, Willow. You've met her family. They live in the house next door to our family home in Maine. Willow and Angie are business partners and own The Krystal Unicorn."

Hannah nodded her head and grinned at Willow. "I've heard all about you and am so glad to meet you. Do you get back home often?"

"No not much." Willow said hesitantly, looking first to Hannah and then narrowed her eyes at Tristian. "Work keeps me pretty busy and my fiancé lives here. He's an artist," she said proudly.

Tristian nearly choked on his own spit, eyes rounded as he repeated. "Your fiancé? But you're just…"

"Just really glad you're not my brother." Willow dissolved into a fit of laughter, joined by Angie. Hannah covered her mouth so Tristian wouldn't see her broad smile at his obvious surprise.

"Yes, Tristian, fiancé. As a matter of fact, we were just about to discuss the possibility of having a double wedding, when you and Hannah walked in," Angie said smugly. *I wonder if Andre would officiate at our ceremony.* She tucked that thought away for the moment, deciding to wait until a better time to mention it. *Maybe I'll talk it over with Matiah first.*

"We were?" Willow sputtered staring at her friend then repeated. "We were." Willow bobbed her head emphatically.

"Double wedding," Tristian repeated cutting his gaze to Hannah. "Who else is getting married?"

Hannah shook her head and shrugged.

Tristian glanced around the room, then his gaze settled on Angie. "Ok, someone needs to bring me up to speed on what's going on around here. Hannah and I were just on our way to the airport, when I decided—" He paused and glanced at Hannah." I mean we decided, it was time to introduce Hannah to all of you before we left. She is an important part of my life now."

This time it was the others turn to stare in shocked silence at Tristian. Such a personal declaration from him was uncharacteristic. Just a few months ago, no one even knew he had a sister.

Angie was the first to find her voice. "I am so happy for you." She rushed back to Tristian and threw her arms around him then Hannah. "It's about time. You've spent way too much time trying to take care of me, while putting your own life on hold. The double wedding is for Bruce and I, and Willow and Caleb. You'll receive an invitation when we've ironed out all the details."

"Settling down huh?" Bruce reached his hand out and shook Tristian's. "Maybe it would be a good idea to stick around and let Angie and Hannah get acquainted, Willow too. I can make the apartment available to you for a while longer."

Tristian shook his head. "We gotta get back and check on things at home." Then switched his gaze to Hannah who frowned. Tristian cleared his throat and quickly added. "But we'd like to return in a couple weeks. Would that work?"

Hannah's frown faded and she nodded in agreement, a smile forming at the corners of her lips.

"Sure, let me know the time frame and we'll make arrangements. We can send the jet for you." Bruce slid his arm around Angie's waist again and pulled her into him brushing a kiss across her forehead, in a rare show of affection in public.

Tristian frowned but kept his voice pleasant. "Will do." Tristian and Hannah waved as they left through the door.

No sooner than the door closed behind her brother and Hannah, Angie winked at Bruce and glanced at Willow. "We better decide on a date and get started on the guest list for our wedding." Angie leaned over and whispered to Willow, "Did you know Bruce's mother is an angel? She'll be attending the wedding along with Bruce's father, Andre."

"That's a nice thing to say about your mother-in-law to be." Willow whispered back wondering why they were whispering.

"No, really, an angel with wings and everything." Angie whispered.

Willow's eyes rounded and she just stared at Angie.

"Well, that's the first time I've ever seen Willow speechless." Bruce grinned. "It's undoubtedly going to be an interesting few months."

A word from the author...

With the majestic Rocky Mountains just outside the window, I sit at my computer with vampires, demons, witches, faeries, and a variety of paranormal creatures gathered around telling me their stories! I am an author of paranormal romance novels and cozy mysteries with magic spark. The everyday world is mundane, but sprinkle a little magic and you have fantastic!

Colorado is home. I share my life with a wonderful husband of many moons, our brilliant Chow Chow, a terribly spoiled companion parrot, and a forty-year-old box turtle. We enjoy hiking, biking, and camping, also love water sports including kayaking and whitewater rafting, especially on the Arkansas River through the Royal Gorge.

Another passion of mine is reading a good novel. You can find me any winter evening curled up in front of a crackling fire with a good book, a mug of hot chocolate, and a big bowl of popcorn. While growing up, if I didn't like the ending of a book, I'd rewrite it, which led to writing my own books.

http://www.tenastetler.com

Thank you for purchasing
this publication of The Wild Rose Press, Inc.

If you enjoyed the story, we would appreciate your
letting others know by leaving a review.

For other wonderful stories,
please visit our on-line bookstore at
www.thewildrosepress.com.

For questions or more information
contact us at
info@thewildrosepress.com.

The Wild Rose Press, Inc.
www.thewildrosepress.com

Stay current with The Wild Rose Press, Inc.

Like us on Facebook

https://www.facebook.com/TheWildRosePress

And Follow us on Twitter
https://twitter.com/WildRosePress